For My Father, the Hero

Mister Shah

Christian DeFeo

To Ha,

With best wishes,

[signature]

GreenSunsetBooks
www.greensunsetbooks.co.uk

First published in 2010 by
Green Sunset Books
92 Mosse Gardens, Fishbourne
PO19 3PQ
www.greensunsetbooks.co.uk

Cover design: © 2010
by Andrew Reaney and Danny James
www.club70design.co.uk

A catalogue record for this book is available from the British
Library

One

Three quick breaths, then a long exhale. The pulse, in response, briefly accelerated and then settled back. A sure sign that one is alive, and according to the imam, it is *mubah*.

A sea of faces entering the mosque: Wahid was one of them, again breathing quick, quick, quick, then slow. He wore a white cotton *kurta,* which draped down to just above his knees, and a small knitted hat that covered the top of his head. Important: the hat concealed the two white ear buds extending from his iPod. Ahmed, the boisterous butcher from Brick Lane, with a beard extending from his chin to the top of his enormous belly, did not see them. He said, "*Salaam*, Wahid!"

Wahid read lips well enough to understand his greeting. He nodded his head, his neatly trimmed beard dipping in time, took another three quick breaths, and gingerly placed his fingers on his wrist to check his pulse. Fortunately, it was still there.

"Steady as a drumbeat," Dr Al-Haq had said.

Hmmm. Following the tide of other men, he made his way into a vast ivory marble hall, lined with red carpet bedecked with a pattern of blue Turkish tulips; the scent of black tea simmering in the distance filled the air. He found his spot, slipped off his soft, black shoes and pushed the toe ends up to the wall.

"Little better than slippers," his wife Rania had said. "Your feet will get wet in the rain!"

He had assured her that he would wear an extra pair of socks.

"Isn't it a beautiful morning, Wahid?" Ahmed said from behind, loud enough to penetrate the Mozart Clarinet Concerto

1

serenading him on his iPod. Wahid turned and nodded, his vision slightly blurring as his gold wire frame glasses juddered on his nose.

There was little point in arguing with Ahmed; he was the type of person who believed that dead animals were a sign of wealth. Anyone sensible knew the morning was not beautiful: this country was far too cold. Wahid had a genetic memory which gnawed on him: the rain, moisture and chill were wrong, an abomination; he was not made for this.

There had been a July day in London when the temperature hit 30 degrees Celsius. Wahid switched on the old black iron ceiling fans in his office. The sun had momentarily distracted him from long lists of sums. He stood in front of the window as the light and heat blazed through the glass. Yes. The requirement for three quick breaths and an exhale was temporarily forgotten.

Wahid wandered into the great hall in his socked feet, carrying his prayer mat rolled up underneath his arm. He reminded himself: "Must pick up some antiseptic later." It went into the wash for his socks, and he made sure he sprayed the prayer mat with it every evening.

Picking a spot was always difficult. There was no way he could kneel down next to someone who was coughing; Allah knows what disease they could have. Bird flu? He'd been reading in the newspaper about it spreading in Suffolk before going on to the obituaries. This was the largest mosque in Britain: it was possible that someone would drive all the way from there.

Where was a surgical mask when one needed it? The imam had preached that all Muslims were brothers, indeed, but one wasn't obligated to pick up whatever disease they might have.

He looked further: ah, an empty spot in the third row, perfect. Wahid rolled out his mat; the sharp scent of disinfectant rose from it. An old man was perched in front of him, kneeling. The call to prayer sounded out in the distance.

Wahid pressed a button.

God did not say anything about iPods to the Prophet. Wahid found that prayers worked better to a beat and time, namely that of Strauss' "Blue Danube." Its strains quietly filled his ears as he followed the man in front of him in the waltz before God.

And bend over, two three, and up, two three, and over, two three, and up, two three. *Allahu Akbar.* God is great.

And over, two three, and up, two three, and over, two three and up.

God is great. As great as the mighty waters of the Danube and the rushing of the blood through the veins which yields the glorious pulse.

And over, two three, and up, two three, and over, two three, and up. Repeat.

Done. The imam began to speak. Wahid turned up the volume slightly and drew his face into a mask of concentration.

The imam was immaculately groomed; he had a sharply trimmed black beard and wore a pair of tan tinted glasses. His black tunic fascinated Wahid. It was free of dust; there was not a speck of lint on it. It was a tunic worthy of complete admiration. Wahid wondered what lint brush he used, and did he use the same dry cleaner…?

He assumed the imam was speaking about the usual themes of brotherhood and maintaining morality. This was more appropriate for his brethren working in the entertainment industry. One of the disadvantages of being an accountant in Wahid's view was the sheer lack of opportunities for moral indiscretions. He thanked God for arranged marriages, as he had never had to work out a "pick up line" with such unpromising material.

At long last, the sermon ended. Wahid pressed the button on his iPod again and rose to his feet, bending over carefully to roll up his mat. An unwelcome hand clapped him on the back.

Ahmed again. "Have a good day, my brother. *Salaam!*"

"*Salaam*," Wahid replied.

Three quick breaths.

3

Brick Lane was not an ideal place for an accountant's office; Wahid had chosen it because it was close to much of his clientele. In the morning there was the scent of the previous night's cooking from the various restaurants. The stench of overcooked Balti Chicken hung in the air, the wrappers from multitudes of takeaway restaurants and old wet newspapers littered the street. The council's street cleaners were always late and never did a job that Wahid approved of; there was far too much muck, never enough glistening tidiness.

More breathing. Wahid put his hand to his heart; he could feel it beating through his *kurta*. That was more reassuring. Sometimes his pulse was elusive. A few times he had managed to convince himself that his heart had stopped, and indeed, that he was already dead.

This was better; this confirmed all was well.

"One day, I will die," he thought as he paced down Brick Lane, carefully navigating through the rubbish of the previous day's market: cardboard boxes, sheets of plastic, scattered clothes hangers. As he proceeded, the narrow lane grew narrower, the restaurants more densely packed together. He passed a man in a forest green parka and knit cap who was rapidly sweeping his doorstep.

"One day, I will die." He wondered how many other people - the man sweeping, the loud Australian tourists in his path who were drunk at 8:30 in the morning, the community parking officer writing a ticket to put on the windscreen of an old white Vauxhall Nova - were thinking about the fact that they were going to die too. Did it not occur to them, ever? Did they just carry on with life until one day it wasn't there?

How blissful that would be, Wahid thought. Ever since his mind could get around the concept of life being over, he had wondered when it would all end. Today? Possible. He could take a wrong step and end up under the tyres of a Vauxhall Nova. Or, more likely, through the windscreen, and he'd be cut into mincemeat by the broken glass.

4

He smacked his lips. He had told Rania not to prepare his food with too much ghee, but she didn't listen. He could still taste it lingering beyond the flavour of toothpaste and antiseptic mouthwash. He could have heart disease. His veins were filling up with fat right now, and he'd collapse, dead of a heart attack. He'd seen an American television programme in which the lead character, a dapper, middle-aged man with thinning blonde hair, was walking through the woods at night, and then cried out, clutching his heart.

Horrible. But if one had to depart, perhaps that was the way to go: collapsing in a heap amidst the leaves and the scent of autumn trees. Looking up through the branches of the trees, the sky might start to spin, picking up suction as the rotation took hold, dragging the soul up to heaven.

That was unlikely to happen in Brick Lane, however. Rather, he'd get to his computer, compile a spreadsheet and then die. His neighbours would say it was the shocking state of the figures that killed him. Wahid Shah, aged thirty-seven, dead of accountancy.

He got to the door of his office; it was heavy with ornate nineteenth century woodwork, painted bright green with gold numbers. While the restaurant next to his door was no prize (it had been shut several times by health inspectors), at least his door was clean. The mortise lock yielded to his key. He held his hand over his heart as he ascended. There were twelve steps: one, two, three, four, five…his heart was pounding harder now. Yes, all the fat in his veins was clogging his bloodstream, his heart felt like it was going to burst. Six, seven, eight, nine, ten, deep inhale, almost there. Eleven, twelve. Cough. His heart beat faster, a thin rivulet of sweat made its way down his back. Slow, slow, slow. The rate mellowed, and he opened his door.

His eyes focused on a framed poster hanging on the wall next to the window. It featured a chalet in a meadow filled with daisies and heather in bloom. A paved road of impeccable tidiness bisected the scene. A red flag with a white cross, crisp, with no stains or rips fluttered in the breeze. In straight red letters the poster said, "Visit Switzerland".

Switzerland. A land so precise, so pristine, that it required cleanliness inspectors to visit one's house before one was able to sell it. Wahid remembered when he moved into his Hackney home: Rania had found a colony of cockroaches living in the cellar.

Clean and hygienic, what a land of wonder it was. Staring at the poster calmed him. However, it was time to plunge into the numbers and discover who was bankrupt and who was solvent. This was as close as he dared to hold the power of God.

Click, click, click. The numbers correlated, added up, divided, subtracted across the vast territory of his spreadsheet. It was rather like a set of mechanical soldiers marching in a row, battling their way towards a result.

Ah ha, Basir the car mechanic had a tidy profit of fifty thousand pounds and forty-one pence last year. He could now afford to go on the *Hajj*.

Wahid clicked the mouse to load the next spreadsheet.

Hmmm, Ahmed was wealthier in dead animals than money. A loss of thirty thousand pounds. For shame, such profligacy; he had bought an additional butcher's shop in Bradford and it was sinking fast.

Wahid pursed his lips, breathed quick, quick, quick, and slow. The sunlight trickled into his office and gathered into a growing pool of brightness on the bare wood floor.

The radio softly let out six beeps. "This is BBC Radio 4, it's twelve o'clock."

The day was half gone already. He sighed.

What else did he have to do? He opened his green leather day planner that sat next to his keyboard. The pages were thick; its pleasant texture communicated through his fingertips.

Ah yes, at 2 o'clock he had a meeting with Basir the mechanic. Though the news was pleasant, it would require a trip to Highbury. That meant the Tube. Germs and filth.

Was it Highbury where the tunnels were winding because

victims of the Black Plague were buried in pits around the station? Was that Green Park? Or was it most stations in London?

Given what a dirty city it was, probably most, he reasoned. He would pray again. Then he would have lunch; a light vegetarian meal chased by purified spring water, he thought, would unclog the fat in his arteries. Following this, he would go expose himself to the plague, deliver the good news to Basir and return home to die, covered with pus-filled sores.

Two

God be praised. Wahid found a place to sit, even though the London Underground was deep in the throes of the lunchtime rush. He laid out a sanitised handkerchief on the seat before he sat down. He had a small plastic bag in his briefcase. Once he arrived, he would carefully insert the infected cloth into it, and then wipe his hands with antiseptic; he kept a small bottle in his briefcase for emergencies such as this. The briefcase also contained a bottle of toilet bleach and a flask of ammonia, just in case he needed to use a public lavatory or get anywhere near a dirty surface: one could never be too careful.

He switched on his iPod and pressed play on Brahms' "Ein Deutsches Requiem". He looked up at the advertisements above the windows across from him. Apparently he could have a new career in computing, save money on his car insurance, and be verbally disciplined by young, leather clad girls by ringing an 0900 number. Once he had read the advertisements and their fine print (who really paid fifty pence a minute to chat on the phone?), he read them again. It was far better to do that than to think about the train rocking and swaying, to listen to the sound of its metal wheels grinding against the rails and the occasional crackles of electricity, or worse, to look at his fellow passengers.

Today he sat opposite three executives from the City. One could unfailingly tell who they were because of their ties which were always made of high quality silk, but the colour and patterns were obviously designed to give everyone a headache. One glance at a City type with a pink and red elephant patterned tie was a form of aversion therapy.

As the train buckled and swayed between Oxford Circus and Warren Street he felt his stomach do a back flip. He could never share in his father's love of the Tube, God-forsaken, *haram* place it was.

Father was not unfamiliar with long, uncomfortable trips by train. After Independence and Partition, Father had ridden on top of a passenger train from New Delhi to Lahore, fleeing the persecution that a Muslim could have faced in a Hindu state.

It was a story that Father never tired of telling: hired by a British export firm as a bookkeeper, he was wrong-footed by the departure of the English. He put all his worldly possessions in an empty rice sack and went to the train station, pressing his way through masses of shouting, screaming, crying people. Women in tousled *saris* and men in *kurtas* stained with dirt and blood were pushing on each other with their families in tow, waving crumpled rupee notes in the air as they pushed towards the ticket counter.

Babies cried, children demanded to be fed, adults shouted and argued. Father's description of the scent of sweat, excrement and the odour of lentils and onions cooking always made Wahid's nose wrinkle in disgust.

Father was able to buy a Third Class ticket. Pushing on to the old steam train, he found there were neither seats nor room in which to stand. The carriages vibrated with the fear of the passengers; their desire to escape the impending slaughter was palpable. The only place to go was the roof; every square inch was occupied by the time the train coughed into life and lurched its way out of Delhi.

The Tube, in contrast, Father said, was a pleasure: even when it was crowded, it was never full to bursting with seething people. One was indoors in the cool and the dark, not burning with thirst as the sun scorched one to a cinder on an expanse of sizzling black metal. When one got out, it was never far to a place where one could sit, have tea, and reflect on the moments of silence.

Wahid knew that it had taken Father some time to distance himself from the past. Having escaped to Pakistan, Father had prospered through bookkeeping in Lahore to the point where he developed the money and connections to move to the little cream coloured Victorian terraced house in Edgware. Father thanked Allah every day for having been brought to such a paradise, where little dabs of heaven were to be found in Sainsburys, Debenhams and British Home Stores in chilled pots of strawberry yogurt and neatly folded piles of fresh cotton towels. Such wonders had made him careless. He was blissfully unaware of viruses, bacteria and eventually, cancer.

Denn alles Fleisch, es ist wie Gras, the iPod mournfully droned. Wahid had looked up the phrase: "For all flesh is as grass".

The Tube train shook. Wahid sighed. One of his strongest memories of Father involved a train like this one. It was late April, 1975. Father was dressed in pressed tan English trousers and a white cotton shirt, standing in the vestibule and riding the waves of motion as the Tube swung around violently on the Central Line.

"Come on, Wahid!" he said, encouraging him to stand up with a gesture. Wahid remembered the bright smile on his clean-shaven face, his hair slicked back with some English concoction, the scent of cologne overpowering the compartment.

"No, *Baba*, I am afraid," Wahid replied.

"Come on, you cannot be afraid all of your life!" he said. The train swayed, the lights briefly went out, and there was a sound of grinding metal. Father teetered to the point of collapse, but pulled himself back up, his grin even more radiant.

Wahid trembled. His mother, seated next to him, wore a floral silk scarf around her shoulders and a beige silk dress. A glance from her dark eyes warmed him as she took his small hand in hers. Her scent was of lilies and roses.

"It's all right," she said, gripping his hand tightly. His fears

11

eased; he did not have to stand.

Poor woman, when Father had gone into Allah's embrace, she had wasted away, spending her days singing to herself while sitting in the cream-coloured lounge of the cream-coloured house, rocking back and forth in a cream-coloured easy chair. She had held a black and white photograph of Father smiling, the wind whipping his hair back rakishly like a Fifties movie star. He had gone to eternal paradise, but he was her paradise. She followed as soon as she could.

Still, she had been correct. It was all right. He would protect himself by avoiding danger and staying close to the embrace of Allah. He did not drink, did not smoke, he had been true and faithful to his wife. His sole vice, if it was one, was classical music. He attended mosque, he had been diligent and honest to a point that earned him respect, expressions of which he swatted away like a fly, lest it bring the sin of pride into his heart. Surely Allah, the Merciful, the Compassionate, would shield him from all the horrors of the world, from germs, to cancer, to running for one's life and hearing the wailing of a displaced people in his dreams till the day he died. *Denn alles Fleisch, es ist wie Gras.*

"Next station is Highbury and Islington," the driver said over the intercom.

God be praised.

Three

Holloway Road was nearly as disgusting as Brick Lane. Worse, traffic roared by without any regard to pedestrians. As he walked to Basir's garage, Wahid saw a small elderly woman with an aluminium walking frame position herself hopefully on the kerb across from Waitrose. Her porcelain white hair was curled tightly, she wore thick glasses and a heavy bright purple overcoat. She looked right, and then finding nothing promising, looked left.

White Ford Transit vans, the scourge of humanity, blasted by and honked at her each time she dared attempt a step. One of the drivers, a young, blonde, pockmarked man smoking a cigarette, leaned out the window to shout "Wanker!" at her as he passed.

As Wahid passed her, he detected a scent of liniment and lavender. He thought about stopping and helping her halt the traffic. He took a step to approach her; she saw him. Her hopeful demeanour soured; her eyes scanned him up and down.

Of course. This was one of the "Old English", as Father would have called her. Her age, her scent, her manner of dress suggested she had been alive for the War and liked the country better when the only takeaway was fish and chips, all the pubs served only warm dark beer and the BBC issued weather reports through the hiss of the wireless that were only useful to a merchant marine that no longer existed.

Probably, given half a chance, the old woman would shout "Paki" at him or claim he was assaulting her if he tried to help any further. Best to leave it alone. Fortunately, the driver of a

13

large, silver Land Rover spotted her and pulled up to a halt. He reached out an arm and waved her on. She smiled, nodded, and proceeded slowly. At least there was only one lane remaining for her to worry about.

Basir's garage was at the intersection of Tufnell Park Road and Holloway Road. "Crescent Moon Motors", it was called; it was a corrugated iron garage painted a dark green, with a large white crescent moon and star, the symbols of Pakistan, painted across its large door. A large yellow sign hung above the door informed the visitor in clear lettering, "All Repairs Undertaken and Guaranteed, Specialist in Ford, Vauxhall and Maserati (the presence of the last make was a symptom of Basir's sense of humour), MOTs Done Within An Hour". The scent of oil and petrol permeated the air along with the sounds of machinery grinding and drilling against metal.

"Wahid!" a voice said.

He turned and there was Basir, coming around from the back of the garage, wiping his hands with an oily rag. A tall, skinny fellow, he had a bright white smile that was too wide for his clean-shaven face. His blue coveralls and forehead were stained with black axle grease.

"Basir." Wahid said.

Basir reached out his hand to shake his. Wahid reluctantly shook it. Hopefully the petrochemicals on Basir's hands had killed any germs.

"Come in."

Basir ushered him into the garage; inside, his apprentice, a dark-skinned teenage boy, also in dark blue coveralls, was working on a burgundy red Ford Escort. The front end was a smashed mass of glass and metal; personally, Wahid would have written it off and claimed it as an expense. However, one of the reasons why Basir had been doing well was his remarkable ability to make something out of nothing.

"My wife's car," Basir explained. "She got lost on the way to Bradford and decided to correct her mistake by taking a detour through a lamppost."

14

"Ah."

They entered a small office, which overlooked the rest of the garage through a pair of dirty windows. A coffee maker, its "On" light glowing orange, sat in a corner. Wahid grimaced as Basir offered him a seat on a dusty grey plastic chair.

Three quick breaths. Wahid hesitantly sat.

Basir sat behind his desk, which was covered with car magazines and manuals. It was a tired piece of Seventies office furniture; an old beige personal computer rested on a corner. Pictures of family were pinned to a corkboard on the wall behind Basir's head; most were of Basir and his wife and children smiling broadly in various scenes, some in restaurants, others at home, some outside. The most prominent photo featured Basir alone, holding a rifle in the wilderness. Wahid recalled the story behind it: Basir had been on a hunting trip in Pakistan, unsuccessfully trying to shoot some supper. Still, the sky in the photo was a perfect turquoise, which contrasted with the dry brown earth.

"Coffee?" Basir offered.

"No, thank you."

"Thank you for coming today."

Wahid shrugged. "It is my work."

"So, my friend, how am I doing?"

Wahid opened his briefcase and pulled out a pristine manila folder; he delicately placed it on Basir's desk. Basir picked it up, and to Wahid's annoyance, immediately began to cover it in greasy fingerprints.

"You can afford to go on the *Hajj*," Wahid said.

The smile became almost blinding. "Wonderful."

"You can also afford to open an additional garage."

The smile dimmed. "I don't think so."

Surprising. "I thought you wanted to open a similar garage near Bethnal Green?"

"Actually, my wife and I are planning to move back to Pakistan. My brother just wrote an e-mail to me this morning: he has offered us a place to stay in Karachi while Dina and I get

15

settled."

"But…why? You are doing well…healthy profits, a big house in Tottenham…didn't you buy that satellite package so you could watch all of the cricket in High Definition?"

Basir smirked. "Don't you pay attention to the world around you?"

"I try not to," Wahid admitted.

"I could tolerate being called names from time to time…God knows, the English do it to each other. But now…it's worse."

"Oh."

"They hate us… more than before. Some of us hate them just as much in return." Basir's smile faded completely. "I don't want to be here…I don't want my son to grow up with this. I just want to go home."

Wahid swallowed. Politics was not something he thought much about. Indeed, he could not remember the last time he bothered to vote; he assumed his constituency had been Labour since the beginning of the world. An interesting thought that, "And Allah said let there be light…and gave Hackney's seat to Labour."

Politics was irrelevant because it mostly dealt with far away danger. How could one even give a moment's thought to that when even more peril was always close at hand? Would Tony Blair get cancer for him? Would Jack Straw disinfect his house? Would John Prescott eat his wife's cooking? Well, maybe…

Basir broke his reverie. "You don't see," he said.

"No…I don't."

The smile flashed again. "My good friend Wahid, may God always keep you as you are."

"Thank you," Wahid replied. He stifled the urge to shrug.

Four

To get back to Highbury and Islington station, all Wahid had to do was turn right off Tufnell Park Road and walk in the direction of the London Metropolitan University tower block.

He tried not to strain his neck to look up at it. He had gone there to learn his trade when it was the University of North London. Some Marketing graduate, he was sure, could explain why the name had to change when nothing was accomplished by it changing.

Beyond the University, on the opposite side of the road, were the grounds of St. Mary Magdalene's Church. It was a strange bit of green in the middle of such a built up area. The church itself was made of alabaster stone, the gardens surrounding it were well trimmed and filled with brightly coloured irises and pansies which seemed incongruous with the grey March weather; the garden was protected by a black iron fence. Beyond St. Mary Magdalene's was the Georgian restaurant, which was followed by Barlow and Company's Surgical Goods shop.

The shop was the best part of the journey. The counters inside were a taste of Switzerland: they were a sterile, dazzling white. The cabinets displaying the various goods from alcohol swabs to scalpels were made of a clean grey metal that gleamed whenever a touch of sunlight hit them. He had never stepped inside, lest he was disappointed by some stray mark or ball of lint. The closest he dared go was right by the entrance. One day, someone had come out; the intoxicating scent of lemon and

17

disinfectant followed the departing customer. It was difficult to believe it was of this earth.

He smiled as he glanced in the window; this day, a grey-haired man in a black suit was gesticulating forcefully to a thin young man who stood behind the counter dressed in what appeared to be a white lab coat. The younger man listened, nodded and then disappeared into the back of the shop. He returned, clutching a brown cardboard box. He opened it and lifted out a container of disposable surgical masks. The grey-haired man smiled, nodded; he paid the young man. He stepped out of the shop, the door swinging open so smoothly with no squeaks or rattles, the scent of lemon following him.

This was impossible to resist; Wahid stepped inside and approached the counter. The young man looked at him quizzically.

"Can I help you?" he asked. The look in his grey eyes was one of mild surprise.

"Yes," Wahid said, "a box of surgical masks, like that other gentleman."

"Are you a surgeon?"

"No," he said, struggling, "just I am around *people*."

The young man brightened. "Ah yes, the flu going around?"

Relief. "Yes." Then, panic: the flu?

"Just one moment."

The young man again departed for a few moments and returned with yet another cardboard box. Wahid wished he had his iPod on to listen to something triumphant as it was opened.

"Here you are." The young man said, holding out the box. It contained fifty disposable surgical masks; the box had "sterile" printed on it in bright red letters.

Beautiful. "It's…good."

"That will be nineteen pounds fifty pence, please."

Wahid pulled out his old black leather wallet and handed over a twenty pound note. The young man rang the register and held out three coins.

Wahid hesitated. How many hands had touched that

18

money? It had probably come from doctors and was covered in the germs of their patients. Who knew what pestilence was in it.

"Fifty pence change," the young man prompted.

Wahid sighed and reached out his hand. "Thank *you*," he replied.

Wahid could not stop toying with the box. He pulled it out of the bag, raised it to his nostrils and could detect the faint scent of antiseptic. Oh how tempting it was to put on one now.

A mother passed by him on the street, just outside a small florist shop. She had her little girl in tow: she was dressed in a blue school uniform, her blonde hair done up in pigtails. The little girl sneezed.

Ah ha, there it is. Time to put on a mask.

"No, no," he chided himself. It was just one little girl in the open air. Far better to wait for a real opportunity to put one on, these were far too precious to waste. He replaced the box in his bag, letting it swing like a pendulum as he continued his journey.

He arrived at the station. In front of its entrance was a small stand: two men were seated in folding metal chairs behind a card table; Socialist Worker posters were taped to the front. One placard called President Bush a war criminal and highlighted the President's face with a rather ominous glow. The other featured a smiling Tony Blair; it called him a liar. One of the old comrades, whose weathered face was covered in brown and grey stubble, nodded at him, smiled and offered him a newspaper. "Read the truth about the war?" he offered.

Wahid could not help but notice his jacket – it was faded blue and thoroughly spotted with anonymous white stains. He wrinkled his face in disgust. The gentleman might think he was on Wahid's side, but Wahid had little incentive to be on his. He passed on quickly; the scent of stale beer assailed him.

Fortunately, he did not have to wait long in the nether world of Highbury and Islington station, which was not the pride of the Victoria Line. Advertisement posters peeled off the walls as soon as they were put up. The lights were fluorescent and dim, a

19

combination that made the waiting passengers listless. The one exception in the dreary crowd of men in Marks and Spencer suits and women with pushchairs was a young lady of West Indian origin. She was dressed in an outfit of tight bright pink Lycra and sat on a bench enthusiastically eating a hamburger. The stench of its sauce and the mysterious meat whose true flavour it was masking made Wahid sick to his stomach.

At last, the sound of a train rumbled in the distance. He looked down the tunnel: a set of headlights came into view and an old train clattered up to the platform. Again, he was lucky and found a seat; carefully, he pulled out another cloth from his briefcase and set it down before sitting down. The bottles of antiseptic, bleach and ammonia rattled slightly as he shut the case.

"The next station is King's Cross St. Pancras," the announcer said.

Wahid noted that Victoria Line trains were generally empty until they reached Kings Cross station, then they were crammed full of people, then empty again beyond Victoria. It was always the clot in the middle that worried him.

At King's Cross, a group of schoolchildren dressed in grey jackets and red sweaters got on. They were coughing, sneezing and rubbing runny noses on sleeves.

At Warren Street, two Swedish teenage backpackers boarded the train. Their packs were emblazoned with large patches indicating their nationality. They also looked as if they hadn't seen the inside of a shower in six months. Their fingernails had encrusted dirt underneath.

They lazed their way into the seats across from Wahid. Their scent wafted over; they reeked of old tobacco. Worse, they punctuated their odd, lilting language with the occasional cough and sputter.

At Oxford Circus, a bustling group of shoppers got on carrying bags marked from HMV, Monsoon and Benetton. The accents Wahid heard were varied: the West Country,

Birmingham, Scotland. One couple dressed in jeans and leather jackets were definitely American; hmm, the way the woman said "Twenty" like it was "twenny", she was from New York, perhaps? They were laughing, talking, and yes, sometimes coughing.

"The flu," Wahid thought.

The young man in the surgical goods store had warned him it was here. Invisible germs were flying around and bouncing off the walls with every cough and splutter. He could almost see them; in his mind's eye they were like miniature trolls, grinning maliciously as they leapt from person to person and place to place, ricocheting endlessly off every surface as if their feet were made of rubber.

Only God knew what bacteria and viruses lurked under the skin of the Swedes, hid in the mouths of the children, and had been brought from elsewhere by the tourists. Malaria, beri beri, typhus, smallpox?

Quick, quick, quick, then slow. In spite of the breathing exercise, his heart beat even faster. He checked his pulse on both his wrist and his chest. The mass of people seemed to swell within the compressed space, as the train raced through the dark tunnels and ground and squeaked and bumped and clattered. To be sure, the gyration would make the germs bounce more violently. They would come after him next.

No, no, now was the time for the mask. The mask, or he would certainly die.

He grabbed the box and popped it open. He tore desperately at one of the plastic envelopes inside. He pulled out a mask and yanked it over his face, breathed heavily into the sterile paper and sucked down its clean scent. He needed that as much as the oxygen.

His breathing began to relax. Quick, quick, quick, and slow. The pulse decreased. He was safe. He held his briefcase to him; it was comforting. Relief.

"Oi, you!"

Wahid looked. Standing behind the glass next to his seat

21

was the West Indian lady in bright pink Lycra. She had finished her meal: her stomach and breasts were bursting out of her insufficient synthetic restraints. Her brown eyes were wide.

"You!" she repeated.

The other passengers stopped chattering; their eyes turned to him: the shoppers, the Americans, the schoolchildren, the Swedes all hit him with a suspicious gaze. They looked at his mask, his briefcase, his clothing, and his face.

"Me?" Wahid gasped.

"What are you doing?"

Doing? "Nothing!"

"The hell you are!" she said, her eyes flashing.

"Al Qaeda!" the female New Yorker shouted.

Wahid clutched his briefcase like a shield. What?

"Everyone down!" her husband yelled. "He's got a bomb!"

People screamed. The West Indian woman reached the side of the train and yanked down on the Emergency Stop. Instantly, the train began to grind to a halt with a dying screech. The passengers crashed into each other and the sides of the train. Wahid shut his eyes and clutched his briefcase tightly. He heard women crying out, metal grinding.

Strong arms grabbed him. His briefcase was forced out of his hands.

"Take this, you fucking terrorist bastard," a male voice said.

There was a sharp inhale from one of them. Wahid opened his eyes for a moment: all he saw was a clenched fist.

Then, there was shock.

Pain.

Silence.

Five

The world was covered in smoke. Wahid could not smell it nor find the fire where it came from, but everything he saw was enveloped in a shroud of swirling grey.

A few images passed through the murky veil; he saw the face of a man, young, blonde, covered in pimples. He looked concerned and shone a bright light into his eyes.

"Multiple fractures, concussion, broken jaw," the man said. "Get him out of here."

The smoke rose again. Wahid heard the distant sound of a siren; it was much like what Rania and he would hear at night in their Hackney home. The police were always busy trying to clear away the remnants of crime on Clapton Road.

Rania. Was she lost somewhere in this thick, blinding mist? Would he awake to find he was in bed at home? Perhaps it was night and the orange glow of the streetlamps was trickling in through a gap in the blinds. He would get up, descend to the kitchen, make some mint tea and settle his stomach in the darkness.

Perhaps he would awake and find it was morning. Rania would be lying beside him. He would see her dark hair, unbound from her headscarf, spread out on the white pillowcase like long flowing ropes of silk, the threads trailing back from the edges of the pillow to her perfectly oval face. Her eyes would be shut, her full lips set in an "o" as breath slowly passed in and out.

Best not to look. If he looked, then she would more than likely awake, and if she awoke, she would remember what she recalled every morning, that she wanted to have a baby. She

23

would tell him that neither of them were getting any younger and that all her friends had children.

"Do you not want a fine strong son?" she would ask.

Perhaps. There was a chance that a boy would be like Father.

But that was unlikely.

Nevertheless, Rania would reach out to him. She would shed her clothes in the process, wriggling out of her nightdress like a butterfly emerging from a chrysalis. This was pleasant; Wahid liked the curves of her body, even the slight roll that had emerged around her waist in recent years. He enjoyed tracing his finger along the smooth perfection of her skin. He liked the way that her eyes glittered clearly like reflections of the sun on still waters. He liked how she was always so well scrubbed and smelled of fresh soap and vanilla.

Sometimes he would yield to her, sometimes not. The act was not unpleasant, just messy. There was kissing, moving of bodies, sweating, crying out, then secretions.

A good word. Such untidiness was best kept "secret".

Voices penetrated the mist. "Oi, Mark…I think he's smiling."

"Poor sod."

The smoke faded. Lights were passing above his head. So he was dead at last. He was flat on his back and he was moving fast. Allah had reached out the tip of His finger and lifted Wahid onto it like a single teardrop. Now the cosmic hand was drawing back into paradise. The stars were swirling around his head and flowing fast above him in their celestial orbits. A miracle. Allah be praised. *Allahu Akbar.*

"He's coming around," a voice said.

Wahid turned his head slightly. The chariot to the heavens had attendants. The one who had spoken was a dark-skinned man dressed in blue scrubs. He had a stethoscope around his neck.

"Don't try to talk, Mr. Shah," the man warned, "we're taking you into surgery."

24

"Yes, surgery," Wahid thought. "Purge me of all that is impure within me. Make me clean. I am ready."

The chariot stopped.

"Anaesthesia!" the man shouted.

The smoke consumed him.

Beep beep beep. The sound was a thin line of cord leading out of the smoke. His consciousness reached for it and began to pull. Sensations came to him.

Pain.

Fatigue.

He felt as if he had been swept up by the wind and dropped from a great height.

There was warm sensation coming from his right hand. He deciphered it: another hand was holding his. He ran his thumb over the knuckles, then down over a ring. The ring had delicate scrollwork on it and a large stone surrounded by a dozen smaller stones.

"Rania?" he asked softly. The word did not come out as he had expected; it sounded as if someone had stuffed a gourd in his mouth.

"Shhhhh," she said, "don't speak, darling. Can you open your eyes?"

The desire to keep his eyes shut was overwhelming. The lids were too leaden to respond to his brain's commands. He concentrated on his left eye; the lid fluttered open.

The smoke had been replaced by a blur. There was a dark shadow. It moved closer. Death?

No, surely death did not have such a rounded face. Nor did it have beautiful eyes.

"Rania?" he repeated.

Her voice was soft, low, and melodious. "Yes."

"What...?"

"Do not speak. Your jaw is broken."

Broken? Ah yes. The train. The germs. The West Indian woman. The fist.

"You also have a broken leg and several bruised ribs," Rania continued.

His eye drifted from her to the door. There was another dark figure, standing straight and as upright as a minaret pointed at the vault of heaven.

Wahid tried to point. "What…?"

"Shhhhh," Rania said, "don't worry about it now. Sleep."

He complied.

The bed was a rest stop in the universe. Time accelerated, the skies moved overhead, the earth moved, but Wahid's bed remained in a fixed position. Nurses came and asked him to relieve himself into bedpans. Unclean, untidy, but he was sitting on the linchpin of the cosmos and he had to remain on this delicate perch. He remembered being a boy in school, wearing a bright green blazer and hunched over a desk, reading an ancient Greek myth about a man who bore the weight of the world upon his shoulders. To a boy with twice-daily washed hair and pimples on his nose it seemed ridiculous. But now, Wahid had some idea how the Greek felt; the man was a fixed point while the world turned, now it was as if Wahid was riding on his shoulders.

Allah had put him here as a challenge; yes, that had to be it. Whenever the impression faded, and the bed seemed to be moving back into time's natural flow, some nurse would come to his bedside and fuss with his IV, and the swirling motion around him would return like waves crashing into the shore.

He heard things. As they came from outside this crow's nest of Creation, he let them pass; however, he could not help but eavesdrop.

A tinny sound, from a distant television: "Police are continuing to investigate a suspected terrorist plot to release chlorine gas on the London Underground. One of the accused was seized on a train by passengers and is now in hospital with severe injuries. Police Commissioner Sir Ian Blair had no comment to make at this time…"

Voices, close up: "I tell you, Inspector, he is in no position to be questioned. His jaw was shattered."

"Very well. But we want to speak to him as soon as possible."

Rania: "Feeling better today, my love? Basir sent you a fruit basket."

He had difficulty with focus. The movements of the planet were a tumultuous rumble and pitiless like the drumbeat of war. Sometimes its pounding was as loud as thunder, sometimes quiet like his heartbeat or the beep beep beep of the machines surrounding this tiny oasis in time and space.

He would not be moved. He had to hang on.

"Mr. Shah."

The voice was male, upper-class English, insistent.

Rania's voice joined in. "Darling, wake up."

"Mr. Shah," the voice repeated.

Wahid opened his eyes. The world was in sharp focus. It had stopped moving around him; or rather, the bed had landed in a modern hospital room. Sunshine was streaming through the window. He had fallen back into the ebb and flow of the world; events could once more come crashing in.

There, at the side of his bed, was Rania, her eyes gazing at him intently. At its foot was the man who was beside his chariot to the heavens; he was writing on a clipboard. Next to him stood a tall figure, a middle-aged man in a black suit and white shirt with a red tie.

Behind him stood a policeman in a blue sweater; he had a radio clipped to his shoulder.

"Good morning, Mr. Shah," the man in the suit said.

"What...?" Wahid began to say. Pain silenced him.

"Be careful, Mr. Shah," the man with the clipboard said, "your jaw isn't healed up yet."

Wahid tried to nod but his head fell back onto the pillow.

"He's quite weak, Inspector," the man with the clipboard stated.

"So I surmised, Doctor," the Inspector said.

27

The Inspector bent closer to Wahid. His blue eyes glittered. He needed a shave. He smelled of a recent cup of cheap tea, probably obtained from a vending a machine in the hospital lobby and consumed in a hurry. "Do you understand me, Mr. Shah?"

Wahid gave a slight nod.

"You are under arrest on suspicion of participation in a terrorist conspiracy."

What?

"Do you understand?"

Wahid tried to shrug to indicate his confusion.

"He has no idea what you're talking about, Inspector," Rania pleaded.

"Please be quiet, Mrs. Shah," the Inspector said. "Mr. Shah, we found ammonia and bleach in your briefcase. We know as well as you do that combining those makes chlorine gas."

What?

"You are going to be placed under guard while you are here at the hospital. Do you understand?"

Wahid nodded.

"Good."

The Inspector and the policeman left the room.

Rania held his hand. He tried to choke back a sob.

"I'll get you something for the pain," the Doctor said.

"It's all right," Rania said softly.

Hot tears flowed down his cheeks.

Six

The art of walking had to be relearned. Wahid was unsteady at first; Rania positioned herself by his bed, her arms wrapped around him in case he fell. A good idea: the burly male nurse who was supposed to be helping her stood by the door and looked like he would be indifferent if Wahid jumped out the window.

Wahid shuffled on his backside to the edge of the bed. Slowly, delicately, he swung out his right leg, which was in a cast, down to the floor. Underneath the cast, the leg had begun to itch; Wahid had asked the Doctor if this was a sign of infection.

"No," he had replied, "it is a sign of healing."

Hmmm.

Just as carefully as the first, Wahid swung his other foot down to the floor. The sting of the cold linoleum, the sound of clicking cartilage, the false lemon scent of cheap disinfectant, these were his first impressions as he stepped back into the world.

"I am under arrest," he thought. He could not bring himself to say it aloud, partially because it still hurt to speak.

Rania gave him his metal crutches. With one effort he hoisted himself up. A sharp pain shot through both legs.

Under arrest! It was preposterous. He had never broken the law. Yet, he could see the dark outline of a policeman through the glass portal in the door of his room.

Perhaps it was not as bad as it appeared; it may have been merely a misunderstanding. Outside the confines of the hospital, surely forces of righteousness and justice would be at work. The

Inspector would return, his pale blue eyes heavy with remorse, and say, "So sorry, Mr. Shah, it's all been a ghastly mistake."

"Try to focus," Wahid thought. He lifted his left leg; he looked down and noted that the purplish black bruises there were rapidly fading into a less ominous yellow. He made a shuffling step, dragging his broken limb behind him. There was the pain of impact as his heel moved slightly up, then down. It felt like someone had injected boiling water into his veins.

"You're doing well," Rania encouraged.

"Think about something else," he told himself. According to Rania, the name of the Inspector was Fredrick Willows. She brought articles from the *Guardian* for him to read; they said that the Inspector was educated at Eton and Cambridge. He was the son of Cecil Willows, the Duke of Crawley; he should have gone to the House of Lords. However, he had been diverted from a promising career as an idle geriatric by changes to the House of Lords which discriminated against hereditary peers. He had decided to spend his time instead pursuing an interest in criminology. His passion for the subject, unfortunately, was not matched by his aptitude: he had been responsible for five false accusations in the past five years.

Yes, surely the avatars of justice would see to it that such a stellar record of incompetence would not continue. Rania had hired a solicitor, some fellow named Hassan. It would all be sorted out.

Quick, quick, quick, then slow.

"Take another step," Rania said.

Wahid tried another shuffle. He fixed his eyes on a sink in the far corner; there was a pink bottle of antiseptic liquid soap on a shelf above it. He pushed himself towards it.

The leg burned.

"Very good," Rania commented.

"Don't tire yourself too much," the nurse advised.

Righteousness, mercy, justice, they were in the world; Allah had told the Prophet that contrary to what people believed, he was not uninterested nor supine in the face of the suffering of

His people.

Unless of course, this was a test.

Once more. He shuffled again, the crutches clanking with the heaviness of the step. He could visualise the bone in his thigh: it was white, cracked, and as brittle as old porcelain. It would shatter into a dozen pieces if he moved further; he gasped.

"Please," Rania said.

The nurse caught him in his arms and put him back into bed. Wahid lay flat on his back and caught his breath: quick, quick, slow, slow.

Rania took Wahid's hand into hers and caressed it.

"Rest."

It took two weeks for the short, shuffling gait to evolve into a walk across the room. Wahid celebrated the triumph of his exertions by washing his hands; the soap by the sink, to his delight, had no particular fragrance except that of pure cleanliness.

His jaw slowly healed; bit by bit, he began to converse with Rania and the doctors. The latter development was particularly critical; his GP, Dr. Al Haq, had always prevented him from going to hospital. At last, he could have as many checkups and consult as many specialists as he liked.

Disappointment followed disappointment. No, his blood pressure was fine. No, his heart was fine. No, his cholesterol was fine. His veins were not filling up to bursting. The headache he had a week before he was assaulted was not due to an impending aneurysm. By every last single measure, apart from his injuries, he was healthy.

It cannot be, Wahid reasoned. He merely needed a second opinion. He would get it once this silly business of arrest was behind him. Then he would discover truly what a sick man he was. Still, even if he was healthy now he was probably running a risk of catching some hospital-infesting superbug which would likely finish him off.

Rania forbade Wahid to watch the news. She tried,

31

unsuccessfully, to have the television removed from his room: it was positioned high in a corner and bolted to the wall. The porters could not be bothered to unscrew it. Instead, she stole the remote control, sliding it deftly off the night table and into her handbag.

"You don't need to worry," she said softly.

Wahid raised an eyebrow.

After she had left for the day, he pressed a button to call for a nurse. A few moments later a slim, red-haired young woman entered. Her uniform was starched white and her face was covered in freckles.

"Do you need something, sir?" she asked in a broad Australian accent. Her eyes scanned him up and down and up again.

"Yes, please," Wahid said. "I can't seem to find the remote, and I'd like to watch the Ten O'Clock News."

She exhaled. "Certainly."

She reached up and pressed the on switch. It began to hum as the picture tube warmed up.

"Will there be anything else?"

"Very polite, this hospital," Wahid thought. "No, no thank you," he said.

She left.

The picture came into focus, and a grim-faced female newsreader appeared. Wahid noticed that her pencil-thin eyebrows rose as she inhaled.

"Tonight, on the News at Ten…" the newsreader said, "London Underground poison gas attack; new evidence of a conspiracy, police say. Another suspect is under arrest."

Wahid's ears perked up.

A clip of a standard-issue blonde Australian pop star dancing and singing appeared; fortunately, the music had been excised. "Sadie, the Queen of Pop, retires; she announced she is going to become a Buddhist nun," the newsreader said.

"Well that's unexpected," Wahid mused.

An image of Team Pakistan practicing at Lords followed.

"…and in cricket, Pakistan was defeated by Isle of Man in the World Cup."

"I must be dreaming," Wahid thought, "or I'm living in Basir's nightmare."

The image switched back to the newsreader.

"Good evening. Scotland Yard announced the arrest today of one Abdullah Basir, a mechanic living in North London…"

Wahid gasped.

"…this follows the arrest of Wahid Shah, a Brick Lane accountant, who was captured…"

Captured?

"…by passengers on a Victoria Line train, who feared he was part of an impending terrorist attack. Inspector Fredrick Willows, who is investigating the case, had this to say…"

The image cut to a press conference. Willows was standing in front of a blue background that bore the symbol of the Metropolitan Police. Flashbulbs were popping as he spoke. He gesticulated to the press to indicate they should settle down. The flashes receded.

"We are at an early stage of our investigation," Willows said. "We suspect that we have foiled a terrorist plot to bring fear and death to the people of London. We will not rest until justice has been served."

The broadcast cut to a picture of a smiling Basir seated around a table with his family: his wife's and children's faces were digitally blurred. "Abdullah Basir has been described by his friends and associates as a mechanical genius, able to build or fix anything. He also has a First in Engineering from Imperial College. The police say his vast knowledge could have been turned to sinister purposes. Suspicion of Mr. Basir has been heightened after police found evidence that he had been preparing a hasty move back to Pakistan."

The image returned to that of the newsreader.

"The families of the accused have objected to police tactics, saying that the arrests have been made based on hearsay and circumstantial evidence. Neither Mr. Basir nor Mr. Shah, they

33

point out, have a criminal record. Nevertheless, the investigation continues."

"Sir?" The red-haired nurse's question broke his momentary paralysis.

Wahid looked down; his thumb was pressing hard on the call button.

"I'm sorry," he said. "Can you please switch off the television?"

"No worries. Just remember next time, you only have to press the call button once."

Seven

"Is he well enough, Doctor?" Willows asked.

The Doctor finished writing and flipped the metal lid of his clipboard shut.

"Yes, I'm afraid he is," the Doctor replied.

Wahid tried to be impassive as he watched the discussion. He was dressed in his *kurta,* cotton trousers and cap, and seated in a soft chair. His broken leg, which was still in a cast, was elevated and resting on an ottoman. Rania stood beside him, holding his hand. On his other side stood Hassan, the solicitor that Rania had hired. He was distressingly young; he could not yet grow a full beard or moustache, and had to be satisfied with thin wisps of hair covering his chin and upper lip. At least he had a tidy haircut; also, his suit, shirt and tie were very clean, and all three buttons of his jacket were done up correctly.

"Good," Willows said. "Mr. Shah, you'll be coming with us then….if that's all right with you, Mr. Hassan?"

Hassan nodded. He had explained that "today was not the day to fight".

With a flip of his fingers, Willows indicated to Wahid, *get up*.

Leave the hospital? So long as he was sick or hurt, Willows could not hurt him. Yes, he could go on the news night after night and make ridiculous statement after ridiculous statement about evidence which he could not possibly possess. The hospital however, kept Willows just outside his door.

Now he was well. The Doctor said "afraid so" when he was asked. Afraid. What would Father say, would he be afraid?

No, Father would have smiled at Willows. He would have looked him straight in the eye and said, "Let's go." The subsequent march to freedom would have been short.

Wahid looked up at Rania. Tears glistened in her brown eyes, like flecks of silver in an ebony sea. He turned to Hassan. His dark eyes were downcast; he nodded.

"I'm coming," he said quietly.

With some effort, he hoisted himself onto his crutches. He could move without pain, but walking was still difficult, as if his limbs were moving through honey rather than air. Given these infirmities, Willows had assured him that he would be going directly to a prison hospital.

"Why leave this one?" Wahid wondered.

Perhaps it was because Willows thought he might escape.

Wahid winced as he got to his feet. No, surely the Inspector was not *that* stupid.

Perhaps Willows was fastidious to an unnatural extreme.

Or perhaps he wanted Wahid to *appear* to be arrested.

The Doctor opened the door leading into the hallway. Wahid saw two tall policemen, dressed in identical dark blue sweaters. They positioned themselves on either side of him as he hobbled out. Hassan and Rania followed.

The hall: it had been the same one he had wheeled down on the day he was brought in. Perhaps it would have been more merciful if he had died then. Where had Allah been that day? Where was He now?

"Keep going," one of the policemen said gruffly.

He willed his crutches to press on; they clattered. The boiling sensation bubbled up his tendons again.

They passed a nurse's station; the red-haired Australian was working today. She gave him a quick glance and then turned back to talk excitedly to a West Indian colleague. They were discussing Queen of Pop's conversion to Buddhism and her newly shaven head. One of the policemen chuckled.

They passed patients in various states of distress: an old man in a wheelchair with a tube in his nose, a younger man, thin,

36

gaunt, losing his hair, rolling an IV on a metal frame towards the bathroom, a young girl in a nightgown, clutching a teddy bear. All looked at him. He could not avert his eyes.

The doors leading out of the hospital loomed ahead. The sunlight streaming through the glass was so bright that what lay beyond was obscured.

Quick, quick, quick. Slow.

The doors opened with a creak.

As he stepped out, Wahid was assailed by a memory. He was twelve. He had just finished school for the day and had stepped out into a cold January afternoon. His scarf was tied tightly and his coat was buttoned up to the neck, as his mother had advised.

The skies above were grey, heavy and damp. Wahid decided he would run to the bike shed and pedal home as fast as he could before their threat was fulfilled. He jumped down the stairs, one, two, three, and dashed to the red and rust-stained enclosure. It was open; there was no door. It was dark inside and the scent of earth and oil was overwhelming. Some miscreant had sprayed on its interior his wish that others would go forth and multiply.

As soon as Wahid stepped inside, it began. First, a couple of drops bounced off the tin roof, then more, then a flood. The rain sounded like a torrent of marbles was pounding its flimsy roof. Wahid crouched down; he wanted to leave but not get wet.

"Please God," he said, "let it stop."

The storm replied by getting worse. The drops were trying to drill through the roof, pounding the metal till it gave in. Bang bang bang.

"Please, God," he said, "I will be good, let it stop!"

The rain was relentless. Wahid could see his fellow students still inside the school. Some laughed and pointed, others just watched, looking at him with some pity. One boy who was convulsed with mirth pulled a camera out of his bag and snapped a picture of him. The flash made him wince. Lightning struck, followed by thunder. He crouched lower.

"God...." he pleaded.

The rain did not reply.

The cameras at the hospital steps fired at him like well-trained artillery. Snap snap snap. Click click click. The reporters shouted, "Mr. Shah! Mr. Shah! Mr. Shah!"

He swallowed.

"Move along," one of the policemen told him. He grabbed Wahid by the elbow and pushed him a step forward towards their goal: beyond the gaggle of faces, cameras, lights and microphones was a van sitting next to the kerb.

"That way," the policeman urged.

Wahid struggled towards it. His heart pounded.

The torrent was relentless. "Mr. Shah! Mr. Shah! What do you have to say about the accusations against you?"

Hassan, from behind him. "Mr. Shah has no statement to make at this time."

"What is his reaction to the arrest of Abdullah Basir?"

Hassan again. "He is certain that the accusations against Mr. Basir will be proven as false as those against him."

Wahid took another painful step. Rania caressed his hand in hers over the handle of his crutch.

"Mrs. Shah! Mrs. Shah! What do you have to say about all this?"

Wahid looked at his wife. She ducked her head, trying to avoid the glance of the multiple, glassy, lidless eyes that stared at her.

"Mrs. Shah! No statement?"

"No..." she said softly. Her voice quivered.

The back of the van was opened; inside it was white, with two hard metal benches. One of the policemen leapt into it. He turned and reached his hand down to Wahid.

"Come on," he said.

Wahid staggered towards the entrance. The torrent remained focused on his back.

Click click click. "Mr. Shah! Mr. Shah! Mr. Shah!" The

beep of mobile phones was going off, playing various cheap melodies that added up to a symphony of mindless noise.

A reporter shouted, "There's Inspector Willows!"

"Come on," the policeman repeated.

Wahid reached up, in the process letting one of his crutches dangle around his wrist. The policeman grabbed Wahid by the hand and pulled him up.

Rania pulled up her skirt slightly as she climbed in. They collapsed on one of the metal benches, breathless and sweating. Wahid blinked as he stared out the back. Some of the cameras were continuing to stare.

"Please God," he whispered.

Rania clung to him.

"That's it!" the policeman shouted.

An unseen set of hands swung the doors shut.

The noise was reduced to a dull roar. The van revved up, and they drove away.

Eight

Wahid concentrated on a crack in the ceiling above his bed. It was a long fissure, extending about a foot from the wall, and it pointed towards the centre of the room. The paint around the crack was peeling: a large flake of eggshell white was dangling, poised to drop onto his face.

He sighed.

He could feel every spring of the mattress through the thin sheet. The point of each spring poked into his back; it reminded Wahid of an Indian *fakir* lying down on a bed of nails, rusty nails which would give him tetanus to be sure. The blanket, made of coarse grey wool, was probably impregnated with all sorts of bacteria. The room stank of old sweat and cheap disinfectant. The fluorescent lights hummed and flickered.

"What you in for?" The question came from the bed next to his.

How he wished for privacy. After one week in the prison hospital it had become an obsession. He would have traded a limb or two for some seclusion.

"Oi, you, what you in for?"

Wahid turned. The question came from a young man dressed in a sweatshirt and a pair of faded and ripped blue jeans. His shaved head sported a bandage which covered his forehead: a spot of blood had formed and dried in the middle of it. His brown eyes had a dull glaze to them. He had been wheeled in last night after what had been described as a "minor disagreement".

Wahid did not want to reply. However, he guessed that this fellow would not be satisfied with silence.

41

"Nothing," he said and shifted his eyes back to the ceiling. A spot of damp was gathering near the crack; it had grown at least a centimetre since the previous day. Probably this room was saturated with typhus too.

"Ha ha, everyone says that. Seriously, what'd you do?"

"I said, nothing."

"You one of those Al Qaeda bastards?"

"No, I'm not one of them."

"Like hell you are. I saw you...you were bowing on the floor this morning."

"I was praying. I am not a terrorist."

"The fuck you are, mate, the fuck you all are."

Wahid rolled over onto his side. There was little point in continuing the conversation. The man's pallor and his glazed eyes suggested years of drug abuse. Wahid had seen people like him hobbling along Upper Street in Islington, wandering in lazy circles as if caught in a dream from which they could not escape. The lucky ones sat down and began a career holding out empty paper coffee cups to collect any loose change that fell from the hands of middle class liberals. The unlucky ones ended up in a place like this.

"I'm not done talking to you, you bastard," the young man continued. "You hear me, you're a fucking terrorist. Just wait till you heal up and they get a taste of you, mate!"

Wahid shut his eyes.

Footsteps.

"What's this?" a booming voice asked.

It was the nurse, Mr. Watson. He had the look of a professional wrestler, complete with a shaved head and a large handlebar moustache. Tattoos of intertwined roses were scrawled up and down his forearms; they resembled thick bramble bushes. His burly appearance, however, concealed a set of near-perfect manners. Wahid could imagine him as the enforcer at a school of etiquette, wearing a morning suit and wielding a large bamboo cane as a tool to bring miscreants into line.

"Nothing, sir," the young man replied at last, "we was just

42

having a chat."

"Right," said Watson severely. "You all right there, Mr. Shah?"

Wahid kept his eyes shut. "Fine, thank you, Mr. Watson."

"He's a terrorist shit, isn't he?" the young man said.

"Innocent until proven guilty," Watson replied with a note of caution in his voice. "Didn't you learn that during your trial?"

"But I was guilty."

"And you've got what you deserve," the nurse said flexing his beefy right arm. The brambles expanded and shrank. "But what Mr. Shah deserves is yet to be determined. Let him alone."

Wahid heard the young man swallow. "Yes, sir."

The daily routine in the prison hospital helped to blur one day into the next. Wahid awoke at dawn, and under the watchful eye of Mr. Watson, he prayed towards Mecca. Then, physical therapy: fortunately, Watson had a minor qualification in the subject. He helped Wahid with his exercises. Over time, Wahid limped across the room with increasing strength.

After exercise came breakfast: usually it was tea and porridge, with a glass of orange juice. After the meal, recitation: Watson borrowed a well-thumbed copy of the Qur'an from the prison library for Wahid's benefit. Wahid wrinkled his nose at this at first; he was in the habit of buying a new one the moment he saw a single fingerprint on a page. However, even though the pages were covered with smudged fingerprints, it was a comfort: Wahid sat by a window overlooking the prison yard, his leg elevated, and read quietly, his lips moving in a whisper to the words.

Often after recitation, there were visitors; one of the few privileges of being an "unconvicted prisoner" was that there were no limits on their number. At these times, Watson led Wahid to a grey concrete room with a bare wooden table in the centre. The sole window was covered with a steel mesh; only a trickle of daylight could penetrate it. The sole bit of colour was a single light bulb covered by a metal lampshade: both were a soft pink. The folding chairs were made of a cold steel which had obviously been designed to encourage short visits.

Rania came as often as she could. On one visit, she related how she and Basir's wife, Dina, were evading the media; they kept a watch on the press, then picked the house that had the fewest reporters surrounding it. Running from those jackals in human form and leaping over back garden fences, strangely enough, did have benefits.

"I've lost weight," Rania announced.

"Oh?" Her modest clothing wasn't designed for a proud slimmer to show off.

"Yes, all the running I've been doing; I've lost a stone."

It had been a while. "I would like to see that."

She reached across the table and held Wahid's hand. "Have faith."

Faith? Some days it was easy to come by: when the sun shone and the therapy went well, and the porridge had been cooked long enough to kill any potential pathogens, it was easy to believe that this period of confinement was nothing more than a way station in life. Perhaps he would be transformed by it. Perhaps it would make him into a great man. He would emerge, flinty-eyed and toughened by his prison days, his hair suddenly turned stylish like Father's. Maybe he would write a book and expose the injustices of the British legal system towards Muslims. He would be a guest on Radio 4 and go to a reception at the Pakistani Embassy and regale the Ambassador with tales of his imprisonment.

No, no, that was pride, he chided himself, false pride, phony pride, based on dreams, not achievement.

And indeed, there were other days, when the rain came, and the porridge had a thick skin on the top, concealing the chilled congealed mass underneath, and the walking was painful, and he could see nothing but the endless filth of the prison. He wanted to crawl deep within himself and use his diseased flesh as a shield from the endless pestilence. When this happened, he thought Faith was not enough. This experience could be the death of him.

"I will die here," he often thought, looking at the raindrops streaking the windowpanes.

He once was brave enough to reach out and touch the glass; a chill communicated back through his fingertips.

Hassan's visits were a further challenge to Faith. The sun could shine, he could walk with ease, the porridge would be sufficiently hot to be germ free, a Sura could move him nearly to tears, but then Watson would appear at the doorway during recitations and announce the solicitor's arrival.

"Mr. Shah," he'd say, "Mr. Iqbal is here to see you."

Quick quick quick and slow.

The visiting room took on a chillier aspect when Hassan came. Perhaps it was the very cleanliness and precision of the man, qualities which were admirable in and of themselves. Once, Wahid noted, Hassan's shoulder pads were sharpened with starch to unnaturally crisp points. Wahid could picture Hassan shrouded in a cloud of steam and attacking his clothes with the iron and a plastic spray can. The result of such fastidiousness, however, was that the room's corners and deep shadows were enhanced by his presence.

Perhaps. But it was more likely the room was colder because every visit brought information Wahid would rather not hear.

Basir had been beaten up in prison.

Willows was spouting more nonsense.

The BBC had run a documentary on the activities of Muslim radicals in London; the latest opinion polls showed a spike in the demand for the police to take "strong action" in response.

There was a bill in Parliament to extend the period of detention for terrorist suspects. It had support from both Labour and the Conservatives.

Wahid wished he could plug his ears and prevent the news from permeating his brain, but he knew the information would trickle through with or without Hassan telling him. The prison grapevine communicated every nuance of events through its constant stream of messengers: inmates who had teeth knocked out, got in knife fights, overdosed on heroin, or had all too convenient accidents. It was much more pleasant to roll over in bed and say, "I know," to any inquisitor who wanted to leer and laugh along with delivering the latest blow. At least they would be denied the pleasure of the agony being fresh.

"There will be a trial," Hassan told him as he gazed at Wahid over the top of his black-framed glasses.

How ridiculous. "Why?"

Hassan raised an eyebrow. "Well, in addition to you carrying the ingredients for chlorine gas around with you, it would seem some of your associates have been less than careful."

"Like who?"

"Remember Ahmed Mirza?" Hassan asked, raising an eyebrow.

The Butcher from Brick Lane. "Yes?"

"Did you know that he gave money to the Brotherhood of Eternal Jihad?"

"Who are they?"

"They're on a Home Office watch-list. Apparently they have been helping Sunni rebels in Iraq buy weapons."

Wahid swallowed. "But I barely know Ahmed, he's just a client."

Hassan gave a small smile. "No doubt. But he too is now under arrest. Salim Al-Maliki, is that name familiar?"

"Yes," Wahid said cautiously.

"The imam," Hassan prompted.

Oh. "What about him?"

"Did you know that he visited the Finsbury Park mosque on several occasions?"

"So have I," Wahid said. He had gone there to pray during his lunch hour. It was convenient when he paid visits to North London clients like Basir, but surely…

"I know. And Willows knows. But the imam was seen in that mosque with a group of radical preacher."

"But all this is just a bunch of coincidences," Wahid protested. Even if the imam had been preaching violent *jihad*, thanks to modern technology and his vast collection of classical music, Wahid hadn't been getting the message for the past two years.

"To you," Hassan replied. "To Willows, to the Crown Prosecution Service, it looks like conspiracy."

Wahid put his head in his hands. Quick, quick, quick and slow.

"I'm ruined."

Hassan's voice softened. "Not yet."

There was a knock on the door; it opened with a creak.

"Sorry to disturb you, gentlemen," Watson said, "but the guard has informed me another prisoner requires this room."

Watson withdrew, carefully shutting the door behind him.

Hassan stood, picking up his brown leather briefcase which was resting on the floor beside him.

"One further item," the solicitor added. "Willows is going to be here tomorrow. The police have decided you're well enough to be interrogated."

Oh, joy. "What should I tell him?"

"The truth."

"What if he doesn't accept the truth?"

"Tell it to him again."

Wahid swallowed.

Hassan read his disquiet. "Have faith," he said.

Wahid exhaled. Quick quick slow.

"*Salaam*," the solicitor said.

"*Salaam*."

Nine

"Are you sure, Mr. Shah?" Watson asked.

"Yes, thank you, Mr. Watson," Wahid replied.

Watson had just offered Wahid a more comfortable chair for the interrogation. Willows had been amenable to the request. But if this was going to be torture, Wahid reasoned, he may as well get the full measure of it. No amount of personal comfort would be able to counteract the forthcoming unpleasantness anyway.

Watson led Wahid down the narrow staircase to the visiting room. Upon opening the door, they discovered it had been transformed. With just two people in it, the chamber had seemed cosy, intimate. A slight chill greeted him on this occasion.

The Inspector sat at the table with an associate flanking either side. To the Inspector's right was a young blonde woman, her hair drawn back tight and tied up at the back. A set of black-rimmed glasses magnified her bright blue eyes, making her stare particularly penetrating.

To the left of the inspector was a young man, his red hair cut short and slicked forward into a single, sharp point. There was a slight gleam of freshly applied aftershave on his recently shorn cheeks and the antiseptic scent of hair gel.

The only thing that could be said in their favour was that none of them showed signs of requiring a handkerchief. None coughed. None spoke. None smiled.

On Wahid's side of the table stood Hassan, standing as upright as his stocky frame would allow. He had gone so far as to use his hair gel in such a way that ensured that he had an additional half inch of height.

"Good morning," Willows said.

Wahid bowed his head.

"You can go," Willows told Watson.

"Yes, sir." Watson shut the door behind him.

"Take a seat," Willows said, motioning to the chair.

Wahid complied. Hassan took the chair next to him.

"This is an informal interrogation; as is your right, your solicitor is allowed to be present."

The words seared Wahid's ears. There was sweat forming on Willows' upper lip, his lower lip glistened from flowing saliva. Hidden underneath the table, Wahid's hands trembled.

"Shall we begin?" the Inspector asked.

"Yes," Wahid said quietly.

The questions were insistent and precise. They began with the mundane, such as asking him to confirm his address. Then, they became increasingly ludicrous:

"Did you plan to release chlorine gas on the London Underground?"

"Are you part of a conspiracy to release chlorine gas on the London Underground?"

"Who were you working with?"

Wahid tried to insist he was a normal man, doing normal things on a normal day. But Willows was trying to turn every nuance of Wahid's demeanour and opinions into weapons to be used against him.

"What do you think of the Iraq War?"

"Do you support the anti-terror policies of the Government?"

"How do you feel about Al Qaeda?"

The Prophet did not say that God's message was "Butcher each other and be happy about it." Did he have a strong opinion on Iraq? He was against the war, just as he was against abusing children and sealing kittens in trash bags and throwing them into the Thames.

No, he did not support Al Qaeda, particularly since their

50

attack on the World Trade Centre had meant that paranoia had apparently become a civic virtue. As he spoke, Wahid wondered why terrorists always apparently blew up women and children and never got anyone, well, like Willows.

As for the anti-terror policies of the Government...he bit his tongue and said, "Detaining genuine terrorists is necessary. But I'm not one of those."

Each answer elicited a smile from Willows, a nod to the young woman on his right, who could apparently write without looking at the page of her notebook; the red-haired man simply stared at him, motionless. Wahid's hands kept shaking. A bead of sweat collected on the middle of his forehead.

"Are you nearly finished, Inspector?" Hassan interjected.

Wahid exhaled. Slow slow slow. He hadn't realised he had been holding his breath.

"For now," Willows replied, "just one further question."

Wahid trembled more violently.

"Why do you have a bag of explosive ammonium nitrate, in your potting shed?"

Ammonium nitrate? Wahid thought of his back garden: that quiet little expanse of green amidst the noise of London had been one of the reasons why they had purchased it, at Rania's insistence. In spite of being constrained by her modest clothing, she liked to kneel amongst the plants; she sowed geraniums, lilies, white irises along the perimeter, and left a small section for tomatoes and cucumbers. Wahid could bear sitting out on the patio: he enjoyed sitting on his wooden chair, reading the newspaper, and occasionally glancing up to admire his wife's industriousness. However, he could never join her in digging in the dirt. There was always a risk that ants would crawl up his sleeve, and he'd never be rid of them. Worms too, lurked in the earth, and they were truly filthy creatures: they actually *ate* dirt.

The potting shed was Rania's territory, not his. But ammonium nitrate, he recalled, was not just something used for explosives. There was a schoolboy fact that rattled around in his memory. Ah yes.

51

"You mean fertiliser?" Wahid asked.

Willows' smile turned sour. "Yes."

"It's to fertilise…the garden…we grow tomatoes."

The Inspector nodded. The young woman next to him wrote a final note and shut her notebook.

"Thank you, Mr. Shah. You've been most helpful."

The Inspector stood, nodded to his coterie, and they proceeded in a single column out the exit.

"What just happened?" Wahid asked Hassan.

The solicitor shrugged and frowned.

Watson got a hold of a television. It was a replacement; the previous television, according to the nurse, had a very brief lifespan.

"Some of the football results caused too much consternation," Watson explained.

Apparently a cure to the angst caused by Tottenham losing to Arsenal was to destroy any large smashable object, including the one that had caused such offence.

The television arrived when there was a brief period during which Wahid was the only inmate in the ward. In spite of the crumbling decay that characterised the entire facility, with privacy, the prison hospital had become almost civilised.

Wahid was scared to switch on the television; he was afraid that opening that particular window to the wider world would reveal more horrors. The screen leered at him. Unfortunately, it was positioned right in front of where he would kneel to pray to Mecca. In the absence of his iPod, he would think of Strauss' Blue Danube: one, two, three up and down, *Allahu Akbar*, up, repeat. The grey screen was watching the entire time, blank, silent in its reproach.

After a week of letting the television sit there unwatched, he resented it. Its presence meant that he felt like he was in a television commercial at times; a photographer would have had a field day with the image of a man kneeling before the almighty telly five times a day.

Patience, forbearance, Father had counselled at times, usually when Wahid was about to face anything unpleasant, like a test. Maths had come to him easily, but history A levels had made him vomit five times the night before the exam. He wore pinstripe pyjamas, the pattern shuddering along with his body as he was sick. His mother heard his retching and stroked his back as he kneeled over the sink, as he tried not to gag further on the strong scent of cleaning bleach.

Courage, Father had counselled too, when Wahid had to go to the dentist. Wahid winced and pushed back the memory of dentist chairs and iron hooks.

Courage. A strange word, Wahid rolled its syllables over in his mind. He tried it in Urdu - *himmat*. "Caution" in both languages was much more pleasant to the ear.

Rania was glad to hear he had not been watching the television. On her last visit, she was wearing a strange perfume which she said she had borrowed from Dina; her normal scent of vanilla had been replaced by that of an overripe fruit salad. She told him not to worry about money; all that cash he had put into the savings account had finally come in handy, and anyway, her Uncle Naseem from Karachi had wired her five thousand pounds and said he'd send her more if she needed it. No, there was no need to worry, no need to worry at all. Soon he would be out and all would be as it was before.

Wahid returned to the ward, looking down at the four empty beds, his own more neatly made than those which were vacant. The sun streamed through the window, only slightly dimmed by the regular pattern of iron bars. He set down his crutches on the edge of one of the beds.

"Courage....and forbearance," Wahid said aloud.

He stepped over to the television. His hands trembled again. Not today.

Ten

A dream came to him.

It was murky at first. He was in an unidentified landscape: it was blurry. It slowly came into focus. Ah yes, the brown earth and turquoise sky were right out of Basir's holiday snaps. He was in Pakistan.

The landscape was barren with the exception of a railway track running through the middle of it. There were two small wooden shacks, hastily erected and made of untreated wood. The light colour of the wood indicated they were fresh and new. A fence separated them, with a gate extending over the track that could be lowered and opened at will.

Over one of the huts flew a saffron, white and green tricolour. India. Over the other, the familiar soothing green and white banner with the crescent moon and star. Pakistan.

Wahid heard a loud whistle. In the distance, he saw a black iron steam train, coughing, puffing, storming towards the two huts. He walked towards the barrier. People clung to the train like a multitude of ants clinging to a leaf. The train was chugging hard, using all its might to pull the weight.

Wahid reached the barrier. He looked down the track as the train steadily came closer to barrelling through. An Indian guard, wearing a crisply starched Army uniform, rushed out of the shack and lifted the barrier. Correspondingly, his Pakistani counterpart also stepped outside.

Point of crossing, point of no return.

The train was almost there. The whistling was loud, a scream for anyone in the way to get out. The train to freedom would not be stopped for anything; no flimsy obstacle that India put up could stand in the way.

The train blasted through. Wahid looked up; unlike most of the passengers who were hunkered down, there was a man standing on top of the train – his arms outstretched, his fists clenched, his hair flowing in the breeze like he was on a film set.

"Father," Wahid said.

He looked down at Wahid and gave him his familiar brave grin and a wink.

Wahid awoke; it was dark and quiet in the prison hospital. The light of a full moon streamed through the window. A teenager of Bangladeshi origin had been wheeled in the previous day after getting in a knife fight; he had a long gash across his chest. The boy was used to sleeping on his stomach, so when sleep first overtook him, he rolled over: the pain of his wound awoke him with a yelp. He found peace by sleeping on his side and was snoring.

Wahid listened. The sound of the wind against the window was soft and flickering. There was the clatte0r of a London Underground train in a distance. Not quite midnight then, unless it was a train heading back to the depot.

There was too much to think about to sleep, he mused.

He stood and paced over to a chair; he flexed the tendons in his leg. It had returned to full strength. Watson had kindly got him an extra week just to ensure there was no remaining soreness in the limb. He could now walk normally. He could climb stairs normally. He could be treated as a normal prisoner.

The moonlight hit the television; Wahid saw the reflection in its screen. It was the only time he thought of peace in relation to the appliance.

Watson had switched it on for him. From the news, he learned that the British National Party had found out where he lived. His part of Hackney was not particularly Muslim, so there was little solidarity from the neighbours; most of them were Eastern Europeans who had been cast onto the great sinking wreck of London and were clinging on any way they could. They did not understand these shaven-headed men who waved Union Jacks and shouted "Muslims Out! Muslims Out!" The residents spoke to each other in Polish or Lithuanian and hid behind their locked doors and drawn curtains.

A squad of policemen, wearing blue uniforms and fluorescent vests, hooked arms and formed a perimeter in front of the house. Whenever one of the protestors got too close, a policeman would push back, sending the miscreant spinning like a top back into the mass of his brethren causing it to swell and push forward again. The lines buckled and swayed but did not break.

The leader of the protestors was interviewed.

"We think this case of the London Four…" he began.

London Four?

"…proves that the Islamic community is totally incapable of living peacefully with its neighbours. It's not a race issue, it's a culture issue."

Wahid noted the gobs of spittle forming at the corners of the BNP man's mouth. "Perhaps it's a rabies issue," he mused.

Over the man's shoulder, Wahid could see his house. The butter yellow paint was largely intact, but there were red splotchy stains near the doorway. Rotten vegetables? Paint bombs? On the upper floor, he saw the curtain flicker in the window. Just a brief, blurry glimpse: there was a woman in a headscarf. Rania? Dina? The curtain closed.

Later, Rania tried to deny all knowledge of the event. "You do not need to worry!" she insisted.

He took her hand in his. "You know better than that."

She started weeping.

There had been phone calls. Letters. Anti-Muslim graffiti painted on their doors and walls. Swastikas. Once, someone had left a pile of excrement on the doorstep.

"Did you clean it up?" Wahid asked.

No, no, Dina's cousin Imran had done that. He had also treated the doorstep with antiseptic. Good.

57

Quick quick quick, slow.

The police had suggested she go elsewhere. However, Basir's place had been similarly violated.

"Should I..." she began to ask. Her tears were flowing profusely.

"Should you what?"

"Should I go back to Pakistan for a while? To Uncle Naseem, I mean."

Wahid exhaled.

"If it's too much, go to Uncle Naseem."

"But will you be all right here...alone..."

No. "Hassan will handle matters."

"Are you sure?"

No. "I'm sure. Do what you think is best."

"But the house, our lovely house...."

"It will probably be burned to the ground," he thought. "It will be lovely again," he said.

"If you're sure."

No. "I love you, Rania."

The words surprised him. She ran into his arms: the impact of her body on his chest knocked the wind out of him.

"I love you too."

She remained in London for the moment, as far as he knew. As the days progressed, he noted that sleep came with increasing difficulty. He was spending more and more evenings looking at the moonlight, listening to the sounds of the ward. There was a slight static hum of electricity. A pipe gurgled with water; it was probably someone flushing a toilet somewhere in the bowels of the building. The young man in the next bed switched from snoring to soft breathing.

Freedom. Wahid had seen it in Father's eyes in the dream, his outstretched fists, the smile on his face, the flag of Pakistan fluttering against the turquoise sky. Perhaps that was what Basir had been driving at for so long.

"Go through the barrier, Rania," Wahid willed her in his

58

thoughts. Break through the hated blockade, whether it had a Union Jack or a Saffron tricolour over it. Be free, fly away. Fly into the moonlight on the wings of angels and be set down amidst the good, dry earth and sunshine of our country.

"I will," he thought as he shut his eyes, "die here."

Slow slow slow.

Eleven

A blue jumpsuit replaced the *kurta*. The official rationale was that it would make him stand out less. Wahid looked at the garment critically. He poked it with a borrowed tongue depressor. He lifted it up as close to his nose as he dared. It smelled as if it had been boiled. There was a hint of cheap laundry detergent. Beneath it, there were traces that it had been worn before. Was that sweat?

Disgusting. But according to Watson, this was what he was to wear.

"I can't say I think the garment is particularly useful," Watson stated.

No, it was not "useful" to be treated like a prisoner without actually having committed a crime. Worse, he was going to be detained in a regular cell; only God knew what kind of people would be there. Would he end up laid out like so many of the young men that he had seen in the ward? Perhaps that would be a small mercy: to be injured again and return to the hospital, to his tea and his routine, was preferable to having criminals breathing their virulence on him or taking their rage out on him with their fists.

One last prayer to Mecca. One last breakfast. One last recitation. *Allahu Akbar*. Wahid handed back the borrowed copy of the Qur'an to Watson with great reluctance. Memory was fallible. Supposing there was no copy at the detention centre? Would he be able to recite the Suras by heart?

Slowly, Wahid shed his *kurta,* pulling it gingerly over his head. Rania was right: he had lost weight. His ribs were more clearly visible than ever before. His bruises were gone; what remained were a few small scars on his formerly broken leg.

Deep inhale. The air seemed too cold for it to be late May; the chill penetrated his body from the tips of his toes to his shoulder blades. He shivered. His heart beat faster; he put his hand over his chest to still it.

He stepped into the jumpsuit and pulled it up over his legs. There was a minor itch of discomfort as it progressed up and over his boxer shorts. He would have to keep the shorts buttoned up tight. It was entirely possible that the jumpsuit had the sort of germs which could give him a urinary tract infection. He'd read about how awful that could be in men; urinating clots of blood did not appeal.

Deep inhale again. He pulled the jumpsuit over his shoulders and began to button it up. One, two, three. He reached up for his cotton cap and gently pulled it off his head. He ran his fingers through his hair to keep the top of his head warm.

"They're here," Watson announced.

Wahid turned to him; the nurse was standing the doorway, his sleeves rolled up, revealing the elaborate rose tattoos. His large moustache was drooping.

"So this is good bye, Mr. Watson," Wahid said.

"Indeed, Mr. Shah."

"Shall we?"

Side by side, they proceeded down the stairwell.

Two policemen took custody of him. One was ginger haired and spoke with a Scottish brogue; he smiled as he put the handcuffs on Wahid. "There you are, laddie, your new bracelets," he said.

"Say nothing," Hassan had advised.

They piled him into the back of their van. Fortunately, the prison did not allow cameras or reporters into the loading area, but Wahid could see their spying eyes in the distance, beyond a high wire fence. His anger boiled.

What did rage look like on television? He could imagine himself: eyes sullen, mouth set in a firm line, hands cuffed. It was not an image of pristine innocence, perhaps. But he was innocent. He wanted to scream it from the rooftops. Somehow, he doubted anyone would listen.

He thought Rania was probably watching at home: he hoped this premonition was false. Hopefully she was getting ready to go to Pakistan. Hassan told him she had bought a ticket, but had changed the date once, twice, three times. It was costing money.

"Tell her to make up her mind, the next time you see her," Hassan advised. Every penny spent on Pakistan Airways was one that the solicitor could not get in legal fees.

"But I don't really want her to go," Wahid thought.

"I will tell her," Wahid replied.

He got into the back of the van and the door slammed shut with a metallic thud.

The jolly Scottish policeman kept on saying, "You'll be there before long, laddie."

Laddie. "You stereotype," Wahid thought.

There were the sounds of police sirens as the van brushed aside traffic, the click click click of cameras as the vehicle stopped en route.

The van accelerated. It swerved around corners and the brakes screeched. Quick quick quick, slow.

At long last, it came to a halt. There was a brief conversation between the driver and a guard: "Here with the prisoner", "Ah yes, we're expecting you, come in", "Righto".

There was a sound of metal and squeaking gates. The engine again accelerated briefly, then the van coasted to a stop.

"We're here."

The sun touched Wahid's face briefly as he emerged from the van. He wanted to keep his eyes shut, absorb the warmth for a moment but hands were guiding him away. He had to open his eyes and focus on the great gate ahead of him.

The detention centre was made of brick: a tall tower loomed over the complex. The windows were opaque; one could not see if there were people inside. The ever watchful eyes of the guards, Wahid assumed, were concentrated inside.

Ahead of him was an iron gate. It stood at eight feet high; the dwarfing effect made Wahid's heart pound harder. His memory echoed with Brahms' Requiem - *Denn alles Fleisch es ist wie Gras.*

"Oh no," he thought.

The gates swung open. The prison relied on loose gravel to provide the surface around its perimeter. Each step, his own and that of the guards' resulted in a crunching sound.

Wahid began to gasp. The shadow of the centre leaned in his direction, thanks to the angle of the sun. There was no need to be afraid of shadows; they were merely natural phenomena caused by the angle of light and the position of objects. But maybe the science was wrong. Perhaps they were a physical extension of evil in the world. Was there not something called "dark matter"? This might be it: the embrace of shadows, the physicality of them.

He took shorter and shorter steps, not wanting to step into the darkness.

"Come now," the Scottish policeman said. "It's your new home till the trial."

Home? Never. Home was a place full of conventional worries like being concerned about taking the rubbish out on time or ensuring that the toilet was well scrubbed. It was full of fears that could be soothed by disinfectant and cups of mint tea.

One step, then another into the shadow. His body temperature dropped. His heart felt as if it had turned into a solid lump of ice. The handcuffs prevented him from checking his pulse on his wrist; he held up both hands to his chest to ensure his heart was still beating. He dragged himself on.

"I will die here," he thought. *Denn alles Fleisch es ist wie Gras.*

"Not far now," the policeman encouraged.

Ahead, there was a black metal door; it was an irregular entry point for such a uniformly brick building. It opened; at first the space behind it was as black as the shadows. A light switched on: at the door stood a prison guard who regarded him critically with a set of beady eyes. He was, Wahid guessed, in his late fifties. He wore a blue cap and uniform. In this outfit he was more reminiscent of a train conductor than a guard.

"Bring him in," he encouraged.

All aboard.

Wahid felt as if he were in a black hole, a place where matter was compressed and compressed again till all was density and dark.

The walls! He thought that the prison hospital had been dire, but here, the paint was peeling everywhere. Cracks were in every ceiling. The smells of damp, sweat, cheap disinfectant and excrement assailed his nostrils as soon as he entered.

The voices! He heard voices laughing, gabbing, cursing. Every other word was apparently to do with fornication. Fornicate this, fornicate that, fornicate you.

The sounds! There was metal banging against metal, the hiss of rising steam, the whir of unseen machinery.

What was the correct Sura, he wondered. His mind drew a blank; he wanted to remember the one to keep away evil. He needed it desperately. His heart felt compacted, as if a fist was squeezing it to the point of bursting.

He coughed. He had a strong temptation to sink to his knees and bow before Allah. "Forgive me all my sins, oh merciful God," he thought, "just please deliver me from this."

His memory responded with the hundred and thirteenth Sura. He said softly:

> *"Say, I seek refuge, with the Lord of the Dawn*
> *From the mischief of Created things*
> *From the mischief of the Darkness as it overspreads*
> *From the mischief of those who practise Secret Arts*
> *And from the mischief of the envious one, as he practises*
> *envy..."*

65

"Quiet," the guard told him. "Keep moving. Your cell is further along."

Quick quick quick. They proceeded into a narrow, cream coloured corridor, with iron doors on either side. There was a small portal on each, which could be swung open or shut. At this time of the day, they were open.

The guard reached the door he was looking for. He pulled out a large key and opened the lock.

"You'll be sharing a cell," he told Wahid.

One of the policemen undid the handcuffs.

The door swung open with a loud creak. Wahid turned to look inside.

The cell was lit by a single fluorescent bulb and a window that was sealed over with metal grating. Mould was growing at the join of the ceiling and the far corner of the cell. Seated on a thin grey cot, reading a copy of the Qur'an, was a stooped figure of a man. His shoulders were hunched forward. He had a trace of grey in his hair. The face was scarred, swollen around the eyes, but…familiar.

"Basir?" Wahid asked.

"Hello, my friend," Basir replied. His familiar broad smile struggled to emerge, but finally, it won out.

Twelve

"Come on Arkie, kick him again!"

Wahid watched helplessly as Arkie, a prisoner wearing baggy denim trousers and large work boots kicked Basir across the floor. Arkie's shaven head glistened as he delivered the blow: he grunted slightly with the effort. Basir cried out and collapsed face down.

"God!" Basir gasped.

"Stop it!" Wahid shouted. His arms were held back by Arkie's accomplice, a fellow armed robber named Stan. The stench of body odour from the man made him sick to his stomach.

"Shut your noise," Stan advised. The slang was all the more cutting with a South London accent.

Wahid stared at the floor. It was made of cold black and white tiles. The grouting had gone dark: it was utterly filthy. Basir had to get up, otherwise he might die. He was gasping, reaching out a trembling hand towards the wall.

Arkie grinned and paced after him. "You're a good little dog, aren't you?" he said. He winked at the dozen other prisoners standing around them in a circle. There was a nervous chuckle. It was advisable to laugh at Arkie's jokes.

"Yes, what a precious little doggie you are," Arkie said.

Another blow to the stomach. Basir collapsed again. Wahid wanted to clutch at his own abdomen in sympathy; he could feel blood vessels bursting, filling his duodenum up with fluid.

"Stop it," Wahid said softly.

Basir's shoulders shook; he was sobbing.

67

"What, you crying?" Arkie asked.

Basir did not reply.

"You answer me!" Arkie shouted.

Another kick. Basir hollered in pain.

"Yes!" Basir yelled.

"That will fucking teach you to smile, you toothy bastard. You only smile when I give you fucking permission to smile."

The grip on Wahid shifted.

"The pigs," Stan warned.

Sure enough, heavy footsteps sounded in the distance: thank God, the guards.

Arkie nodded. "Let him go."

Stan pushed Wahid away from him. Wahid turned; Stan raised an eyebrow and gave him a small wave.

"Have a nice day," he said in a faux American accent.

Disgusting. Wahid turned back. Basir was gasping, his hand pressed up against the wall. Blood ran out of his mouth into a small puddle on the floor. A wave of nausea shook Wahid; he could almost detect its metallic taste, its warm scent was impossible to escape, even beneath the steamy clouds of detergent released by laundry day.

Basir coughed.

"Come on, my friend," Wahid said softly. Tentatively, he stepped over to Basir and knelt down. Basir's odours assailed him: sweat, stale coffee breath, tears.

God.

But.

Do what is right.

Wahid swallowed. Reaching underneath his rancid armpits, he hoisted his friend's limp body up. Basir used his limited strength to assist. They got to their feet shakily; both sucked in a gasp of air. Wahid put an arm around Basir's waist. Basir threw his arm over Wahid's shoulder. They began the long walk to the infirmary: Basir's head rolled back, they staggered. A trickle of blood flowed out of Basir's mouth onto Wahid's shoulder, rolling down his neck; the hot fluid stung with the pinpricks of a thousand bacteria. Quick quick quick and slow.

Onward, onward. They stumbled and righted themselves. Do what is right. "Almost there," Wahid said.

"Thank you," Basir replied. He coughed.

Wahid winced and gulped. Quick quick, slow. Brothers. It was a word that Wahid had heard before, but its meaning had been lost on him. All Muslims are *brothers*, the imam had said. Wahid had thought that it was a platitude. Now it was clear; Basir and he were the *Dar al Islam* – the house of peace. Surrounding them was the *Dar al Harb*, the house of war. Brothers.

The Infirmary was run by an ageing doctor named Perkins. He had probably held the post since leeches were considered an excellent remedy for virtually everything. Every last white hair was perfectly slicked back on his head and a pair of silver-framed glasses were delicately balanced on the end of his nose. He wore a white coat which had been treated with so much starch it appeared as stiff as a board. He moved with a slowness that suggested that he knew his time was short, and every moment was worth stretching. Wahid could sympathise: there was a simple beauty in enjoying walking across the room and wanting to relish every sensation.

The Infirmary itself was an anachronism. It was painted a dark green; the cupboards and instruments looked dated. Wahid was glad that the Doctor was unlikely to do any surgical procedure.

Whenever he and Basir entered the Infirmary, it was usually the same story. Doctor Perkins would say, "Got into a bit of a tussle, eh?"

One could say that.

"Well now, let's see what we can do."

Alcohol swabs were delicately applied, wounds were bound up, painkillers given. Basir's face would relax as pain receded; he often said the bruises radiated a warm glow.

"There now, as right as ninepence," the Doctor said. "Off

you go."

Hassan complained about the beatings to the authorities. He said there were promises that the guards would be more watchful. But rules were not part of the *Dar al-Harb*, particularly when it came to Arnold "Arkie" Arkwright, the man who had robbed ten banks in three weeks.

The meeting room at the prison was much more unpleasant than the one at the prison hospital. It was smaller, there was no window and the coarse wooden table gave off splinters with a brush of the hand. The light came from a solitary forty-watt bulb that flickered in time to the guards' radio in the next room; unfortunately these guards were fond of hip hop played at top volume. A scent of dampness, old orange peels and rotten semen shed on conjugal visits permeated the scene.

"The prisons are overcrowded," Hassan explained. "They have nowhere else to put you."

A vein in Wahid's forehead began to throb insistently. "When are we going to be put on trial?" he asked.

Hassan shrugged. "I haven't been given a date yet. The Crown Prosecution Service claims it's still building its case."

Basir spoke up. "This is ridiculous. We are completely innocent."

"I know. The good news is that the *Guardian* is running an investigative report on this case. There have been a few questions in the Commons from the Liberals. I also have hope that other political pressure will be applied."

"What are you talking about?" Wahid asked.

"The Socialist Workers Party is holding a 'Free the London Four' demonstration next Sunday."1

"Is that a good thing?" Basir asked.

Wahid wondered that himself. He recalled his encounter with their Islington representative.

"I don't believe it will hurt," Hassan said. "What harm could it do?"

There was little to do but wait and pray. The cell was too small to accommodate their prayer routine; they were forced to stack their beds. Fortunately, the window faced east. This made it relatively easy to figure out where Mecca stood.

Wahid imagined during his devotions that the sun was shining not in the sky, but from that point on the map. *Allahu Akbar*, he whispered as he bent towards it. Merely reciting the words filled him with warmth. *Allahu Akbar.*

Perhaps he was here to discover God. He had been filled with the letter of ritual, but perhaps none of its spirit. He had said "God is Great" so many times it was beyond counting, but maybe not until now he had felt its full force. How else, except through the mercy and grace of the Compassionate One, had he survived?

He had been or was going to be stripped of everything. Rania, Hassan had told him, had finally set a date for going back to Pakistan. Willows had said that it was all right. Of course it was. Wahid was closer to God and he understood more now; Rania's departure was *helpful*. But what did it matter in the end. *God* remained *Great.*

Basir interrupted his thoughts. "Wahid."

Wahid's eyes were shut. "Yes, Basir?"

"We're done with morning prayers. You can stop kneeling now."

71

Thirteen

"Your wife is here," the guard told him.

"At last," Wahid thought.

He tensed and flexed his leg muscles as he made his way to the visiting room. His gait was not perfect; prison life had aggravated his aches and pains. He caught sight of his reflection in the cafeteria window as he walked; he hadn't realised he was hunched over. Grey had made a sudden appearance in his hair. His dark eyes had sunk back into his skull.

The guard led him into the room and shut the door behind him. It took a moment for Wahid's eyes to adjust to the darkness. Rania was looking him up and down.

"Darling?"

"Yes, Rania," he said.

She ran over to him and threw her arms around his waist. "Wahid," she sobbed.

Best not to worry her further. "There there, now. I'll be all right."

"You don't look like…you," Rania said.

Wahid suppressed the urge to laugh. "No, I suppose I don't."

She patted his stomach. "You are so thin…have you been eating?"

"Yes." Wahid was unable to resist a surge of nausea at the thought of the prison's idea of a *halal* meal. He had no idea why, but the other prisoners had looked sharply at him when he received it. But then again, the prisoners thought that the authorities put dust in their custard.

73

"When you get out, I will make you your favourite supper."

"Probably with too much ghee," he thought. "I look forward to it." He changed the subject. "Are you ready to go, Rania?"

She turned and faced the table, balling her hands up into fists and leaning on it. Her shoulders trembled slightly.

"I have my ticket…I am packed….Cousin Imran boarded up the windows to the house."

"Are you *ready*, though?"

She turned. Trails of tears glistened on her cheeks.

"No, darling."

Wahid took her into his arms. "You have to be." He thought of the train of his dreams, Father, the Pakistani flag. He could imagine her arrival, the sunlight, the clear sky, relatives rushing to meet her and take her to Uncle Naseem's house. "You are going to be free," Wahid said quietly.

She sobbed.

"And when all this business is behind us…you will come back. We will repaint the house. You will replant the garden."

In his mind's eye, he could see it: he would get a gallon container of butter yellow paint and a roller, and attend to each wall and corner of their house. The first time had been a pleasure of precision: he had gone so far as to utilise a fine paintbrush, more useful for a canvas and oils, to paint the smallest corners. He could envisage the gentle spring sun, Rania kneeling, watering and cooing to a petunia coming into bloom.

Her sobbing became more vehement.

Give her a dream, Wahid thought. He took a deep breath.

"And I promise, once I am free, we will try again for a child," he said.

That he could see too. He could imagine them alone, the making of a child, her clothes distending as the months progressed, the emergence of a tiny person from her womb. He fought down the image of himself changing diapers.

She wrapped her arms around him even more tightly. The impact nearly knocked Wahid off his feet.

"Darling," she cried.

"Go, Rania…go home."

"Yes, Wahid."

"I love you," he whispered.

The walk back to the cell was slow and painful. The guard followed silently.

"I am alone," Wahid thought. This was new. Mother and Father had passed the baton on to Rania; though he might be away from home, he had never thought of it being empty.

His mind was reeling at the thought of Cousin Imran nailing rough wooden boards over the windows. Rania was thorough: she would have taken out the old sheets from the linen closet and thrown them over the furniture. All the old food would have been stored or thrown away. The gas would be turned down to a minimum, the refrigerator switched off, the lamps unplugged from the wall. The scent of mint tea and spices would recede. A chill would seep through the walls. Very shortly, his home would become an empty shell.

"I am alone," he repeated in a whisper. His steps slowed further. Yes, he had his friend Basir, but there were limits to friendship between unrelated men; Basir was not family. Basir could not comprehend the entire chapter and verse of his heart, not any more than Wahid could look into his.

God knew, but God was silent. He had His Purpose, but that Purpose did not involve words of comfort, being called "Beloved" or being told "I love you" in a soft voice.

The pressure of hot tears made Wahid blink. He passed by some of his fellow prisoners in the corridor. He held back on letting his emotions show, lest he be an automatic choice for persecution that day. As it was, a few "Wotcher, Paki" sounded out from some of the cells.

"Wotcher, Paki!" Normally the jovial remark would have stung. This time, it was as distant as the stars.

The guard opened his cell. Wahid stepped inside, the guard shut the door behind him. Basir looked up from the Qur'an.

"How is she?" Basir asked.

Wahid collapsed on his bed and stared at the ceiling. The fourth damp stain of the week was spreading through the alabaster paint. He turned his back to Basir.

"Gone," he replied.

Fourteen

There was a television in the recreation room. By no means was it perfect; a bird flying overhead was sufficient to knock out three of the five channels it was meant to receive.

Sunday. Wahid and Basir tried to treat it like a normal day. Wahid felt a gnawing in the pit of his stomach. If the demonstration was big enough, if the media covered it favourably, if the Liberals kept asking questions, maybe, just maybe, the Government would act.

If if if. It was best not to confound oneself with unfulfilled expectations. Wahid and Basir prayed as normal. The skies beyond their window were clear: a good sign; favourable weather might encourage turnout.

They would learn nothing until five o'clock, however. They were locked into the same rhythms as the rest of the nation: the television would be the harbinger of bad or good news.

Distractions. Basir told Wahid about how he had once fixed a Reliant Robin with a rubber band and a coat hanger. Wahid talked about painting the house: perhaps he ought to change the colour from butter yellow to old cream?

No, Basir advised, cream would show dirt more easily. Best to stick with the yellow, but perhaps a softer tone. Yes, Wahid had seen a shade called "Buttermilk" which he quite liked.

They looked out the window regularly, checking the position of sunlight and shadows to tell the time. The concrete prison blocks cast a short shadow into the cement yard. Not yet.

Wahid asked Basir about Ahmed and the imam. Had he

heard anything prior Wahid's arrival? Basir knew they were not in the same prison, but they probably had to contend with much the same conditions.

"God help them," Wahid said.

"Yes," Basir agreed.

They talked about the cricket. Had Basir seen the results from Lords? Oh yes, what an utter tragedy that was; Pakistan losing to the Isle of Man. The Isle of Man, of all places!

"How many people live there?" Basir asked.

"I think about eighty thousand," Wahid replied.

"Good God," Basir exclaimed.

Well, Al Massoud's bat was definitely questionable; no, it was time for changes throughout the starting line-up.

"They may have to anyway," Wahid said.

Basir caught his meaning. "Yes, they probably got lynched as soon as they got off the plane," he joked.

They paused.

"But there's always next year," Wahid stated.

"Yes."

They looked out the window again. Not yet.

The sky changed from turquoise to a deeper shade. Clouds began to shift in colour from white to purple. Shadows lengthened. Birds lazily flew from one roof to another, switching positions, bobbing their heads in the fading light.

"Now?" Wahid asked.

Basir nodded.

They stepped out of their cell and walked to the recreation room. Fortunately, most of the other prisoners were occupied by playing a game of snooker. They placed bets using torn off strips of paper instead of money.

Basir stepped over to the television and switched it on.

Quick quick quick. Slow.

"…this is the BBC News, it's five o'clock…." The television intoned.

The programme always inserted two heavy bangs of a drum

before each major item. "Thump thump," the television blared.

"…more carnage in Baghdad. Ten are killed in a car bomb explosion outside a Shi'a mosque."

Thump thump.

"…oil prices set to reach a record high tomorrow according to economists…but the Chancellor won't be moved, no reduction in petrol tax to compensate…"

Thump thump.

"…in London, a demonstration calling on the Government to free the London Four turns into a riot."

No.

Wahid held his breath. The broadcaster, a man in his forties, wearing a grey suit and red tie, spoke far too slowly. Iraq? Oil? Who cared?

Come on, come on, come on. In his mind, Wahid was staring over the edge of a precipice. Gravity beckoned.

Finally. "…police have made seventeen arrests today in central London, after a demonstration calling on the Government to free the London Four turned into a riot. George Castle has a report."

The image shifted to a middle aged man in a trench coat standing at Trafalgar Square with Nelson's Column directly behind him. Also in the scene were a group of policemen speaking to each other. Red buses carried on in the distance.

"Thank you, Michael," Castle said. "Police are just cleaning up after what has been described as the worst violence since the Poll Tax riots."

The image shifted again to show a group of people marching with signs in their hands: "Free the London Four", "Free Palestine", "Stop the War", "End the Blair Dictatorship". The protestors were laughing and smiling as they passed the camera. They were a mixed group. There were some young people, students, Wahid presumed. Others were Middle Eastern in appearance and of various ages. Others wore a *kaffiyeh*. One held up a large Palestinian flag.

"The demonstration started peacefully enough," Castle's

79

voice said. "It was an event designed to protest the Government's continued detention of the London Four, and broadcast a wider political message."

The image changed to a white, middle-aged man with thinning hair and a greying beard. He wore a tweed jacket with several buttons on the lapel which echoed the signs the protestors were carrying. A caption identified him as Samuel Wainwright, a Socialist Worker Party Spokesman.

"This protest is about sending a powerful political message to the Government, saying in no uncertain terms: no, you cannot carry on with your current agenda. The London Four's plight is merely the latest example of the horrible crimes committed by Tony Blair's regime."

"What about us?" Basir shouted.

"Shut up," one of the prisoners playing snooker yelled at him.

"Watch," Wahid said quietly.

Wainwright was replaced by images of demonstrators throwing rocks at police and smashing windows.

"At around midday," Castle continued, "the violence began. Police are uncertain as to the cause, but they believe that some of the protestors have a history of participation in anti-capitalist riots. Officers on the scene have said that it is likely this segment of the crowd which decided to smash in the window of a McDonalds."

"You idiots," Wahid whispered.

"Police fired tear gas, and the demonstration was broken up by their anti-riot squad. So far, the police have reported only three injuries but seventeen arrests. George Castle, BBC News."

"Switch it off!" Basir cried.

Wahid was unable to move.

The image returned to the newsreader. "The Prime Minister had a brief statement to make about today's disturbance."

The picture changed to Tony Blair. He was standing at a podium outside Ten Downing Street. Flashbulbs fired en masse.

"Obviously," he began, "today has been a difficult

80

day…and I would like to thank our police and emergency services for handling it with their usual skill." He cocked his head to the right and inhaled. "We have a great tradition of protest in this country, and this government respects that right….but…when it comes to disturbing the civil peace, engaging in violence, we do not respect that form of protest…" He inhaled again and shifted his head back to centre.

The motion reminded Wahid of a peacock's neck bobbing.

The Prime Minister continued. "…we will not be deterred from our policies by these means. I assure those genuinely concerned about the welfare of these four suspects that justice will be swift and clear. Thank you."

Quick quick quick. Quick quick quick. Slow.

Fifteen

Wahid tried to sleep. He rolled over onto his back; the ceiling appeared to be set lower than it was earlier in the day. Was it an optical illusion? No, it was probably some new torture. Millimetre by millimetre, it was coming down. At some point, he and Basir would be crushed into the floor. He could imagine the moment when bone gave in to concrete; his nose would be flattened against it, the ceiling would move one millimetre more, there would be a single crushing sound, a flow of rushing blood, and then sweet release.

He turned onto his side. In the dark, he could see Basir's back. The soft sounds of Basir's snoring followed the rising and falling of his hunched shoulders. He did not suffer from stress, bless him. His soul was prepared for his body to become a pancake. He would rise to the hand of Allah without difficulty.

Wahid turned onto his stomach. He stared at the wall. Even in the dark, only illuminated by a partial glimmer of moonlight, the crack in the plaster was evident. Peeling, flaking paint was forming into a small pile on the floor. Wahid had swept it up with his hands two days ago, scraped the dusty flakes into his palms, cast them into the sink and flushed them down the drain with water. Afterwards, he washed his hands thoroughly. Now he had to do it again. He sighed.

Why did it crack, he wondered. What made the outer shell decide to give up and fall away? Where did the rot set in? Had someone, another prisoner perhaps, picked at it and then the peeling developed a momentum of its own? Or perhaps there was rot underneath; with the right conditions, damp, humidity

83

created by human bodies, and mould, it found it easy to emerge, destroying the outer layer, scouring it, showing the ugliness underneath.

If the rot was within, perhaps the wall was just as weak as the paint. Wahid positioned his body ramrod straight. He imagined he was a torpedo in a firing tube. He flexed his feet against the rail at the base of the bed.

Fire one. Fire two. Hit the destroyer, captain. Aye aye.

He turned to his other side. This wall was also moving inwards. Perhaps it was not just the ceiling then. Space and time could be compressing in this small space, pushing inwards into a temporal enigma which would suck himself and Basir into a different dimension. What a journey that could be. It would likely be better than here, he mused. Anywhere would be better than here.

Pipes rumbled in the distance. He heard a splash of water, then the sound of excrement being dumped out of a window: a prisoner's protest through completed digestion. Wahid pulled his blanket up over his body, hugging it to him like a shroud. He softly recited a Sura. He listened intently to the sounds of water flowing through the prison plumbing. The words, the sound of gurgling water lulled him.

Dawn. Wahid detected the golden light through his shut eyelids. He did not want to face the day. He knew, however, that not doing so was only postponing the inevitable.

He sighed.

"My friend," Basir's voice said.

Wake up, wake up.

"No," Wahid said.

"Come on, you must awake," Basir said. "They're opening the cell."

Wahid opened his eyes.

Sometimes, the doors to the cells were opened. This was called "social hour". The phrase made Wahid think of how his mother's friends would visit her; he recalled being a young boy, opening the door, and being pinched on the cheeks by a succession of middle-aged women. Their scarves and blouses were a technicolour procession of reds, blues, purples and browns, each shade a mark of individuality for women who all seemed the same:

"Such a strong boy."

"Such a fine boy."

"Such a good boy."

Pinch pinch pinch. Ow.

"Come on," Basir said.

It was best if he and Wahid took a walk rather than remain in the cell. Basir was right to be nervous: the last time they had tried to lay low in their own space, it had been a prelude to another game of "kick the Paki".

Wahid slowly sat up, twisted his body and planted his feet on the floor.

He put his hand over his heart.

Quick, quick, slow. Not dead yet.

Unfortunately.

He felt each of his tendons tighten as he stood, as if they were made of piano wire and being plucked with the effort. Basir was standing at the open door.

"Glad you could join me," he said with a smile.

Wahid nodded. They stepped out into the hall.

Powerful arms grabbed him from the side; he was pinned against the wall.

Wahid had never looked at Arkie up close. A thin layer of sweat covered his pug nose, his eyelids, his shaved eyebrows. A flow of saliva came out of his mouth with each exhale.

Arkie's breath stank of stale milk. "Well well, what do we have 'ere?" he said.

At once Wahid wanted to cry out; a hand was clamped across his mouth. He let out a stifled scream.

Oh my God!

The guards usually watched the prisoners more carefully

85

during social hour. Wahid cast a glance across the alabaster hall. No one.

A voice to Wahid's right. "Arkie, you sure about this?"

"Shut your gob," Arkie said, "we're going to play some football...get up!"

Wahid shifted his eyes; Basir was similarly restrained. He fought against his two captors, Arkie's colleagues Stan and Stitch, trying to wriggle out of their grip.

"Now!!" Arkie exclaimed.

Basir and Wahid were thrown onto the floor together. Wahid felt hands grab him and tie a cloth around his mouth.

"Now there won't be too much fucking noise now, will there?" Arkie said.

One of the other prisoners began to sing a wordless song. "Da da da da, da da da, da da da da da da!"

"Quit with that Match of the Day shite," Arkie's compatriot hissed.

"Fine, let the game begin!"

A kick to the stomach. Wahid flew upwards. He tried to scream; it felt as if his internal parts came loose.

"Goaaaaaalllll!"

"Lining up on the penalty spot," another prisoner said.

Wahid felt a boot blast him squarely on the backside.

"The keeper would have caught that, mate." Arkie commented.

"Fuck you. I could have been the next Cantona."

"Yes, if you weren't on meth and lost ten stone. My turn," Arkie said, "And now a Beckham special…"

A swift sideswiping kick to Wahid's face. He flew sideways and crashed to the floor. Two of his teeth swam in his mouth.

"Goaaallll!"

Time slowed. The shrinking pressure of the universe, Wahid noted, did not proceed at a uniform rate. Sometimes it was as quick as a movement from Beethoven's Ninth, other times, it was slow as Siegfried's Death March from Wagner's

"Goetterdaemmerung". The galaxy was held together by a variety of play lists, each tune representing a different tempo in which its course could proceed. Allah was Master Composer and Conductor, Maestro of All.

"Kick him again!" they shouted. The words came out slowly; as if a switch on an old-style record player had been set incorrectly, and the music and lyrics came out distorted.

"Kick him again!" How many times was that said? The statements were punctuated with stars going off inside Wahid's head, bright supernovae exploding in distant galaxies. He tried to scamper towards the light.

"Grab him!" a voice cried, "he's trying to get away!"

"No, no," Wahid thought, "I just want to see the wonders of all creation."

He was pinned to the wall, the Barrier of the Universe. The cold scratchiness of the Barrier pressed hard against his face. On the other side, Wahid was sure, lay Allah. His fingernails scratched against it.

"Let me in, let me in," he whispered.

"What's he saying?"

"Paki rubbish," Arkie said, "he can't even fucking speak English properly."

"I'm thinking," one of the prisoners said.

Wahid tried to raise a fist to knock on the Barrier. "Let me in, Lord," he thought. His hand was pinned down; he could barely tap on the obstruction with a fingertip.

"You, thinking? That'd be a first," Arkie said.

"Shut up. These goat shaggers are used to buggering each other. They're probably fucking good at it."

Wahid tried to lift a foot to kick against the Barrier. His leg refused to respond. "Allah, let thy servant in!" he thought.

"What are you saying?" Arkie replied.

Quick quick quick. Slow.

"What's the closest thing to pussy we 'ave around here?"

Quick quick quick quick quick quick. Thump thump. The Barrier would not yield. "Dear God, Allah, Lord of All, let me in," he thought. He heard the rushing of water on the other side, ah yes, an eternal spring from which Allah's servants could drink upon passing. "Quench thy servant's burning thirst, O Lord of the Dawn," Wahid thought.

"I see your point," Arkie said. "Want some dark meat, do you then?"

"I'll shut my eyes and pretend it's my girlfriend. She has really big tits."

"Made out of latex, eh?" Arkie asked.

"Shut up."

There was a tearing of clothes. A cold wind rushed over Wahid's body.

"Scrawny little fucker, isn't he?"

"Beggars can't be choosers."

"Hello, darlin'!"

The universe collapsed again. The singularity it focused on was filth, disease, vermin, disgust. The epicentre of that truth penetrated Wahid to the core of his body.

"OH MY GOD I FLY TO THEE," Wahid thought. In spite of the gag, he vomited violently. The gag only served to push the vomit back into his mouth as forcefully as it exploded out of him.

There were moans.

"Ride that fucking pig!" Arkie said.

"He likes a big 'un, doesn't he!"

The singularity slammed Wahid against the wall repeatedly. The concrete was stained with his blood, vomit, and his face was shoved into it again and again and again.

"Here I come, you little minx!"

A star exploded with a roar. Fragments of its fire scarred Wahid throughout his body. The filth of its ashes contaminated Wahid to every last cell. He wanted to curl up and die, but here he was, spread up against the wall. Allah had not let him pass through. Perhaps he was dead and in Hell.

"My turn," Arkie said.

A whistle sounded. The cosmos ceased.

Sixteen

A bird sang in the distance. It was a lilting melody that warbled and wavered as it travelled through the air, touching his ears like the tickling of a feather.

Wahid became aware of sunlight glowing through his eyelids. Wake up wake up wake up.

Quick quick quick. Slow. The pulse accelerated, dropped back. As the blood travelled, sensations from his body communicated to his brain.

He was damaged; but this was a different sort of injury than those he suffered on the Tube. No bones were broken, but there were bruises. They merged to the point that his body felt like one large sore.

Slow slow slow. There was another feeling to accompany the dull pain; his limbs felt as if they were made of finely worked crystal; the slightest motion and they would shatter. To test the theory, he lifted an arm and lowered it. No breakage, but his fingertips came down onto a surface. It was soft, made of what felt like coarse wool, ah, a blanket.

Did he dare open his eyes? The sun's warmth coursed through him. The Prophet described a Heaven of dazzling light that was impossible for humans to describe. Perhaps the Barrier had opened after all and he had arrived in Eternity.

He exhaled; he opened his eyes. The sunlight initially blotted out the scene; there was a dark, blurry shape in the corner. The shape came towards him, blocking the sun's rays.

The image began to sharpen. The figure was a person: bald head, handlebar moustache....

"Mr. Watson," Wahid said. The weakness in his voice surprised him.

"Mr. Shah," Watson replied.

"Am I...."

"You're back in the hospital."

Another shape hobbled into view.

"Basir?" Wahid asked.

"Yes, my friend."

"Mr. Basir has two sprained ankles," Watson said. "It seems your assailants tried to twist his feet off."

"But....me...."

Basir and Watson were stony faced.

"You will recover," Watson replied.

"I assume you want to press charges," Hassan said.

Wahid looked at him. Hassan was wearing a brown suit that day, pressed to an extreme that meant his figure was all corners and angles. As he sat on the edge of the bed, Wahid noted there was nothing comfortable about his appearance.

"Yes," Wahid said slowly.

"Based upon what Mr. Basir has said, we've established that the ringleader was one Arnold Arkwright, known as Arkie."

Arkie Arkie Arkie. If Wahid willed, he was sure he could make the name devoid of meaning. If it was devoid of meaning, perhaps he would cease to exist. In his mind, Wahid could see a faceless lump in an orange prison outfit. The lump laughed, joked, poked his comrades in the arm. Then with God's help and Wahid's will, just a gentle pop, and he would disappear. After all, as was said in Sura 19, when God said Mary would become pregnant with Jesus, all He had to say was "be!" and so it was. The reverse applied, surely.

"Arkie's already in solitary confinement," Hassan assured him.

"Good, if he was even a real person," Wahid thought. In reply, he nodded.

"...and Willows has said that you can stay here for the

remainder of your pre-trial detention."

Willows? Perhaps if Wahid willed him away, he would go too. Allah would surely not wish such a dreadful person to exist either. "Not be", and so it is not. Yes.

Watson stood in the corner of the room, his arms folded across his chest, crinkling the white starched perfection of his coat. Truly, he could learn something about sharpness of line from Hassan.

"Mr. Hassan," Watson said, "perhaps you ought to mention the counselling that Mr. Shah will get."

Hassan brightened. "Ah yes, the Prison Service is going to get a psychiatrist to have a few words with you."

Oh? "I am perfectly sane. It just the rest of the world that is not Switzerland," Wahid said.

Hassan swallowed. "Indeed," he replied.

"Are you sure that you are still constipated?" Watson asked.

Wahid nodded.

"I'll get you another dose of laxatives," the nurse replied.

It was a daily ritual: the toilet had taken on a holy significance. The evil star had exploded within him, and Wahid had embarked on a Mission, to flush every last remnant of its poisonous ash out of his body.

In this quest, the laxatives were a gift. When Wahid sat on the toilet, and the flow came out of his colon in a massive burst, he was certain it was taking some of the ash with it. But the massive tidal wave was rare, unpredictable. Only the laxatives could ensure that happened on a daily basis. It would take years, Wahid estimated, for all of the filth to be washed out of him. When he shut his eyes, he could envisage it: it had hardened, formed into granules which had embedded themselves into the deepest recesses in his body. Out out out.

The shower was subject to a similarly scientific process. Watson gave him two antibacterial washes and a sterilised cloth before each bathing. Wahid recited a prayer, turned the water to as hot he could stand and applied both soaps to the cloth, taking care to wash underneath his toenails, to cleanse each hair on his forearms, and sterilise the curvature of his lower buttocks, or at least that which remained. This had to be done at least twice a day, sometimes, three times.

Eating was a process best done alone. With Basir, it became unbearable. Basir was a good man, but he simply could not comprehend that when the forks and knives were laid out on the table, they had to be precise before one began to eat. The edge of the knife handle had to be precisely aligned with the straight edge of the table. It could take some time, as Wahid adjusted the knife millimetre by millimetre by small touches of his fingertips. The process was repeated with the fork. Wahid then turned his attention to the plate; he took a bottle of rubbing alcohol and a ball of cotton wool, kindly procured by Mr. Watson, and doused the cotton with the solution. He first flipped the plate upside down and carefully sterilised the bottom, flipped it upright and then sterilised the part which would hold his food.

Basir constantly got in the way; he kept asking if Wahid was all right.

"It is just Switzerland," Wahid replied. The word was the quality and the quality was purity, and purity and purpose and cleanliness were all that mattered.

They insisted that he see the psychiatrist.

"You are not well, Mr. Shah," Watson said.

On the contrary, he had never been better. He was following in the footsteps of the Prophet.

Wahid remembered being eleven years old, and Father reading the Qur'an to him. It was a November evening; the month always scared Wahid because the night rushed in sooner, and somehow there were always clouds that obscured the moon. He cycled home from school and already the shadows of the evening were creeping along the street, the clattering of gears and pedals was the only protest against the dying light, along with the distant din of London's traffic.

Night followed him, he was sure. He cycled a mile, turned a

corner, and there were the shadows lining the street. The sun was fast setting, its power to disperse the darkness fading by the moment.

Father, only Father could face such endless darkness without the need to stifle the urge to cry out in horror.

That November evening, Father lit the gas fire with a long match, and as the blue flames rose up and buckled and swayed in the breeze from the chimney, he reached up for the dark green leather bound volume from the top shelf of their oak bookcase. His crisply starched white shirt crackled as he extended his arm. Mother, wearing a beige silk scarf and dark brown dress, sat in an easy chair facing the fire, reading a *Home and Garden* magazine. No doubt she was looking up what bulbs Father would have to plant in the window boxes. Tulips, daffodils, anything with a lot of light colours.

Father stretched and strained; the book finally popped free into his hand. Still, it was essential to keep it on the top shelf. "Keep the highest book in the highest place," he told Wahid.

Typical Saturday evening. Father reading from the Qur'an or telling him tales of the Prophet, his dark eyes flashing, his hands gesticulating in line with the story. The Prophet suffered humiliation and attack in Mecca, Father said, his hands forming a circle, as if he was strangling an imaginary person. It was absolutely essential for him to leave for Medina. There, he was able to establish the Faith.

England was another Mecca, to be sure. But unlike the Prophet, Wahid wished to stay in Medina. But what was Medina in this case? Where would he find it?

It was not under the bed. Wahid checked, and found only dust and rusty springs.

Perhaps Medina was Switzerland, he mused. Yes, it had to be! Medina was an oasis, Switzerland was an oasis. Logically, they were one and the same.

Wahid looked out the window, and upon seeing a bird floating on a summer breeze, he thought about projecting his thoughts into the animal. Yes, the Prophet flew to Jerusalem on

93

the back of a flying creature, surely Wahid could cast his mind and spirit into some other creature, a lesser one, one that would take him to Salvation.

"You must see the psychiatrist," Watson informed him.

Watson was a good man, but he was not of the Faith. He could not understand the journey that lay ahead for Wahid, the alternative *Hajj* which would purify him, and lead him to sanctuary.

Wahid folded his hands in front of him, examining his fingernails as he crossed his fingers, ensuring that there was not a single speck of dirt beneath them.

See the psychiatrist. What relevance did that have when he needed to see God?

But as Father had explained while leafing through the dark green leather book, and speaking in his warm tones, the Prophet had faced diversions, setbacks, and even defeats. Seeing the psychiatrist was a way station, a diversion on the road to Medina.

Yes, he would see her. It was what God wanted, to be sure.

Seventeen

"I am here to help you," she said.

Help?

The psychiatrist was a woman in her forties, with a few grey strands at the front of her hair. She unsuccessfully hid this by sweeping it back and tying it into a ponytail. Her eyes were blue and slightly magnified by the large, thick-lensed glasses she wore. This gave an insect-like aspect to her gaze; Wahid temporarily wondered if she was a giant fly, who vomited enzymes on its food to digest it, before taking it in. Disgusting, but not unexpected.

Worse, there was a smudge on her oversized blue shirt, right near the cuff. It looked like it was from motor oil; it was dark black and was in the shape of a fingerprint.

"Perhaps," Wahid reasoned, "it is merely ink."

Still, so careless. He found he could not reply to her. He pulled out an alcohol swab from his pocket, which he had borrowed from Watson. He tore open the white packaging. The scent of alcohol brought an involuntary smile to his lips; he pulled out the swap and wiped the table with three sweeping strokes. He folded the swab, and put his hands down on the spot where he had wiped most vigorously, watching carefully that he did not rest any part of them on an untreated area.

"I see you are very tidy," she commented. Her accent was peculiar to Wahid. French, perhaps.

She folded her long, blue denim clad legs, kicking her feet out alongside the table. He wrinkled his nose in reply.

Wahid focused his eyes on his hands and the table beneath.

95

Perhaps he should have wiped the table a bit longer. His skin was too thin to keep any germs out to be sure; he could see the bones, muscles and tendons moving underneath the protective sheath, reminding him of watching snakes wriggling beneath a blanket. The table's grey metal surface probably had microbes which weren't susceptible to the swab. No, only pouring boiling water on the table, then an alcohol rub would do.

No, actually, only boiling the table would do. But how could he boil the table? Was there a vat large enough?

Quick quick, slow slow. He looked up at her.

"Yes," Wahid replied.

The psychiatrist tilted her head. "I am Dr. Blanchard," she continued. "Your friend Mr. Watson suggested I tell you where I am from: I am from Lausanne, Switzerland."

Wahid looked up. She was smiling, her big eyes glittering through the magnification.

"Lausanne?" he asked.

"Yes."

"Is it...*clean* there?"

"Yes, it is," she replied. "It is very clean indeed."

He shut his eyes as she spoke at length about her home. Yes, there were home inspectors which ensured that a home was tidy before it was sold. Yes, Lausanne's pavements were swept till they shone. No, litter was not tolerated.

"Tell me about the air," Wahid said.

"Clean," she said. "It is bracing."

Wahid inhaled. Quick quick quick. The air in the prison was stale and humid; Swiss air surely was hygienic, dry and cold. Yes, breathing it in would be like when his mother rubbed wintergreen oil on his chest when he was ill. The bite was a symptom of germs in retreat, the victory of all that was tidy.

"It is time for me to finish for now," Dr. Blanchard said.

Wahid opened his eyes. She reached out and handed him a tissue. Without thinking, he took it, and dabbed away some tears.

"We will talk again," she said.

Eighteen

Wahid held himself perfectly still. He lay on his back, his hands rested just above his stomach, the palms pressed together. His eyes were shut.

"If I stay this motionless," he thought, "perhaps all will be well."

His stomach was churning over the lentils and rice he had eaten for lunch: filthy, disgusting food in prison, to be sure. The spice was too hot, the rice was too dry, there was probably rat hair in it.

Wahid recited the Nineteenth Sura silently, his lips moving to the words. He did not speak Arabic, but that only lent more power to the recitation. Knowing too much destroyed the mystery, and all things that were important were hidden and unknowable.

He exhaled and his eyes opened.

"Are you all right, my friend?" Basir asked.

Wahid cast his glance to the bed on the other side of the room. Basir's bruises were healing, he noted. The black pits around his eyes had grown more shallow, blood vessels beneath the skin were healing, purple turning to yellow and then disappearing entirely.

"I am fine," Wahid said slowly.

Basir nodded. He had become like that. The broad grin appeared less often; Basir looked at him with some caution, as if Wahid was ready to set himself alight.

Admittedly, the thought had occurred to Wahid. He had dreams about the man whom God said should not be, that Arkie

97

person, and recalled how the Barrier of Creation had not opened. The nightmare of utter filth made him want to find a bottle of rubbing alcohol and set himself on fire. Fire was good, fire was pure, no bacterium could survive its embrace.

The door to the hospital ward swung open slowly; the old brass hinges creaked. Really, how untidy, that needed to be sorted out. Rania knew where the spray lubricant was kept. It was underneath the sink in the kitchen, along with the disinfectant. A few shots of that and it would be as right as rain.

But was rain right? It was right for flowers and trees, but for Wahid it was a precursor to getting his feet wet and being caught out with the flu. It had only been through God's grace that it had not caught him the past three winters.

By the open door stood Watson, holding a few letters. The sleeves of his white coat were rolled up that day, revealing the bramble tattoos which interwove further as he flexed his arms.

"Post for you, gentlemen!" he exclaimed.

Wahid remained still. Basir leapt up and took the letters.

"Thank you, Mr. Watson," Basir said.

Watson nodded towards Wahid. "I noticed that one of the letters is for Mr. Shah," he said. "Hopefully it will boost his morale."

"No doubt."

Watson withdrew. Wahid focused his eyes on the ceiling. Another crack was forming. It had to be the thirtieth or fortieth one in the past two weeks.

Basir placed the letter in front of Wahid's eyes and the ceiling.

"Letter for you, my friend....I think it's from Rania."

Rania, Rania, Rania. He had tried to keep her name out of his head. After all, he was still on the path to purity. She would have to wait for him at the end of it.

The envelope was so thin that Wahid could see light from the other side penetrating it, and the shape of the folded paper on the inside was obvious. A bright green and white stamp, showing the banner of Pakistan flowing in the wind, was covered in ink marks stating "Karachi".

God knew how many hands the letter had passed through. There were dark brown fingerprints on the front. Wahid's name, the address of the prison, were written in precise, clear letters in blue ink.

So perfect, the sweep of the "W", the curvature of the "a", the majesty of the standing "h".

Wahid reached up and took it in his hands. He just had to make sure he washed his hands later before he touched his face. Seventy percent of colds, he recalled, came from people rubbing their eyes with unclean fingers. Naturally, his eyes began to itch.

Basir withdrew his hand.

"Go on, read it," he urged.

Basir was always like that, urging him to take chances. Dr. Blanchard's visits were far preferable to his company. Lausanne, he had found out, was clean to the point of sterility. He could, according to her, eat his meal off the street and only sense cleanliness from the scent of the pavement and the slick shine that was left behind from the soap.

Wahid exhaled. Never mind, the way to Switzerland was very long indeed. He was going to have to wait until God allowed his journey to come to an end.

He tore open the letter carefully. The paper easily gave way to his fingertips. Lucky. If the paper had been caught in a rainstorm in transit, it would likely have dissolved.

There was a slight scent of Rania's perfume as the letter fell into his hands. For a moment, Wahid could recall being close to her, her dark eyes staring up into his upon awakening on a Saturday morning, her lips turned into a smile to say "Good morning."

Odd. Did she really exist, or was she a dream?

He unfolded the letter. Ah, more precise blue writing, lovely.

"Dearest Wahid," the letter began.

Yes.

"I miss you."

Did he miss her? Yes? No? Maybe?

"It's very lonely here, in spite of Uncle Naseem's hospitality."

Wahid cast a glance at Basir. He was reading a letter of his own, his lips turned in an uncharacteristic frown.

"All of my needs are met," she continued. "I have a bedroom that overlooks a garden. Do you remember his garden?"

Wahid shut his eyes for a moment. Yes, he had been there when he was a young man, it was the time when he was introduced to Rania. Father and Mother and he had packed up into a jumbo jet at Gatwick Airport, stuffed into an uncomfortable (and unsanitary!) seat for ten hours and landed in Lahore. Wahid didn't know the purpose of the trip till they were bouncing along in a large beige Peugeot driven by Uncle Naseem. He had picked them up at the airport, embracing Father without hesitation as soon as he emerged from customs.

Uncle Nassem was younger then, his elongated beard had no trace of grey. His black hair was swept back with hair oil, and he gave off the scent of jasmine and dirt. He probably had been working in the garden.

Wahid was jammed in between Father and Mother, the insulation making the potholes and bumps more bearable. Naseem appeared to delight in running over them as quickly as possible.

"Do you know why we're here?" Father asked. He wore his white English shirt, his hair combed in the English style, and he had applied twice the usual amount of cheap cologne.

"We're here to visit the family, Baba," Wahid said.

Mother placed a hand on his shoulder. "That's not entirely the case. We're here for you too."

Wahid turned to her. Her head was bobbing up and down with the car, her purple scarf following her gyrations. She did her best not to appear alarmed.

"Get that Godforsaken piece of rubbish out of the road!" Naseem shouted at a small Japanese car ahead of them.

100

"Yes," Mother continued, "we have arranged for you to meet a girl of a suitable family...we want you to take a wife."

Take a wife? Wahid was all of twenty-one. For him, the idea of having a girlfriend fell down at the first hurdle; he liked an English girl at university named Sally who liked Duran Duran, wore her blonde hair in plaits and smelled of soap and nail polish. She used words like "Whatevah" and "oi" frequently. He could never ask her out because she chewed bubble gum incessantly. Besides where would they go? Not home, surely.

"Don't worry," Father said, placing a hand on his shoulder.

Naseem drove the car over another pothole.

"You will like her," Mother said.

Uncle Naseem's house was on the outskirts of Karachi, hidden among other homes for high-ranking army officers and civil servants.

"What does Uncle Naseem do?" Wahid asked Father once.

Father raised an eyebrow in reply. "He works for the government."

His tone made Wahid silence any further questions.

Whatever he did, it obviously paid well. Whereas the honest bookkeeper had to go to London to ply his trade, Naseem had a large, white house surrounded by an iron fence. A boy dressed in a red shirt stood by the gate and opened it upon his master's approach. The boy was careful to dip his head as Naseem drove past him. Gravel crunched beneath the tyres as they drove up the long, circular drive, and pulled up to a wide entrance, bleached white and shaded by a small balcony supported by two white pillars.

Standing on the steps was a woman dressed in a dark green blouse. She also wore a dark green scarf with a band of gold running through it which was draped over her shoulders. That had to be his Aunt Khadija, Wahid reasoned.

When he climbed out of the car after Mother, she stepped forward and embraced him.

"Wahid! Such a fine boy!" she said.

Pinch, pinch, kiss. Ouch.

Wahid cast a glance at Father, who had opened the boot of the car and was pulling out their luggage. The smile was knowing, and called for forbearance.

Khadija and Mother embraced next.

"Welcome home," Khadija said.

"It's good to be here. Has the young lady arrived?"

"Yes," Khadija said, "she's waiting in the garden. Come inside and we will have some tea."

The lounge in Uncle Naseem's house was decorated with blue sofas and a large oriental rug on the floor. Aunt Khadija clapped her hands; a servant in a long white *kurta* emerged, carrying a tray. He was silent, sullen, and dipped his head before setting the tray down on the glass coffee table.

The tea: Wahid recalled his aunt's fine Wedgwood porcelain set. The cups were small, delicate, white with blue and silver trim along the edges. The teapot matched; Khadija positioned a silver strainer full of tea leaves over its opening and poured hot water from a metal pot into it.

Where did that water come from, Wahid wondered, was it from a well or from the pipes? A brief survey of the drainage system of Karachi during the drive from the airport was not particularly comforting.

"So how are you doing in university?" Aunt Khadija asked.

"He is doing well," Mother interjected. "He is at the top of his class."

Aunt Khadija clapped her hands, the gold bracelets on her wrists clattering. "Wonderful," she said, "he will be an accountant for a large firm....perfect for Rania."

Rania?

Mother waved the suggestion away. "It is more likely Wahid will be an independent bookkeeper much like his father."

Khadija nodded, her heavy gold earrings slightly clinking as she gesticulated.

"That too, is a noble profession."

But the garden. Wahid remained silent as Mother and Auntie chattered about the weather in London, the cost of living, what was happening in the country, and indeed wasn't Uncle Naseem doing well in spite of all the turmoil. They were going to shortly trade in the Peugeot for a Mercedes, and in spite of his love of driving, Khadija had persuaded him to get a chauffeur.

"Good news for all the other drivers in Karachi," Mother said.

They laughed.

Wahid wanted to say something, but was not sure what.

"I exist," he thought of saying. Mother and Khadija kept on discussing his future without asking him about it.

"He will be finishing his schooling shortly," Mother said.

"Excellent, a fine British education has surely made him a well rounded man."

"I exist!" Wahid wanted to interject.

Khadija turned her eyes to him at last.

"Your mother and I are likely to talk for some time, perhaps you'd like to go into the garden, nephew."

Wahid nodded.

She gestured to a set of glass doors behind him. "Just step out there. You'll find a bench by the jasmine and lavender."

Wahid got up and opened the large glass doors. The heat of the late afternoon hit him; the air was humid and still and there was a sound of buzzing insects. In the distance, he heard the sounds of diesel engines and honking horns.

"You can't escape it," Khadija sighed sadly, "the sounds of Karachi are everywhere."

He stepped outside and shut the doors behind him.

The grass was as thick and lush as any pile carpet, and a colour green that was alien to London. Wahid had been to Green Park before on a summer's day, when Father tried to encourage him to run and play. Wahid ended up tripping and falling flat on his face while trying to kick a soccer ball. The green of that lawn seemed terribly pale compared to the verdant grass here. Yet, the air was so oppressive. Truly, it was a miracle from God that anything survived.

Wahid lifted his head, as if to receive the scents of the garden better; there were roses, he was sure, and yes, there was the hint of lavender, and a blast of jasmine. He turned a corner around a bush, following his nose.

There was the bench. It was wrought iron, painted white. Behind it was a large lavender bush, and behind that, a red brick wall. A butterfly floated over the bush, its yellow wings beating furiously to avoid landing on it prematurely.

A young woman was sitting on the bench. She had long black hair with blonde streaks. Her eyes were downcast, and her brown blouse and skirt were crisp in line and contour.

Wahid stepped up to her.

She looked up at him.

"What large eyes she has," he thought.

"Hello," she said.

"Hello," he replied.

Say something else, you idiot.

"My name is Wahid," he said, extending his hand.

She took it. "I am Rania."

Wahid pressed the letter up to his nose. Yes, there was her perfume. Too bad there was no hint of the lavender or jasmine in that garden. He looked at the letter again.

"Do you remember his garden?"

Yes.

"I sat on our bench," she continued. "I remembered how shy you were and how you shook my hand like an Englishman."

Wahid smiled.

"We must come back here someday."

Maybe. Pakistan was so far away. Besides, would the bench be different? It was wrought iron after all. Surely after so many years, the white paint had peeled away, rust had appeared. All things faded and died or fell apart, even the garden and the bench.

104

But then again, perhaps Aunt Khadija had something to say about that.

"I'm trying to keep myself busy," the letter stated.

Good.

"Your Aunt Khadija has suggested that I teach English to earn some money on the side."

Teach English? Well it was not unheard of; Uncle Naseem told them over dinner long ago about how many young girls were actually earning a living in that manner.

"Good for them," he thundered. "Women should earn their way." He hit the table with his fist for emphasis, shaking the bowl of *pilau* rice.

"I'm thinking about it," the letter continued.

Wahid smiled. Yes.

"Uncle Naseem sends his regards. He says what is happening is an absolute disgrace. He says he has been to the British Embassy about it."

Good luck.

"They told him that they have taken his objections into account. You'll be surprised, but I have received some letters from people here. All are supportive."

"Good news?" Basir asked.

Wahid cast a look at him. "Sort of," he said. "Apparently our case is known in Pakistan."

Basir shrugged. "Yes, Dina says the same."

Wahid focused his eyes back on the letter.

"I miss you," she had written.

Wahid blinked. Miss him? He was arrested, disgraced, befouled and they had no children to show for their marriage.

The wedding had been an understated affair, held in a small but elegant hotel near Uncle Naseem's house. The imam had a thick white beard; he wore a pastel turban and a dark vest. He held the Qur'an in his right hand and read several verses. Wahid could hear the imam's words, but was not listening. Mother had insisted that it be a traditional service, so Rania was seated in a separate room.

The imam coughed.

Father tapped Wahid on the shoulder.

Wahid's heart pounded. Slowly and carefully, he recited the Urdu words his father had taught him. The words' meaning resonated in his mind:

I, Wahid, agree to take you, Rania, as my bride.

She was only a few feet away, behind a white door with a polished brass knob. Wahid listened hard as he spoke; there was silence on the other side. He imagined her wearing red silk: a deep, rich shade. Was she listening to what he had to say? Would her big dark eyes widen with expectation or fear? Would she say no?

A chill passed through him, followed by a burst of sweating.

Oh God, I'm dying right here, right at the point of marriage, he thought.

He finished his proposal. The imam smiled.

Quick quick, slow slow.

Miss him? How strange. But then again, he had brought her back to London and they lived with Mother and Father until he was established as an accountant. She was amazed at how small the houses were, yet impressed with the electricity that did not suffer from occasional blackouts. She was also amazed by the size of the supermarkets.

"I love you," the letter stated.

Love? Him?

Wahid felt his back tingle unpleasantly. He shuddered as he recalled coarse hands grabbing him, pushing him, and then the violation.

No, no, Rania, love someone better. Love someone as clean as Lausanne in winter.

"You are a good man," she continued. "Never forget it."

Good? Him?

He was a sinner in a world awash with sin. Rania, sweet

beautiful Rania could never understand the filth of the world. She laughed it off when after each meal he washed his hands in disinfectant. She didn't realise how vile it was for them to make love.

No, he was not good. He was not worthy of love.

"I will write to you again soon. Write to me," she urged.

He shut his eyes and laid the letter down beside him on the bed.

"Good letter?" Basir asked.

"More or less," Wahid replied.

Nineteen

"Have you given up using the laxatives yet?" Dr. Blanchard asked.

Wahid nodded. "Yes, Doctor," he replied.

The doctor had suggested drinking more water to flush all the poisons out of his system. No more than four large glasses a day. Sometimes Wahid was bad and indulged in five. However, when he went to the toilet and saw his urine was clear, he could see the point. Purity. At last there was evidence the filth was washing out of him.

"Progress," she said, putting a finger to her lips.

Indeed.

They were once again seated in the visiting room. The doctor wore an open grey cardigan and a white turtleneck shirt. She wrote on a pad with a black pen, the script looping and arching gracefully as she wrote. Wahid smiled.

"Have you written back to your wife yet?" she asked as she wrote.

"Not yet," he admitted.

Dr. Blanchard looked up. Her magnified eyes were wide. "You need to tell her."

Wahid felt his throat constrict. "I cannot," he said.

Dr. Blanchard shook her head. "You must. You are safe now. You're clean now."

Clean. Wahid wanted another glass of water right at that moment. Yes, he had put the experience behind him through the miracle of the Doctor's water treatment. Thanks be to God. It was not at all strange that His servant was a Swiss woman.

Dr. Blanchard continued writing. Her writing moved like she was conducting an orchestra, and the pen was the baton, Wahid thought.

"And you are sticking to only drinking four glasses of water per day?" the doctor asked.

More or less. "Yes, doctor."

"Good," she said. "I also have a surprise for you."

Wahid tensed. Dr. Blanchard smiled.

"Don't worry, it is a good surprise."

He exhaled. Quick quick quick, slow.

"You are to be reunited with your imam."

Wahid raised an eyebrow. Was this good news?

"Oh?" he asked.

Dr. Blanchard smiled. "I've spoken to him. He will be happy to help in your recovery."

Ah yes, God had sent first the Swiss servant, now a servant in the Faith to help him back on to the road. Amazing, incredible, such miracles: the path was becoming ever more clear all the time.

"Don't worry," Dr. Blanchard said.

Worry?

"This is insane!" a basso voice intoned. "I am going to sue you all once these charges are cleared up!"

Wahid was kneeling in prayer beside Basir on a small square of carpet. It was red as blood, which contrasted sharply with the beige linoleum of the hospital ward's floor.

Wahid tried to resist the temptation to turn his head to listen to the voice of complaint.

Footsteps grew louder behind them. Wahid cast a glance at Basir. His eyes were closed; he was concentrating on his prayers. Basir leaned forward in another surrender to God.

Wahid followed, his nose nearly touching the rug, detecting the acidic scent of the disinfectant he had applied earlier.

The door behind them swung open with a loud creak of the hinges and a bang of the door handle against the mottled beige wall.

"Sorry to disturb, gentlemen."

Wahid and Basir turned. Watson stood before them, a faint look of anxiety crossing his features. The brambles on his forearms were twisting and stretching.

"Yes, Mr. Watson?" Basir asked.

"Your...colleagues have arrived."

Watson stepped out of the way. Two police officers, dressed in dark blue sweaters and with small radios clipped to their shoulders entered first, followed by the imam and Ahmed, the butcher from Brick Lane. Both were wearing handcuffs. They were followed by two more policemen, identically dressed as the first pair.

"This is a miscarriage of justice, I say!" Ahmed shouted. The policemen did not tilt their heads away from the noise.

One of the first pair, who had short cropped red hair and a moustache, turned and fished a key out of his pocket. He unlocked the cuffs on the imam.

The imam's face was expressionless. He wore a blue boiler suit and a white cap. His beard was turning from black to grey, Wahid noticed. Indifferent, the imam stared straight ahead, his lips pressed together with no sign of strain or effort. He offered his bound hands to the policeman without looking at him through his black wire framed glasses. The handcuffs came off with a metallic clink; the officer pocketed them.

The officer turned to Ahmed.

"About time!" Ahmed shouted, forcing his hands out to the policeman.

The same procedure was repeated at the same pace, Ahmed's hands shaking as the cuffs came off. In contrast to the imam's straight and pristine outfit, his boiler suit was stained with sweat, the buttons near bursting where his enormous stomach insisted on intruding on the scene.

The policeman nodded to Watson, and he and his colleagues walked out.

Watson put his hands together. "I presume you will have a

lot to catch up on, gentlemen, I'll leave you in peace."

He shut the door behind him.

The imam turned to Wahid and Basir. "Brother Wahid, Brother Basir, may I join you in your prayers?"

"We'd be honoured," Basir replied.

"Prayers!" Ahmed spat.

The imam motioned to the window and the position of the sun in the sky. "Yes, Brother Ahmed, it is time." He knelt beside Wahid and Basir, and raised his eyes to heaven.

"Prayers!" Ahmed spat again. "Who has time for it?"

He stepped forward and grabbed Wahid by the collar. With a violent yank, he pulled him up till he was at eye level. Ahmed stank of old sweat. His face was covered in perspiration, with a streak of dirt across his forehead. Drops of saliva flew out of his mouth as he exhaled.

Quick quick quick, slow. Wahid shut his eyes, to try and shut out Ahmed's closeness, the rancid odour, and the quaking violence in his demeanour.

"What did you do? What in the name of God did you do to get us locked up, you hypochondriac freak?" Ahmed shouted.

"God, let him not be," Wahid thought. His face tightened in expectation of a fist being crunched into it. He could imagine the feel of Ahmed's knuckles in slow motion, crashing through skin, muscle, blood vessels, bone. The metallic taste of blood was almost in his mouth. This was going to hurt.

God, let him not be, so he is not.

"Brother Ahmed," the imam's voice interrupted. The tone was straight, even, but severe.

Wahid opened his eyes. Ahmed's expression had softened.

"We are in enough trouble as it is," the imam's voice continued. "Do not make matters worse."

"But....it's his fault."

"The fault lies with no one here," the imam said. "Put Brother Wahid down, purge yourself of anger, and join in the prayers."

Ahmed released Wahid's collar.

Wahid glanced at his hands; they shook. He knelt next to the imam.

"In the name of Allah, the Compassionate, the Merciful...." the imam intoned.

Ahmed took his place next to Wahid.

"Later," he whispered harshly.

Quick, quick, quick and slow.

"They waited until after Friday morning prayers," the imam said calmly.

He was sitting on a freshly made bed, his legs crossed. His serene expression oddly contrasted with the story he told. Basir and Wahid were listening while sitting on their beds. Ahmed stood at the window, arms crossed.

"I had just left the mosque when Willows called out to me," he continued. "He then informed me I was being detained according to the terms of the Prevention of Terrorism Act."

Basir's face was distorted by an uncharacteristic frown. "But surely, they have no evidence against you...."

The imam nodded. "No, the evidence is highly circumstantial...with the exception of the materials in Brother Wahid's briefcase."

The imam looked directly at Wahid. What was the word the English used for being unable to determine an emotional state? Inscrutable?

The imam spoke in a slow, clear voice: "Brother Wahid, why are you so afraid of the world?"

Why shouldn't I be? "I...don't know," Wahid replied.

But the question made him visualise his fear. It was like a hard knot, an iron ball at the core of his being: impenetrable, hard, cold, eternal. Wahid shifted his eyes to distract his mind from it. He looked at the imam.

The imam shrugged. "No matter...it seems, however, that none of us have behaved in a manner that is entirely free of suspicion."

Basir exploded, his eyes wide, his hands clenched into fists.

113

"That's outrageous!"

"Oh?" the imam asked, "you were going back to Pakistan, were you not?"

"Well, yes..."

"Say you are English and particularly crude...how does that look to you?"

Basir opened his mouth, shut it, and slowly nodded.

"I, on the other hand," the imam said, "apparently allowed Islamist extremists into my mosque among the countless multitudes who came there to pray. I didn't know that they were there, but apparently, it was my fault they came."

"I have done nothing," Ahmed blurted.

"You?" the imam said. "You run a failing business. You chose that moment to make a donation to a terrorist group?"

"I didn't know it was a terrorist group."

"I repeat – to the crude, there is no difference. To them, it's a case of better safe than sorry."

Better safe than sorry. Wahid could sympathise with the notion, if not the effect. How better it was to aspire to God's love, God's protection, God's embrace than to dare to live without it. He had put on the *kurta*, made sure he prayed five times a day, made sure Rania dressed modestly, putting away her blue jeans and silk dresses which she had brought from Karachi. They stood in front of her open suitcases with a canvas sack; Wahid was going to give her discarded clothes to a local charity shop.

Rania objected at first; she clutched a blue silk blouse to her chest. "I won't be able to be pretty," she said.

No, no, no, it was better to be beautiful in the eyes of God than the world. If she was immodest, God might object and bring misfortune raining down upon them both: her, because she chose to display her hair and body and arouse the baser passions of men, and him, because he had failed as a husband to inform her of God's way.

"I think you look beautiful no matter what," he said.

She nodded, and smiled, and took his hand in hers.

114

"At least more modest clothing will solve a problem," she said.

Her eyes twinkled.

"Oh?" Wahid asked.

"Yes, fewer people will ask me if I am Indian."

Wahid smiled.

"You smile, Brother Wahid?" the imam asked.

"Sorry, I was thinking about something else."

Twenty

"Your trial will begin in two weeks," Hassan told them.

Basir, the imam and Wahid looked at the solicitor intently. Out of the corner of his eye, Wahid saw that Ahmed had his face turned to the damp wall of the meeting room, his arms once again folded across his chest. Beads of water were sliding down the wall and collecting into a small brackish pool at its base.

"I would like my own legal representation," Ahmed said quietly.

Hassan turned his head with a jerk to face the butcher. His jaw muscles visibly tightened.

"Funded by whom?" Hassan asked. "It is only through the generosity of your brothers here that you have my services."

Ahmed did not bother to face him. "Tell my wife to break into my special savings account. I want my own solicitor."

"Very well. I will pass on the message. Kindly leave the room, however, while I talk to my clients."

Ahmed hoisted his overweight frame out of the metal chair, which buckled back into shape as he stood. The chair's groan sounded like a sigh of relief to Wahid's ears.

"With pleasure," Ahmed said with a smile.

He knocked on the door of the visiting room; it opened and he slipped out.

"*Who receiveth guidance, receiveth it for his own benefit: who goeth astray doth so to his own loss*," the imam said softly.

"I beg your pardon?" Hassan asked.

The imam gently shook his head and smiled slightly. "Never mind."

117

"The judge in this case is Lord Justice Oliver Pendleton Hastings," Hassan informed them.

Lord Justice Oliver Pendleton Hastings. Wahid rolled the name through is mind several times.

Basir looked at Wahid, Wahid looked at the imam, they looked at each other.

"You've never heard of him?" Hassan asked, incredulous.

No.

Hassan explained. Lord Justice Hastings was apparently well known for hating "trials by media". He had written a long article in the *Times* or *Telegraph* or some other newspaper that Wahid never read about how the criminal justice system had recently been reduced to a series of pronouncements by the tabloid press, whereby the accused lived or died based upon a thumbs up or down by a howling mob.

"Such a spectacle is not a suitable framework for British justice, rather, it belongs to the era of the Roman Coliseum," Hastings had written, apparently.

Is that good, is that bad, is that indifferent? Wahid asked: Hassan shrugged.

It was perhaps good, because Hastings was unlikely to respond well to Willows' type of investigation. The Inspector's repeated appearances on television would have gnawed on Hastings' nerves.

But perhaps the selection of Hastings was unfortunate. He was over eighty years old, he had served with the Indian Army as an officer and fought in Burma, and he had been around for Partition. Wahid could picture a young Englishman, pale and sweating in a khaki uniform, standing by the train station in Delhi with an Enfield rifle slung over his shoulder, watching people fleeing from the violence. What would Hastings have seen, apart from chaos, the train ready to burst with people, their possessions tied up in little bundles and dragging screaming children in tow?

If only Hastings had met Father, brave and daring Father

who could charm everyone. Father would have given him a hearty handshake, tossed his head back as if he were striding across a film set, and Hastings would have seen the quality of the man. Had they met, Hastings would think better of Pakistan, Wahid was sure.

"He is old school," Hassan concluded. But what did that mean? Hassan shrugged again.

Quick, quick, slow.

"Be calm," Dr. Blanchard advised. She wore a new pair of glasses, which lessened the magnification of her eyes. The pools of deep blue were more warm than glaring.

Wahid gulped down air. Quick, slow, quick, slow.

"You will get through this," she said.

"But, but…."

"But what?"

"What if I am convicted?"

She put down her pen and smiled. "I sincerely doubt it."

Easy for her to say.

The future was plotted before him along two lines. If he was convicted, they would probably send him back to the same prison as Arkie. He would be submerged in filth; the crumbling walls, the intolerable food, the smells of body odour and toilet flowing through the place would kill him. His stomach cramped at the thought of being awake at night, hearing the sound of a prisoner down the hall relieving himself into a pot and then hearing the splash of the fluid being dumped out through the bars.

In that context, death would be satisfying. He could imagine his corpse stretched out on a long thin cot, lying on top of a grey blanket. Death's pallor would make him more pale, almost a faded version of himself. At last, they would allow him to be dressed in white again, the *kurta*, the cap and trousers. He would be free; a stretcher carried by men dressed in black wool suits and top hats would take his corpse to its eternal rest. He had a will: his body would be buried in Highgate, hidden among

119

other generations of Londoners amidst the sad, bending trees and grasping ivy.

Father had taken him there once to see the grave of Karl Marx. Wahid didn't find out why until after Father's death when he found hidden amongst the tidy files in Father's large oak desk a copy of a guidebook. The cover was dark blue, and the print on the title page said, "A Gentleman's Comprehensive Guide to Touring London" and was printed in 1911. Wahid flicked through the pages, discovering the fine engravings of London scenes: Nelson's Column, the Houses of Parliament and Whitehall. Wahid noticed that one particular page was smudged with a fingerprint: a scene from St. James' Park on a summer's day. Ladies and their gentlemen wore fine clothes and walked arm in arm, as children played with hoops and ran.

On the inside back cover of the book, there was a list of tourist attractions that Father had written in pencil: Big Ben, Westminster Abbey, Trafalgar Square. At the end of the list was written "Karl Marx's grave", with a large question mark.

So complete, so pristine, they had gone to a dubious tourist attraction just for the sake of having done so.

Wahid was nine. Mother didn't want to go. Father held his hand for most of the walk through the lines of gravestones. Wahid couldn't help but glance at the rows of grey stone and try to read out the legends inscribed upon them. "William Standhope," Wahid said. "Who is he, Baba?"

"No idea," Father replied, with a sad smile.

"Jessica Itchen?"

"Again, no idea."

Wahid looked at other names. Mother Mary Southall and baby, three. Joseph Davis. Wendell Perkins. All had lived in the same city, breathed the same air, worked, lived, ate, slept, and then fell into the same earth. People perhaps came to visit them shortly after they died. Wahid could picture a man going to Mother Mary's grave, tall, gaunt, with thinning brown hair and wearing a black suit like a character from television and laying a flower there. But he too died. Dirt built up. The gravestone had wild plants growing at its base. Memory faded out: Wahid doubted that anyone could remember what Mother Mary looked like, what colour her hair was or her eyes, whether she was kind or nasty. All that was left were small white flowers blossoming out of the sprouting weeds.

"It will happen to me too," Wahid thought.

They reached Karl Marx's grave, the headstone accentuated with a bust of the man with his great flowing beard and hair frozen in stone. The eyes were firmly focused forward, the mouth set in a grim line. Yet, the artist had somehow put in a touch of benevolence in his expression.

"He looks like Father Christmas," Wahid remarked.

Father smirked.

"You will be all right," Dr. Blanchard assured him.

Really? If he did go back to prison, he would pass on, fade out from memory. He would have been a tiny bump in the vast highway of London's history.

But what if he was freed?

"You have a lot to look forward to," Dr. Blanchard also said.

Did he? No doubt there was an inch of dust on all the furniture in the house, but he could put on his surgical mask and suck that away with a vacuum. But would things be different now?

"I promised Rania a child," he recalled.

No.

He remembered sitting in a sex education class at the age of thirteen. It was a cold winter day, ice formed on the panes of glass and the posters encouraging students to read books in their spare time were peeling off the frozen white concrete walls. Nevertheless, his attention was focused on trying not to fall out of his chair when words like *penis, vagina, intercourse* and worst of all, *ejaculation* were mentioned. Oh dear God. He had wanted to crawl under his desk and put his fingers in his ears. Mother was appalled to hear about this later on, but for the moment he had to endure statements like, "If you must have sex, be sure to use proper birth control, such as a condom. Condoms prevent transmission of venereal disease."

How did that work? Wahid had seen them before; the English boys in the class had bought a packet out of an automatic vending machine. They took delight in filling them up with water from the taps in the school bathroom to the point of bursting, in effect turning them into modified water balloons. Wahid had been attempting to urinate in one of the stalls when one of these missiles landed on the back of his head.

"Condom for a dickhead!" the perpetrator shouted.

With the door closed, it was impossible to see who it was. It could have been any of that anonymous gaggle, filthy, unclean, and evil.

"Just remember before you have sex," the teacher said, "that you're in effect having sex with everyone they were with."

If it were physically possible, Wahid wanted to climb up to the top of his chair, and perch on its back like a cat, cringing away from the words. The teacher was so clinical about it, with his ruddy, glossy overweight face and clipped brown hair; he even smirked as he explained the subject. Suppressed giggles ebbed and flowed through the room like a tide.

"*If you have sex, you're sleeping with everyone else they had sex with.*"

That applied to rape, surely. Rania would be having sex with Arkie; Wahid could imagine his bulky form violating her, her screams of horror and torment at being subjugated by that man. No, no, he could not ever do that again. She was never going to have him to herself again.

Wahid put his head in his hands.

"I can't," he said.

"Can't what?" Dr. Blanchard asked.

"Rania…if I am free, we can't…."

The words constricted in his throat.

Dr. Blanchard held up her hand. The lump in Wahid's

mouth faded. Slow slow.

"Yes, you can. Rania will accept you."

Wahid desperately wanted to drink another glass of water. A gallon, if he could manage it.

"I would like some water, please," he gasped.

"In a minute," Dr. Blanchard said. "I want to tell you something that I heard from a Pakistani colleague in Lausanne."

Wahid's ears perked up. Lausanne: he had never seen a picture of it, however, but on Dr. Blanchard's descriptions he could imagine the mountains, in precise angles standing proudly around the town, the snow-caps neatly trimmed and even around their tops. The city with its magnificent scrubbed alabaster gothic buildings was swept clean by armies of men in pristine orange boiler suits, their brooms pushing the slight hint of dust away into hermetically sealed cans. The good denizens of Lausanne would go out every morning and ensure that their windows were clear, free of streaks, and the only detectable scent was of soap and citrus. Even the birds had to sing in tune. A Pakistani was there?

Of course.

"What did he say?" Wahid asked.

"*A hand that is dipped in mud can be washed clean again.*"

Can it? Were not some stains too deep and too lasting?

She smiled. "You don't believe me."

Wahid shook his head.

"Why?" she asked.

"I don't know," he replied.

She shook her head. "Yes, you do. It's just easier to say that as a reply."

Yes.

Twenty-One

"You have another letter from Karachi, Mr. Shah," Watson said.

Wahid was reading the Qu'an, seated in a chair facing out the window. He nodded in reply.

Watson held out the envelope, motioning for Wahid to take it.

Slowly, Wahid extended his fingers out. The cream coloured envelope made of thick paper, dropped into his hand.

"I'll leave you to it," Watson stated, a smile stretching his bulldog-like features.

"Thank you."

Wahid turned and faced the letter. He had tried to write to Rania in the past week, as Dr. Blanchard advised. He had borrowed some sheets of paper from Mr. Watson, and a pen. He leaned on the windowsill and tested the pen on paper. It worked; a few black lines came out easily.

Damn. He started off with the date. At least that was simple.

"Dearest Rania," That was not complicated either.

"I miss you," he wrote.

But did he? He caught sight of himself in the reflections of the same window he looked out of. He could see the grey hairs, the shaking hands, the hunched shoulders. Surely there was someone better for her in Pakistan.

"Bury my memory," he thought.

No, he had to try. If only to see those eyes again, looking up at him as they did in the garden. Was she still in the garden? Was she still seated there, waiting for him to appear around the corner?

Perhaps.

"I love you," he wrote.

That much was true.

"I am suffering," he wrote.

Ahmed had gone completely silent, and was disappearing frequently into meetings with his new solicitor. Wahid didn't like the look of this new legal representative: he was English, wore a Saville Row grey suit and a pink shirt. His blonde hair was coiffed in a hairdo that was a formal attempt to be casual. After Ahmed spoke to him, the butcher glanced at the imam, Basir and Wahid, smiled, and then returned to his usual solitude.

The imam was patient. He reminded them that Islam meant surrender to God's way. So long as they did so in thought and deed, then all was right with God and thus all was truly right, no matter what was wrong here. There was nowhere to go but God, after all. One could not run away from Him, as He was everywhere. How much better it was to run towards Him.

Wahid felt his throat constrict and glanced out of the window. Patchy clouds were rolling lazily across the sky, a mottled composition of greys of various shades, ranging from those threatening rain to those which suggested the sun was about to break through.

If he wasn't fearful of the flu from standing out in the rain, he would have loved to stand in the open air for a while, perhaps get Mr. Watson to take him to the small courtyard where patients got fresh air. It would be an escape from the scent of rubbing alcohol and boiled vegetables.

Basir's smile was dimming as days passed. Wahid was awoken one night by Basir tossing in bed and calling out to Dina and his sons.

Rania didn't need to know. "You mustn't worry," she said to him.

Neither must you.

The envelope rested in his grip, he felt the thick paper absorbing the oils from his hand. No doubt beneath his fingers the fine black ink with his address was smudging.

He was sure she would berate him. She could get angry.

Once, he wanted to take her out to dinner on Brick Lane for their anniversary. He had picked a restaurant near his office called "The Pleasant Mughal". She had arrived, wearing a dress and headscarf of electric blue silk, and her eyes were glowing as she sat across from him, waiting for him to shut down his computer for the day. Everything about her was pleasing; he could not see a single discordant spot on her clothing, and her hands were folded so prettily around the handle of her handbag.

"Happy Anniversary," he had said with a smile.

"Happy Anniversary," she had replied.

They had slowly descended down the stairs to the exit. When they opened the door, they saw a young man in a hooded sweatshirt retching in front of them into the street. The scent of cheap lager and stale cigarette smoke washed over them.

Wahid slammed the door shut. Quick quick quick, slow.

"What's the matter?" Rania asked.

God, the smell, the disease, who knew what other refuse that young man had lurking in his innards. Wahid gripped the handrail next to the stairway and tried not to swoon.

"You're not going to let some idiot ruin our anniversary dinner are you?"

The sounds of the young man continuing to be sick penetrated the door.

Wahid looked up at Rania. He felt perspiration break out on his forehead. He tried to regain his breathing.

"Rania, I can't."

Her lips set into a firm line. Her eyes no longer had that peculiar light like a firefly dancing among shrubbery in the dark. There was just a hard glint.

"Fine," she replied.

He took a deep breath. He reached his fingers underneath the flap, and began to tear the letter open.

"Dearest Wahid," she had written.

127

Quick, quick, quick, slow. At least he wasn't in trouble. She had not started off with "idiot" or "fool".

"I know it must be difficult for you to write," she continued.

His breathing slowed further.

"I also know that the post to Pakistan is likely very slow," she stated.

Thankfully.

"But I await your letter. I'm lonely without you."

Lonely? Wahid's memories were of her mostly being alone, whether tending to her garden or sitting at a sewing machine in the dining room, making a skirt for herself out of some brown cotton cloth she had bought at the market. Her eyes were always intently focused on the target, her delicate fingers shaping, moulding, guiding. Lonely?

"I've started to teach English to earn some money. One of Uncle Naseem's colleagues, a colonel in the Army, is one of my students. He says he wants to learn English to talk to the Americans. Imagine that!"

Wahid looked out the window. Two sets of clouds, one light grey and the other dark grey, merged into a single pattern in slow motion. It was like watching a collision.

Talk to Americans? That would imply that they listened. Since the Father Christmas of Communism's philosophy had died, they had been looking for someone new to threaten with Armageddon.

They hit on it in 1990; Wahid was still at university then, a boy dressed in khaki trousers and a crisp white shirt, climbing up endless flights of stairs to dimly lit accountancy classrooms. He spent his evenings and weekends up in his room with his calculator, adding sums and reading about tax law.

Father had wanted him to be an engineer or doctor. But engineers got covered in grease like Basir, doctors dealt in death and disease, accountants dealt in the sterility of numbers, the certainty of facts and the symmetry of rules. Easy.

He climbed to the fourth floor on a bright October afternoon. He was on his way to the library, the sunlight

128

partially deflected by the spots on the university's dirty windows, and its yellowish grey beams bounced off the polished light green linoleum floors. He paused for breath in the stairwell, his heart pounding.

"I'm weak, I'm going to die," Wahid thought.

"The Americans are attacking our Muslim brothers!"

What? It was a shout coming from Wahid's left, down at the end of the hall.

"And the British are helping them!"

Wahid turned and followed the sound.

"We must stand up to the West, tell them that the invasion of Kuwait is a matter to be settled between us!"

Wahid found the open door, and looked inside. It was a large classroom, the skyline of Islington, the church towers and tower blocks standing as sentinels outside the large windows. The speaker at the head of the classroom was a young information technology student Wahid knew named Asad. Previously, he had been known for sitting all night in front of a computer, trying to write programmes to make it perform complex quadratic equations. Overnight, however, he had traded his keyboard and glasses for a white knit cap, a *kurta* and white cotton trousers; he was trying to grow a beard which was emerging in a few hairy patches along his chin and cheeks, but still too light to be unified. As he spoke, he raised and lowered his clutched fist. His voice, which had previously been underused, broke and squeaked as he continued his denunciations.

"The evil Bush regime must end!" he said, his statement starting as a bass and finishing on a falsetto. Wahid tried not to smile.

"You, brother, you smile?" Asad shouted.

The classroom turned and looked at Wahid. They were a mixed bunch of students, all of them Asian, some dressed in headscarves, others in jeans. Their brown and hazel eyes locked firmly on his smirking demeanour. Wahid tried not to hyperventilate by thinking about breathing into a paper bag and

129

what a relief it would be to have his breath contained. He clutched his accountancy textbook to his chest, its hard cover shielding his heart.

"No, brother," Wahid mumbled, his eyes downcast.

"Good!" Asad said, his voice drifting down an octave.

One of the audience members raised their hand.

"Yes, sister?" Asad asked.

A girl from one of his accountancy courses stood up. The motion was rather like watching a stream of mercury slide upwards, smooth, elegant, unencumbered and near impossible to believe. She was slender, had a long mane of dark hair which settled over her shoulders, and she wore a white blouse which was open at the neck. Wahid swallowed; in class, she sat two rows over from him, but he never had the courage to ask her name. Indeed, he was surprised to see her there as he thought she was a Hindu.

"Brother Asad, what do you propose we do?" she asked.

Asad smiled, his whiskers spreading outwards. "Thank you for asking, Sister Shehnaz," he said with a squeak. "I propose we demonstrate down at the American Embassy. Many of our brethren at other universities are going to do the same next Saturday. We are going to tell them we want them to stop this insane war."

"Didn't Saddam start it?" Wahid thought. He recalled the images of Iraqi tanks rolling through Kuwait City and the pictures of Saddam Hussein celebrating on a balcony by holding a rifle and bouncing it up and down in his arms like an infant.

Wahid saw that the other students nodding in agreement with Asad. No, bury that thought.

"Isn't that dangerous?" he asked quietly instead.

Again, all eyes turned on him.

"Dangerous?" Asad asked, his falsetto now indignant.

Wahid coughed. "Well, won't the police be there?"

Asad nodded. "Of course, but if we are peaceful, we won't be arrested. Besides, the Americans are not going to stop with Kuwait, my brother. They are going after us, just like they did

130

with the Soviets. We're next. And the British will help them."

Shehnaz was looking at him. Wahid dared not return the gaze.

Wahid turned his eyes back to Rania's letter. Shehnaz had given up the idea of being an accountant in her third year, Wahid recalled, and had moved into fashion design. She now had a shop on the New King's Road which sold traditional Pakistani clothes using brightly coloured silks. English women loved it, apparently, and Shehnaz had been interviewed in the Saturday *Guardian* and confided she had a house in Oxfordshire and drove a champagne coloured Bentley. She mentioned she had a son at Cambridge who was on the rowing team: the father was not identified. Given how powerfully she stood out from the background, Wahid was not surprised the boy didn't want to be seen.

He could picture her now, a streak of grey in her hair, sitting on a dark brown leather sofa and watching the travails of the London Four on a high definition television while sipping Italian sparkling water served with ice and a slice of lime. Did she remember him? Did she still move like unbottled mercury when she picked up the remote and switched to another channel?

Wahid tried to re-focus his eyes on Rania's letter.

"The colonel comes two or three times a week for lessons," she said.

Strange to put all that effort in to merely talk to Americans.

"I do think he rather likes me," she continued.

Wahid involuntarily gritted his teeth.

"I am remaining strong, my darling, waiting for you."

He gripped the paper tightly, his hands trembling.

"Don't make me wait too long, my love, I beg of you."

Wahid put his hand over his eyes.

"Have you written to her?" Dr. Blanchard asked at the next meeting. She wore a grey sweatshirt that had "Université de

Lausanne" printed in black across the chest. There were deep semi-circles underneath her eyes indicating prolonged sleeplessness. Wahid could envisage her awake at one o'clock in her London flat, tidy and pristine, wandering around with a bottle of antiseptic, looking for seepage from the outside world, carefully spraying at cracks, holes, any place where filth could stream in. He could sympathise.

"I wrote three sentences, then the words ran dry," Wahid replied.

"She may think you've lost interest."

Maybe.

"You need to try harder," Dr. Blanchard urged.

But what to say. "I will," he replied.

She leaned across the table. She gave off a pleasant scent of antiseptic soap. Wahid involuntarily smiled.

"Tell her the truth," she insisted.

"Dearest Rania," he began again. He sat in his chair facing the window, positioning a notebook on his knees, his shoulders hunched forward in concentration.

"What are you doing, my friend?" Basir asked.

The words flowed slowly out. "I…have…been…raped…"

Wahid dropped the pen.

Basir's voice contained a note of concern. "Wahid?"

Wahid turned to look at him, clutching his writing hand. "I am writing to Rania."

Twenty-Two

The imam leaned forward, his nose nearly touching the ground, and after a moment, leaned back. There was a precision in the motion that Wahid admired, rather like if well oiled gears and springs had come together in a single, perfect mechanism.

Wahid did his best to follow, but he was consumed with listening to the sounds of his heartbeat, his breathing, and focused on the thought that all the organs were so delicate that assuming the position might cause them to crash into each other.

Dr. Blanchard had told him not to worry. Human beings were resilient, in her view. But did that apply to Wahid? He had heard about a boy in a bubble, a young lad in Shropshire who had such a poor immune system that everything had to be made sterile around him. His bedroom was kept constantly swathed in antiseptics and he had to live inside a clear plastic cocoon which kept germs out. If Wahid had one of those, then he might be comfortable.

Wahid chided himself; he should focus on God. The Blue Danube still echoed in his mind, even though his iPod was long gone. Praise mixed with melody, though melody was technically a no-no. But surely the recitations of the Qur'an represented a kind of celestial harmony. Father recited passages in Arabic from time to time from the dark green book and it sounded like he was singing a long and plaintive melody, the words floating upward as if they were weaving a rope ladder to Heaven.

Wahid pulled himself back up. He had to banish the dissonant thoughts from his mind. It perhaps was because he was not close enough to God that he had come to this.

"What blessings of your Creator would you deny?" the imam whispered. His eyes were shut, his lips were fixed in a relaxed smile, as if he was living inside an invisible sterile suit.

Grace? Would that be the word to describe the imam's state? He was in a "state of grace"?

Perhaps that was a Christian concept which had spilled over from Anglican and Catholic cathedrals, and its slop had landed on his consciousness. Mustn't be like them, mustn't be like the Christians. Asad said so.

Wahid had agreed to go to the demonstration; he then went home. He took a few deep breaths before telling his parents about it. It was dinnertime, and Father had just passed a bowl full of rice to him, the scent of fresh cardamom filling Wahid's nostrils.

Mother was instantly opposed; her dark eyes flashed. He had to help her with making the Saturday meal, which after all was his favourite, curried vegetables, not go off and hang out with some radical ruffians. Father got up from the table and began to pace back and forth in front of the fireplace in the living room, his hands clasped behind his back, the crackle of the flames keeping in time with his stride. He looked down, as if peering into the earth would fix his thoughts. It was a pose Father took up only once before, when that British writer had written a novel attacking Islam and the Iranians had ordered his execution.

Father stopped pacing and took a breath.

"Saddam started it by invading Kuwait," he said finally.

"Yes," Wahid replied, exhaling.

Father continued his reverie. Wahid wondered if his leather slippers would leave a permanent tread mark in the red wool rug. Mother would be much displeased.

"But I think your friend is right too."

That confirmed it: the Americans were coming for them. Wahid didn't know any personally, but he pictured their country, a vast sprawling metropolis with glass towers and corn fields and young men with blonde hair swept back and gleaming white teeth and their wives all hair dye and large smiles. They all owned guns and shot at anyone who was darker or had worse teeth than themselves. Russian dentistry left much to be desired, plus they were Communists. Bang. Now Muslim people to them were little brown folk who ran around in mud huts speaking a strange foreign tongue and deserved to be blasted off the face of the earth for daring to threaten their precious supplies of oil. It was oil that was going to be wasted on giant cars going less than half a mile to the nearest store where Americans could buy cheaply made goods from China, or clothes made by children in Bangladesh who stuck their fingers with needles so many times they had a mass of calluses for hands.

Strange people, so distant, yet so in everyone's face with television and McDonalds and loose women and bad magazines. Not the way, not God's way. Did God ever reach out and touch them, Wahid wondered. The Prophet said that God's message was delivered to every nation in their own tongue. Was the word of God being uttered by someone considered a madman in America? Had he been silenced in the cacophony of idle talk about Jesus? Wahid could imagine their holy man living in a dirty alleyway in some city like New York or Chicago, the winter cold penetrating a grey woollen coat full of holes, his hair greasy and matted with dirt into a spiky shape, but the blue eyes still alight with the Word of God.

Did he go up to people on the pavement, as they carried black leather briefcases and focused ambitious eyes straight ahead, and tell them "God loves you" and "You must obey God". Did they listen? No. It was unlikely they gave him a second glance.

Wahid climbed up the long, narrow staircase to his room and slammed the door behind him. He caught a glance of himself in the mirror. His white shirt was still neat and tidy. His khaki trousers had seams so crisp they appeared to be sharp enough to cut. He wore starched white trainers, which he kicked off.

He looked at his hands in front of him. Brown. He flipped

them over. The palms were slightly lighter, but still brown. They looked incongruous against the whiteness of his shirt.

He undid his shirt buttons quickly and pulled it off. Sure enough, it was from an American chain store and "Made in Mexico", a brown people that Americans probably hated more than him. He recalled that he had seen the item in a store along Upper Street in Islington and impressed by its whiteness and line had begged Mother to buy it. She had relented after a few minutes pleading. Her pink lips twisted down, her eyelids drooped as if weighted down.

He quickly undid his belt buckle and let his trousers fall to the ground. He stepped out of them and picked them up, holding the garment away from himself as if it were radioactive. He looked at the label on the waistband. Ah yes, it was from the same chain store. This pair was made in Thailand. Thailand? Wahid envisaged little children working at ancient sewing machines in a dim grey factory with a roof made of corrugated metal. In the monsoon season, no doubt, the rain belted the roof and the children were made more afraid, bent over their sewing machines, hoping the precise metal clatter of the mechanism would drown out the din of the weather.

He balled up the trousers in his hands and threw it away from him. No, no, no. He had to do better. He had to be closer to God. He went over to his stereo in the corner, and looked at the back of it. Made in Japan. Well at least it was likely assembled by robotics. He opened it and found his Mozart CD still in place. Made in Germany.

He sighed in relief. He may have been in his underwear and socks, but at least his music was still guilt free.

Wahid knelt forward again, following the imam. Asad had known better. Wahid wondered if Asad had gone through the same ritual, abandoning his clothes and trying to find comfort in something else. Probably Asad would rather have gone naked after having had the same revelation; in Wahid's case, Mother convinced him to wear his old clothes while they shopped for

136

new ones. But how they itched. Wahid felt as if he could detect the tiny fingers which had made the garments crawling over the fabric and poking him. The children were probably dead from starvation and exhaustion; indeed, it was likely their ghosts trying to tell him not to wear what had cost them their lives.

How blissful it would have been to be an American; they didn't know and didn't care. They were named Billy Bob and Sue and went to large shopping malls in places like Dallas and Los Angeles. They went to the shiny, air-conditioned stores, picked products made from misery off the rails, held them up and marvelled at the quality and cheapness. They bought them, pennies of the purchase price going to keep the children's bellies filled with rice for yet another day and the Americans went home to watch men clad in lycra and shoulder pads fighting over an oblong ball.

Mother and he went to East London and found a street market selling traditional clothes. She got for him his first *kurta*, a pair of cotton trousers and a skullcap. Just like Asad. Wahid checked: all were made in Pakistan.

They rushed home and Wahid threw off his old clothes. He pulled on the new trousers, pulled the *kurta* over his head and stretched the cap onto his skull. He looked in the mirror, appraising himself and straightening his clothes. He rubbed his chin; he had stopped shaving and the dark hints of new growth itched.

He sighed with relief. He was no longer an American.

Just like Asad.

"What blessings of your Creator would you deny?" the imam said again as he stood.

Wahid and Basir followed in the stance.

If only the imam had been there for the protest against the first Iraq war. His voice was a steady baritone and had none of the shrieking, quirky quality of Asad's.

They had assembled on Oxford Street with students from the

London School of Economics and the University of London. Wahid wore his new clothes. Asad had given him an approving nod, Shehnaz hadn't even looked at him.

Asad's voice competed with taller, more deep voiced spokesmen from the other universities. A young man from the LSE stood on a soapbox amidst the gathered students and spoke eloquently about America's military industrial complex. Wahid assumed he later became a politician because he could recall nothing of the substance of his speech, just that he said it well, and he had good hair.

When Asad took his place on the soapbox, he tried to compensate for his lack of projection and his trembling voice with a bullhorn.

"This is against Islam!" he shouted.

There was a murmur of agreement. Wahid cast a glance at Shehnaz, she was wrapping a navy blue parka around herself tightly and gazing up at Asad, her lips parting and closing, silently mouthing the words "I agree! I agree!"

"It does not matter if Saddam is wrong; this is an issue for Muslims to solve!" Asad shouted.

The murmur got louder.

"We must not let this be an excuse for the Americans to interfere in our affairs! Their way is not our way!"

Perhaps, Wahid mused, the Americans thought that they all wanted to be like them. Yes, everyone did want a warm house, plenty of food and technology to keep them healthy and informed. But what was the point without morality; what of the soul? Wahid recalled seeing a programme on television where silicon breast implants were being discussed. He was fascinated by one of the women, American, with blonde hair that was a colour obviously not her own, wearing a tight sky blue dress which displayed assets God had not originally intended for her to develop. Wahid wondered how much time, energy, innovation and invention were wasted just so women could have that which God did not give them? What blessings of their Creator had they denied?

138

Asad's voice rose in pitch and he raised a fist in the air. "Forward then!"

The mumbling shuffling crowd turned towards Grosvenor Square.

The imam rose to his feet and looked at Wahid and Basir intently.

"That's all for now, brothers."

Wahid and Basir rose simultaneously.

Watson poked his head around the open door. He had deep frown lines on his forehead, accentuated by his baldness. His white coat was open, the collar uncharacteristically dishevelled.

"Gentlemen, sorry for the interruption," he said.

"Not a problem. We've just finished," the imam explained.

"I'm afraid I have some bad news. It appears that Mr. Mirza will be leaving here shortly. He is presently in a temporary holding cell."

"Why?" Wahid asked.

"He's made a deal."

Twenty-Three

"He is damned," the imam said quietly.

Wahid looked at him; there was no change in cadence, octave and expression as he said those words. He stood, arms folded, lips in a solid line, his eyes rarely blinking. Strange how he could be so serene in watching someone slide off an eternal precipice.

"Damned," Wahid repeated, rolling the word over in his mind. It sounded peculiar to him; he tried to disconnect the sounds from the meaning for a moment, undoing learned vocabulary. It still sounded bad even as a noise devoid of meaning. Men of faith would say his actions were *haram*, Wahid thought, which didn't sound any better.

Basir, the imam and Wahid stood at the window; below them, they could see Ahmed pacing across the prison's grey, concrete courtyard towards an open gate. He wore a dark blue boiler suit which appeared to be fitting better due to his having lost some weight on the prison diet. That said, Wahid noticed that his belly still acted like a prodigious advance warning of the rest of his body's arrival.

Ahmed turned to look up at his former comrades. His hair was slicked back, his eyes were brighter than Wahid had ever seen them.

Ahmed grinned. He raised his hand and waved jauntily.

"Truth concealer," the imam said softly in Urdu.

Wahid's throat went dry.

Apparently satisfied with his three-second farewell, Ahmed turned and stepped out of the exit.

As Wahid, Basir and the imam ate their lunch of curried lentils with rice, few words passed between them:

"Pass the water jug, please."

"Pass the salt, please."

"This should be spicier."

The small room they had set aside to eat in consisted of one folding table made of a polished wood that was scratched up with marks from metal implements and cracked due to age. Grey light from the window cast a pale pallor on the scene.

The imam finished eating and set his white plastic fork down on his paper plate.

"He is damned," he repeated.

Wahid looked into the imam's eyes. They were glistening in the semi-darkness. The imam was far more educated about such things than he; however, Wahid remembered Father quoting the Qur'an, "Those who do evil will have the same measure apportioned back to them."

The imam's hands trembled. Were he and Ahmed close? It seemed unlikely. Yet, all the emotion he had been containing so successfully was now seeping out. Was it fear for Ahmed's soul? Or was it simply anger?

Wahid took a guess. "Yes, he is," Wahid replied, "but it is due to no defect of yours."

The imam shrugged. "I know God gave us the capacity to choose…even so, choice…is sometimes disappointing."

The tears in the imam's eyes could no longer be contained. They flowed down both his cheeks.

Wahid dared not watch the television; the imam and Basir did so in his stead. They told him afterwards that it was briefly mentioned on the BBC that Ahmed had become a "witness". Willows had made an appearance and described Ahmed's "marginal involvement in the conspiracy" and said "a deal has been struck". For his testimony, all charges would be dropped.

Quick quick slow. Not only did they have the bleach and

ammonia in Wahid's case, now they had someone to testify against them.

"This changes little," Hassan reassured him at his next visit. The solicitor was dressed in a black suit; he reached out with a hand so tightly clenched it looked like he was wringing the neck of an imaginary chicken.

"I can't see how," Wahid replied.

He wondered what Ahmed was doing now. He was probably in a hotel rather than a prison: a guard at the door to be sure, but Wahid could imagine Ahmed stripped to his stained white boxer shorts, and flopping on a queen sized bed with dark brown silk sheets, his hairy belly undulating as gravity rolled through his flabby form. His smile was likely a model of insincerity as he picked up a remote, switched on the television and heard about the upcoming trial of the London Four.

What blessings of his Creator had he denied? Wahid's stomach tightened at the thought of Ahmed letting fly with some noxious gasses stored in his colon and relishing in the sensation of release. A fat man on a silken bed, he perhaps had found respite. The imam said it was not forever; he would have to face them in court.

But would that matter? After his departure, Wahid had a nightmare in which Ahmed had been cleaned up, given a grey wool pinstripe suit and starched white shirt. He stood in the polished oak dock, pointed at the accused and said, "Yes, they did it, they plotted to murder many innocent Londoners." There was no trace of sweat on Ahmed's forehead in that vision, no trembling of the hands, no faltering of the voice, no shifting of his deep black eyes. The Prosecutor, dressed in a white curled wig that sat awkwardly on his oblong head, frowned, nodded solemnly and said, "Thank you, Mr. Mirza."

Hassan could cross-examine, no doubt, but what was truth to someone who had no conscience? Would saying, "You're lying, you're damned" mean anything to him? Ahmed could return to his home and his business and pick up where he left off. Perhaps he could sell his story to some tabloid newspaper and

143

stave off the impending financial disaster that Wahid had seen in his future. "My Life As An Islamic Radical": Wahid could imagine the lurid headline, with a picture of Ahmed dressed in a *kurta* with his arms folded across his chest, if they were long enough to join up in such a manner across that vast territory.

"It is my business to destroy his testimony," Hassan reassured him. "Lies have a tendency to come unravelled."

Wahid noted that a thin trickle of sweat was making its way down the right side of his forehead.

"Don't worry," Hassan said.

Wahid's lips pressed together. He tried to breathe through his nose: quick, quick slow.

"Don't worry," Hassan repeated.

Another letter from Rania arrived two days later. The envelope had obviously been in out in the rain: small circular watermarks dotted the surface of the cream coloured envelope. Wahid impulsively pushed the edge of the envelope up to his nose. No hint of vanilla and soap, rather just the vague scent of damp paper.

He gently opened it, releasing the flap, which made a tearing noise as his fingertips worked their way through the adhesive. His fingertips were growing dull, he noted, he couldn't feel the texture of the thick paper; when the time came to feel something smooth like Rania's cheeks, or something delicate like the nape of her neck, perhaps that would be lost on him.

"Don't worry," Dr. Blanchard had told him.

Wahid had fixed her with a stare.

She had stirred uncomfortably in her metal chair, the "Université de Lausanne" sweatshirt sagging as she moved. Her wide blue eyes had shifted to the left, avoiding the gaze.

"Try to get some exercise," she had advised.

Wahid paced in the room, clasping his hands behind his back like his father used to do. Ahmed's betrayal, the imminent prospect of being imprisoned, Rania so far away, he let his footsteps fall heavily, almost stomping the floor till he awoke Basir from a nap with the noise.

"My brother, stop worrying," Basir assured him.

"Indeed," the imam added, looking up from his copy of the Qur'an, "you have done all that you can do, all that remains is in the hands of God."

But had he done all he could do? Perhaps he should have been less hesitant in securing Ahmed's friendship; he had never made an effort to be sociable at the mosque. Ahmed had clapped him on the back, wished him well any number of times and his response had been muted. He did not shake his hand back, knowing that the blood and entrails that animals smeared across Ahmed's hands probably left him covered in ungodly amounts of bacteria which no doubt would have killed him earlier.

But what if it hadn't killed him? A remote possibility to be sure, but still. Perhaps Ahmed would not have betrayed a real friend?

Or perhaps he would?

Wahid pulled the folded paper out of the envelope and opened it. The longed-for scent of vanilla and soap rose from the paper, he pressed his nose up to the deepest crease and inhaled deeply. Good girl, she probably washed her hands before sitting at Uncle Naseem's desk to write. He recalled it clearly: it was a luxurious desk made of oak with a grey marble top and fountain pens that one dipped into a pewter inkwell. Light came in through the French doors leading out to the garden.

"Dearest Wahid," the letter began. The script was long, forward sloping. Wahid pictured her leaning her head to one side as she wrote, as if she was trying to create seriousness with each stroke of the pen.

"Thank you for writing to me," it continued.

Wahid's throat constricted. He tried to swallow, but couldn't.

"At first, I didn't know what to say. I took the letter and went to our bench in the garden to read it again."

Wahid glanced out of the window, more grey clouds were rolling in from the west, as if they were ready to accumulate and rain down yet again. Did it ever stop, would it ever stop?

Rania, he reasoned, must be in sunlight, the yellow light permeating a blue sky so clean and pure that the only clouds were the faintest wisps at the top of the atmosphere. Rania would wander among the jasmine plants and tiger lilies and find the bench, their bench, her eyes rolling over the words he had written in this odd grey country and filling up with tears. Perhaps she clutched the letter, held it to her chest?

"I know your fear of being unclean, darling," she wrote.

Yes.

"But I have thought about it. You're not unclean to me."

Wahid felt his throat grow tighter.

"Don't worry," the letter said, "I love you still."

At that moment, his fear subsided.

However, she changed the subject.

"I want to tell you happy things. My English teaching is going well. I have a steady income. The colonel I mentioned in my last letter is my most able student; he brings me sweets from time to time."

Wahid's fist clenched.

"Uncle Naseem has invited him around for dinner with the family this coming weekend. We should all have a lovely time; I wish you were here. You would like him."

No.

"Please write to me, darling. Tell me all, good and bad. I want to know....All my love, Rania."

Wahid folded the letter and put it in his lap. He again peered at the sky outside. A gentle rain had begun to fall; drops streaked down in a slow and steady path along the window panes. He picked up the letter again and re-read it.

"Don't worry…you are not unclean."

Wahid raised an eyebrow.

Watson was surprised when Wahid asked to be let out into the courtyard.

"Are you sure, Mr. Shah?" he asked.

Wahid nodded. They proceeded down the staircase. Wahid

barely noticed the peeling institutional green paint, the dirt stains on the stairs, the metal edging which was showing signs of rust. Normally, he would have trod carefully around or over them.

He had to get outside. Watson was puffing behind him.

Rania, Rania, Rania.

His loose white trainers flapped in time to Wahid's steps. He was sure he would get a blister which would become infected and perhaps they'd have to cut his foot off. Yes, he could see the operating theatre, the leg under local anaesthesia and himself sitting up as men in aquamarine robes and face masks used a wood saw to cut it off. The contrast of his dark brown foot, covered in sores and tinged slightly green, against the white sheets would be hideous. The saw would go in, the surgeon working against the leg as if he were a carpenter and the leg an ordinary piece of wood, and a sound like cutting timber would be heard, blood spattering everywhere.

Quick, quick, quick, slow.

"We're here," Watson said. In front of them was a metal gate; behind it was a wooden door. Watson fumbled with the keys in the pocket of his starched white coat and drew out a sliver of tarnished brass. He unlocked the gate and it swung open, squeaking loudly as it turned on its rusty hinges.

Wahid shut his eyes for the moment. The long mournful sound of the gate swinging was like a single note of sadness, a deep ending like finishing a passage of *Ein Deutsches Requiem*.

Watson opened the door. Wahid stepped out, shut his eyes and tilted his head upwards.

"Let me disappear," he thought. He recalled wishing for Arkie not to exist. How magnificent to think that it would be true, if nature and God were somehow at one's command, and that reality itself would bend to the will of a single man. However, he was just one man and as the imam said, God is all that is real. Pride had made him think that God could delete parts of the universe at his convenience, as if he were the Eternal Accountant who could put in or remove an entry on the cosmic spreadsheet.

Wahid opened his eyes.

"It's raining, Mr. Shah," Watson said.

Wahid felt the drops of rain hit his eyes. Good, rainwater contained acid, dust, germs. If it was acid, then perhaps the drops would dissolve through his eyeballs, hit his brain and erase his mind.

He heard the sound of a jet flying in the distance. Sure enough, in a space between two clouds, he saw the shadow of the plane. Was it flying east? Was it going to Pakistan?

Ah yes, Pakistan. No doubt Rania had been shielding him from her real opinion, finely calibrating her letter while sitting at Uncle Naseem's desk to start the long slow impact of her decision to divorce him. First, tell him that things are well. After all, things at Uncle Naseem's were well. Not only was the desktop marble, but there were fine marble tiles on the floor, and silk drapery in an array of colours. The grounds around the house, the gardens, were kept neatly trimmed. There wasn't the cold and smoke of London which went into the lungs, hastening cancer and leaving grime and grit on the skin. Showering didn't make it any better; Wahid had tried standing under boiling hot streams of water and scrubbing himself with disinfectant soap. However, the moisture in the air carried dirt and the dirt worked its way into every pore, right into the bloodstream, attaching itself to every cell and conspiring to use his body as a giant Petrie dish for more pestilence to breed.

Rania had no such problems. She probably slept in the guest bedroom which overlooked the garden. Every morning, she likely stirred from a bed with sheets edged with gold silk, and was awoken by one of the servants, a man in a white jacket carrying a cup of tea in a white porcelain cup on a silver tray along with a thin glass vase containing a single slim stemmed red rose. Wahid was sure that Uncle Naseem got the best servants for her; no doubt he had ones that had a gleam in their eye as they asked, "is there anything I can get for you, Madam?"

Rania could pick up the cup, savour the rich scents flowing up from the hot tea and sip it back. Would the servant be as

148

impressed by her dark eyes as he was?

How could he fail to be?

Wahid gestured at the clouds with a clenched fist. Come on, come on and pound me into the ground.

"Mr. Shah, you're getting soaking wet!"

Hasten a heart attack; that's quicker than the flu.

Wahid started walking around the perimeter of the cement courtyard. The water wasn't draining properly, so his trainers slapped against half an inch of water, the damp permeating the canvas and sliding over his feet. He walked faster. Come on heart, give out, he thought. He recalled watching *Dr. Zhivago* late one evening on the television set in the living room. He was sipping his peppermint tea and leaning back in his leather chair when Sir Alec Guinness dressed as a Soviet general said the fatal line:

"He must have known how ill he was...the walls of his heart were as thin as paper."

A grey-haired Omar Sharif, dressed in a pinstripe suit, boarded a trolley car and spotted a young blonde woman walking on the streets outside. He pressed through the crowd to get off, his face glistening, his eyes hollow, and then began to run after the woman, sweat pouring down face. After a couple of seconds, he clutched at his heart and collapsed.

Wahid began to run. Yes, his heart was the key. Rania had killed him anyway. Too much ghee in his food. The arteries were ready to clog; his heart was ready to constrict and collapse. He could envisage the arteries, a clot of yellowy fat lodging amidst the healthy red veins and blood cells, then the entire system shutting down and red turning to black.

"Mr. Shah!" Watson shouted.

Rania could then go on, Wahid thought. She would receive a letter written from the prison authorities stating that he had died. Watson no doubt would send her his personal effects, what remained of them, his white cap, his *kurta* and his slippers. He could see her opening the package at Uncle Naseem's desk. Yes,

149

it would come in a dark brown padded envelope. After she opened it, her nose would wrinkle at the stench of damp and death and she'd hide it in a magnificent closet with eight-foot high ceilings, sticking it behind a row of hatboxes from the finest boutiques in Karachi. Or would they be from England? Uncle Naseem was wealthy enough and he liked Rania: he would send off to Harrods for her hats, after all the money went into Muslim coffers.

Then this colonel she mentioned, taller than Wahid, broad shoulders, dressed in an olive green tunic and black beret, would come to pick her up in his shiny black Mercedes. There was pleasure and wealth to be found in Karachi if you knew where to look. Restaurants as fine as those as in London or Paris were available, with service just as impeccable. On the streets, the ordinary populace knew but didn't know. This world was hidden, discreet, pushed behind iron bars and security guards.

"No Admittance" signs were written in English and Urdu, the English being a sign that this was a place for upper classes. No doubt the colonel had access to an officer's club. He could take Rania to places long since abandoned by the British, with Victorian red flock wallpaper, the heads of animals slaughtered in the nineteenth century hanging off the walls and staring at the club members with a blank, glass eyed expression of impending doom. Even in the middle of summer they used the grand brick and marble fireplaces to burn wood, just for the scent of it and the sound of flames crackling. No doubt the colonel had arranged a table overlooking a private cricket pavilion, an intimate setting with clear, clean water glasses, sterilised silverware and a crisp white tablecloth.

The colonel no doubt was a well man, firm of limb and of a hearty constitution. He would crack jokes and smile at Rania. His smile would make her smile, dip her head modestly and blush, the tinge of red beautifully accenting the warm sepia of her cheeks. No doubt the impending gravity of their relationship would cause the distance between them to diminish as the moments passed; they would first move their chairs closer

150

towards each other by a few centimetres. As conversation progressed, they would start leaning over the table. Then hand gestures as they spoke would come close to intertwining. The colonel could not fail but to notice the scent of soap and vanilla from her, the warm glow that her skin gave off in the firelight, the curved perfection of her cheek. What chance did a memory of Wahid have in such a scene? His voice would be diminished to a slight echo of conscience, "Your husband has just died."

What did that mean in this scene? In the back of the Mercedes at the end of the evening, the colonel no doubt would press his lips to hers, with no fear, and she would be enchanted by his lack of hesitation to the point where she would throw her arms around his neck and run her hands through his hair.

Wahid ran harder. Come on, come on, give out.

"My brother, stop running." It was the voice of the imam.

Wahid turned his head. Watson stood at the door with the imam, whose usual expression of calm showed a hint of worry for the first time. He was clutching a copy of the Qur'an, his finger acting as a bookmark.

"Lord, let me not be," Wahid thought.

He kept on running.

"My brother, stop running..." the imam said more loudly.

Wahid couldn't. He needed to die, right then. His clothes were completely soaked through, his hair greasy from the mixture of lingering soap and rainwater, and cold streams of droplets ran down his stomach, his back, his legs. His knees ached. His heart was not nearly pounding hard enough. Damn breathing exercises; they had kept his heart going.

Quick quick quick.

Yes, exhale faster.

No doubt the colonel would ask Rania to marry her. Uncle Naseem would likely approve, his connections in the military having been enhanced by the match. A widow with no sons and radiant beauty? A miracle; again, no doubt Uncle Naseem would be invited down to the officer's club to share in a cigar and a chilled glass of lemonade at their dark oak panelled bar. Wahid was merely an accountant in London; what a gain for the family to bring in, by marriage, no doubt, a man of power. The officers, all dressed in identical olive green tunics and black berets, would buy him drink after drink, cigar after cigar and clap him on the back.

"Fortune landed you a niece, but now you've gained a son!"

Wahid ran harder.

No doubt the wedding would be a beautiful affair. Auntie would adorn Rania in gold and her finest silks. They would get the imam from the local mosque, a man conspicuous by his lack of ostentation, to recite the Qur'an and ask the colonel to propose and Rania to accept. No hesitation on her part: no doubt she would respond with enthusiasm.

At the reception, white rose petals would fall from the ceiling once the vows had been made and perfume and incense released into the air. Her lips would meet those of the colonel, drawn into a smile of pleasure knowing that this man would not hesitate, held nothing back, and would provide for her for all of her days, from a luxurious house, to a large garden, to fine strong sons. London, Hackney, their small garden, the endless bills, their life together scrimping and saving and doing repairs of plasterwork where damp intruded, were all behind her. Wahid was behind her. He was nothing.

Watson shoved Wahid to the ground, pinning him. Watson's words were muffled as he had run his face right into Wahid's shoulder. "You've got to stop now, Mr. Shah!"

"He's right, my brother!" the imam shouted. He grabbed Wahid's ankles to prevent his legs from flailing.

The imam and Watson turned Wahid on his back and lifted him up.

"He doesn't weigh much," the imam noted.

"Gently now," Watson urged.

Wahid's eyes focused on the heavens as the rain continued to gain intensity. The future was there in pristine glory, but he could not die to make way for it. "Not be," he had willed for himself, but he was still there. He was there, this slender reed of an accountant, washed out by the rain, ready to be condemned to prison, and covered in the filth of the rainwater, and his back now likely smeared with the dirt from the courtyard. He could not make his heart stop, he could not force his lungs to shut down.

He shut his eyes. Rania would have to wait a little longer.

From what part of his lungs or larynx the sound emanated, Wahid did not know, but as the sound of rain drops continued to increase in tempo, he howled.

Twenty-Four

Wahid lay on his side, facing the wall. The plaster in front of him had recently fallen victim to cracking: symptomatic of the rot throughout the building. He could not bring himself to pick up the scattered pieces on the floor. All he wanted to do was lie down.

Twice, he had been summoned to a session with Dr. Blanchard. Wahid merely waved Watson away with a backwards gesture of his hand, as if he was swatting away a fly that was buzzing around his lower back.

The imam called him to prayer. He gestured again.

"You cannot run from God," the imam told him, "you may as well run to Him."

Another gesture.

Run towards or run away, the only inevitable consequence appeared to be collision. Accident and disaster were the guiding principles of the universe, to be sure.

The imam called him again. Wahid brushed him off once more.

"You may think God has abandoned you, but He has not," the imam told him.

No, abandonment would indicate a lack of interest. Certainly there was too much happening for God to be uninterested. God created the world supposedly because He loved to be known. Perhaps He also loved to be entertained: if so, Wahid was a character on a cosmic gag reel, performing pratfalls and sight gags for His pleasure. Every time he rose up, the heavens knocked him down, landing him on his ever-skinnier

155

buttocks, weakening him with every massive blow. The film did not cut away. The music didn't rise. The scenes did not fade to black.

"Brother, do not feel sorry for yourself," the imam said. "It is a miracle to be alive."

A miracle? To think, feel, see, taste, touch, all the mechanisms that man could not devise in any artificiality came together in human beings. That indeed was miraculous, but the miracle was of dubious worth when the touch of the world was rough concrete, iron bars, cracked plaster, the tasting was of food whose bitterness surely hid a bit of rotten meat, the seeing was limited to the grey skies, rain, and dim concrete shoeboxes of the London skyline, the feeling was of utter doom and thoughts wandered in a vortex between pain and the hell of his wife in paradise without him.

What was the resolution? Run to God, run away from God, as the imam suggested, it was running in circles; the process of running away was running towards, because He was inescapable. Standing still only meant that he was a fixed point on the circle as it rebounded upon him. Perhaps it was better to be passive, and to wait for what was to come rather than actively seek it. Perhaps lack of motion would mean there would be a pause in the flow.

"Not be," Wahid wished for himself, but he was.

He lay there a day and a night. His eyes remained focused on the cracking wall. He was glad that not eating or drinking meant that he did not have to take the long walk to the restroom, his muscles felt frozen, as if the slightest movement would break them into pieces. At least he was spared the fiction of his purification ritual; four glasses of water per day indeed. Despite what Dr. Blanchard said, Switzerland was probably just as dirty as the rest of the world, and Lausanne likely had its dim shadows and corners filled with the muck and ooze of ages. Zurich might be filled with prostitutes, and the meadow pictured in the poster on his office wall had probably been paved over to become a car park housing grimy little Renaults with windscreens opaque with dirt.

Sunlight poked over the horizon and penetrated the window; the shadow of the security mesh cast a diamond shaped pattern across him and the bed. Wahid traced the outlines of the mosaic of light and shadow with his fingertip. The blanket was coarse and was either warm or cool, depending upon the light's presence or absence.

"Wahid, my friend, you need to stop this," Basir said.

Wahid continued to trace the patterns. If only it was Rania's skin he was touching. She was so smooth, so clean, so well scrubbed, and her patterns were the various shades of her skin, from the exposed surfaces of her hands, over the pale flesh that was hidden by clothing, to the dark peaks of her nipples. Even sacrificing his cleanliness to be with her didn't seem too high a price to pay.

"Do you really think Rania would want you to be this way?"

Wahid thought about the dark silk of her hair against the white crisp pillowcase, and looking down at her face. Would her dark eyes respond with an answer, or just another question?

Wahid rolled over. Basir was wearing a white t-shirt. His usual smile had been upended into a frown, and his eyelids drooped over his sad dark eyes.

What was that, concern?

"You must get up," Basir said. "Stop feeling sorry for yourself."

Get up, get knocked down, get up, get knocked down.

"I'll get hurt," Wahid said.

"You don't know that," Basir replied. "You must get up, at least try."

"Rania's gone."

Wahid shut his eyes, tears squeezing out from between the lids as if they were being pushed out due to high pressure. Rania, Rania, Rania. Perhaps she was with the colonel now, walking in the same garden where they met, holding the colonel's hand as they strolled among the jasmine and discussed the spring.

157

"She's waiting for you," Basir said.

Was she? Could she be standing at the French doors looking out onto the garden, the distant sunset, and as the orange and gold faded into the purple and dark blue of night, did she cast her thoughts like blossoms onto a pond? Humming, buzzing insects briefly sat upon the blossoms floating in circles around the pond's circumference before they leapt off, loudly exclaiming the thrill of launch in their short lives.

"She loves you," Basir added.

Did she really? Did her lips part and the words flow out on a whisper, or in the soft melody of her voice?

"My friend, be strong for her," Basir said.

"How do you know she does?" Wahid replied, his eyes remaining shut.

"Not every blessing turns to dust."

Wahid opened his eyes. Basir's smile slowly emerged, like the sun poking out from behind the clouds.

"Dearest Rania," he wrote. He sat up in bed, a hardback book perched on his knees, a piece of paper on the book and his cheap ballpoint pen pushing hard into the surface. The pen was borrowed from Watson; Wahid had him rub it clean with an alcohol swab before handing it over, same for the book.

"I am not sure what is going to happen," he added.

He inhaled; the air was cool to the point that inhalation felt like he had just sucked on a cough drop.

"I have only this to say: I love you. If you can, please wait for me."

He held his pen back. His hand trembled; he wanted to write out his fears in a single burst: "Don't run off with the colonel, wait for me to die and get married and have a lot of strong sons."

No, no, no. Not all blessings turn to dust.

"You are my hope," he wrote.

"You will always be my hope," he wrote for emphasis.

"All my love....Wahid".

"It's good to see you again," Dr. Blanchard said. "I hear you've been worried about your wife."

Wahid nodded. Watson had brought them two paper cups full of tea. Bloody teabags, God knew if they were stuffed with sawdust rather than real tea leaves. He dipped his slowly in and out using a white plastic spoon. After the liquid turned a deep brown, he set the bag aside and approached the cup with an apprehensive sip. It probably contained cholera, he thought. He sipped and winced. No, it was Earl Grey.

"You do know that your trial begins next week?" the Doctor asked.

The trial? Hassan had been conferring with Basir and the imam in private; both told him, "All will be well," but that was the kind of statement that doctors would tell a dying man, using a phrase and a tone that he had heard many times before. He had been beaten up. All would be well. He had been charged. All would be well. He had been violated. All would be well. Now the trial. All would be well.

"Have you been continuing to drink the water?" the Doctor asked.

"What for?" Wahid asked, "I'm not getting closer to being clean."

She surprised him. She smiled.

"That is positive," she said.

What?

"Rituals are important, but true cleanliness comes from how you think, how you act, and your sincerity," she explained.

Wahid paused.

"Do you harm others?" she asked.

No, he did not.

"Do you help others?" she asked.

Wahid recalled picking Basir up off the ground after he had been beaten. He shrugged.

"Do you love your family?"

Father, Mother and Rania...dearest Rania, who was casting

159

thoughts out to him perhaps right now. Perhaps she was looking at the moonlight above the smoke and din of Karachi and sending those thoughts on a breeze drifting westward. If only the vapour of those thoughts could take form and shape for him to clutch to his heart.

He shut his eyes.

"You are a good man, Wahid," Dr. Blanchard said.

Wahid felt tears well up. What did she know? The evil he had refrained from in his life, and the good he had done for others, had that been because he was genuinely good, or because he had been afraid? What was genuine good then, good acts that only came from being sincerely generous? Was generosity merely an illusion that people made for themselves to validate their existence and to hide the fact that they were afraid?

"I am afraid," he thought. God was out there, after all, and he feared Him; he feared Him and nearly all that had been created by Him.

But did he love his family? The yes in response flowed like warm honey through his veins. Quick quick quick, slow. His heart beat faster and fell back. Yes, he loved his father, he loved his mother, he was still in love with Rania. Yes, he still loved her to the point that he loved God for making her.

"You are a good man, Wahid."

He put his head in his hands.

"I have something for you, just in case you start to feel as if things are hopeless again."

Wahid looked up. Dr. Blanchard reached under the table and picked up her thin brown leather valise. She unzipped it, pulled out a postcard and examined it quickly; she reached out to him, holding the card out for him to take.

"Go on," she urged, the card flapping slightly as she pushed it toward him.

Wahid presumed that as a doctor she scrubbed her hands with enough antibacterial solution that the card would be germ free. He took it and flipped it over.

The postcard featured a picture of a European city arranged

along the shore of a lake with a set of snow capped mountains in the distance. The photo was taken on a sunny day with blue skies. The buildings were straight, noble, and appeared to be from the eighteenth century at the latest. The apartment blocks looked as if they had been whitewashed till no dirt remained. A tall Gothic church tower stood proud. It looked healthy. It looked clean.

The caption, in bold red letters, said, "Greetings from Lausanne."

Wahid looked up at her.

"I told you," she said.

Yes, yes, she had.

Not all blessings turned to dust.

Twenty-Five

Hassan brought him a suit. He laid it out on the visitor's table for Wahid's inspection; this was part of a "dress rehearsal" before the trial. Wahid bent over it, taking the fabric of one sleeve gingerly between his fingers.

With his other hand, he opened the jacket and looked at the label. Typical, the suit came from a mediocre department store; it was brown and the pattern laid out in its polyester fibres was a poor attempt to impersonate tweed. From a distance, perhaps it would fool some people.

"A proper English gentleman," Wahid thought. Something Father would have said, to be sure. If the people in the court were far enough away, and if Wahid shaved his face, no doubt he would look like a swarthy facsimile of an Englishman. All he required was an ascot around his neck, a monocle, a tweed cap, a pair of green Wellingtons and a rifle with a polished oak stock and a blackened barrel freshly oiled for shooting game.

Yes, from a distance, perhaps they would say, "What a decent, pleasant looking chap." Wahid pictured the people as being like the patrons at the Fountain Restaurant at Fortnum and Mason's. The last time Father took Mother and him there, everyone seemed ancient, as if the scene had not changed since before the First World War. Old ladies who wore floral print dresses to hide the ravages of gravity and time sat with old gentlemen who wore yellow v-neck sweaters from Pringle. They ate small biscuits off floral print porcelain plates and sipped weak tea and said "Lovely, how lovely" in response.

The scene was so monochrome, the colours washed out by

163

the harsh, cold light of a January afternoon. Father indulged in eating the biscuits, sipping the tea, popping each of the bland sweets into his mouth with a smile. He buried his reaction to the restaurant's idea of tea beneath a forced grin but there was no audacity about it, no "devil may care" adventurousness: he was just trying to fit in. The old ladies and gentlemen looked at them: Mother in her beige dress and scarf, Father in his white shirt and brown jacket, and Wahid dressed in his green and navy school uniform. Alien, unwanted, a loud burst of colour in a grey world that demanded no change.

"The world needs to see you as a man, not a radical," Hassan said.

Wahid let go of the sleeve and glared at Hassan. Easy for him to talk: the solicitor bought wool suits obviously tailored to him; his shoulder pads were as sharp as ever, his blue silk tie straight and pointed. He fit in. The old ladies and gentlemen might even think him Italian from a distance. While he was not "one of us", he certainly brought a "Continental dash".

Wahid wrapped his arms around his body. The small cloth loop at the top of the jacket, useful for hanging it off the back of a door, read "Made in Indonesia".

Indonesia was the largest Muslim country by population. Their little children had been putting their tiny fingers into the various pockets and buttonholes, working their stitching through. Did they get a chance to pray during the day? Unlikely. It was a suit made by businesses who did not fear God, and that was more than enough.

"I can't wear this," Wahid said.

"You must wear this," Hassan said, his eyes flashing. "The imam has also agreed to wear a suit."

"It's probably made by sweatshop labour."

"Probably," Hassan agreed, "but now is not the time for this."

Wahid picked the trousers up and examined them critically. He found a slight dust mark on the back of one cuff. Ah ha.

"It's dirty," Wahid said.

"What?"

"Look," he said, pointing at the mark.

Hassan looked at it. "I barely see it."

"Nevertheless, it's dirty."

"It's clean enough. No one is going to look at the bottom of your trouser leg when you testify. You have to look respectable and this will do it."

Wahid raised an eyebrow. Respectable? Father had tried so hard to achieve that word and had never arrived at that particular destination. He had built up his professional reputation to the point where even white British clients were knocking at his door; though he may have also got them by charging them twenty percent less than the competition. But none of them invited him to their homes for dinner and cigars. He never was admitted into the trade bodies. He was never invited down for drinks at the Institute of Directors; Wahid could imagine Father drinking a glass of orange juice out of a wine glass, looking so clever in comparison to the drunken English who flopped into overstuffed red leather chairs.

Respectable, indeed. Where was the respect for Father working until three o'clock in the morning in his study, bent over his desk, writing figures with his fountain pen into a leather bound ledger? Did anyone ever work as hard as he did and get so little recognition? Only five people showed up to his funeral, including Wahid and his mother. Uncle Naseem sent a bouquet of white roses which lay on the grave until the wind carried all the petals away and there was nothing but dry brown stems and thorns resting on the patchy grass.

"Try it on," Hassan said hopefully.

Wahid raised an eyebrow.

"Do it," he urged. "If you want to see your wife again, you must follow my advice."

Blackmail. Rania stood in the moonlight waiting for him, perhaps, but the marriage to the colonel and their fine sons could not be postponed forever. What would he do to ensure that she did return to him and they did try to pick up their lives in the

165

pale yellow house? Anything? Nearly anything? Everything?

Wahid pulled off his cap and placed it on the table. He slowly undid the buttons on his blue boiler suit, the cold air hitting his body as the buttons unfastened, and then as the garment fell to the floor.

Hassan held out a white shirt for him to slip on. The cloth seemed immensely broad, a virtual continent of cotton fabric. Wahid heard his joints click as he reached out to put it on. As he did up the buttons, there was a large pocket of air trapped beneath. He sighed; it was almost as spacious as the *kurta*.

Next came the trousers: he slowly pulled them up over his legs. There was a slight sound like tearing fabric; the polyester grated against his skin. His throat began to swell up. Beads of sweat popped out on his forehead.

"I think I'm allergic to the fabric," Wahid gasped.

"You'll be all right," Hassan urged. "Go on." He handed out a tie to him.

Wahid recalled his father teaching him how to tie a tie for school purposes. They stood side by side in front of a long, polished mirror in his parents' bedroom. The mirror was inside the door of their white built-in cupboards. Wahid recalled focusing his gaze on Father's hands, the long fingers stained with ink from writing in the ledger, pulling the wide end of his red silk tie downward, and approximating where the skinny end should go. Wrap the long end around the skinny, or was it the other way around?

"Watch me, Wahid, and learn," he had said with a smile.

"You've got it backwards," Hassan cautioned.

Wahid reversed himself, then pulled the tie into the knot.

"Tighten it," Hassan urged.

Father always said that a good knot was essential: a bad knot indicated that you were an "actor or a journalist". He always tied the knot so tight; Father would slightly grunt at the moment of completion and smile, as if he knew that pain was a sign of quality. Wahid pulled the knot up to his neck, feeling it compress his Adam's apple and constrict his breathing. Close enough.

He turned to Hassan, who held out the jacket.

"The final touch," he said.

Wahid slipped the jacket on, his fingers crawling through the sleeves like grasping spiders and then emerging. He looked at Hassan. Hassan reached out and straightened the collar.

"There now," he said. "Was that so bad?"

Wahid could feel the little Indonesian fingers poking and prodding him in the legs. It was as if they were street urchins demanding money so they could buy a bowl of rice or whatever it was they ate in Indonesia. All Muslims were brothers, but he was going to hide himself behind his brothers' misery to look...respectable.

"You ought to see yourself," Hassan said.

"There's no mirror," Wahid replied.

Hassan paused for a moment then opened his leather briefcase. He pulled out his laptop and undid the latch; the screen was dark, but it reflected the light reasonably well. Wahid squinted and caught sight of himself. From that diminished perspective, he saw a very thin man in a suit. Apart from the beard, there was no indication of where he was from. The suit fit well enough to suggest Hassan and he were distantly related.

"Is this what you want?" Wahid asked.

"It's what is required."

Wahid changed out of the new clothing as quickly as possible.

"We haven't had as much time to prepare with you as I have had with the imam and Basir," Hassan said, "but it's important we get our facts straight."

Wahid folded his hands. "There is nothing to get straight. I was beaten up on the Tube, the charges are ridiculous, and I am completely innocent."

Hassan exhaled.

"Is that wrong?" Wahid asked.

"Factually, no. But you need to answer some questions....like why did you have ammonia and bleach in your

167

briefcase?"

"To clean surfaces. If I had to use the toilet, I was not going to sit on a filthy seat."

Hassan exhaled again. "Do you have any idea how insane that sounds?"

"It's not insane. Public toilets are not clean. I read in a magazine how people don't wash their hands in pub toilets and how the mixed nuts bowl always contains traces of human urine."

Hassan winced. "Disgusting."

"Most diseases are spread through dirty hands, dirty surfaces. I am not insane."

"Most of us don't carry ammonia and bleach everywhere we go, Wahid!"

"The fact that you want to die is not my problem."

Hassan shut his eyes and massaged his temples with his fingers. "At the very least, can you accept that carrying those chemicals around is atypical behaviour?"

Wahid shrugged. "Only because people don't know the danger."

Hassan opened his eyes. "Well, we'll tell them the danger as part of your testimony."

Wahid nodded. "Good idea."

"Now as for the surgical mask...what do you intend to say about that?"

"People around me were coughing. I don't want the flu."

"You do know that the young man you bought the masks from said that you acted suspiciously?"

"He was the one who told me that there was a lot of flu around!"

Hassan picked up his notebook and pencil. He made a mark on the paper as if he had scored a point. "Good. Next, what are you going to say if you're asked about any tendency towards radical Islam?"

"I'm not a radical. I never have been."

Hassan pulled out a file. "Does the name Asad Choudhry

168

mean anything to you?"

What? "Yes, he was a student leader...I was with him during one protest against the first Iraq War."

Hassan bit his lip. "Do you know what happened to Asad afterwards?"

Wahid tried to remember. Asad had asked Shehnaz out on a date, and she had accepted. The next semester, the war was over and Wahid didn't share a class with either of them. However, he did recall someone saying that Asad and Shehnaz had become a "serious item". Later that year, he had seen Shehnaz at the university cafeteria. He was five people behind her in the queue, but that particular wave of dark hair had to be hers. As she set the tray loaded with rice and lentils in front of the cashier and turned to the side, he saw that it was definitely her: he had studied the shape of her nose and her lips for long enough to tell. He glanced down. She was disproportionately and surprisingly...fatter, the flesh of her belly extending so far outward that her blouse couldn't cover the distension of her light coffee coloured flesh. Oh.

"I think he got a girl pregnant," Wahid said.

Hassan smiled. "That's not really what I expected you to say."

"Oh?"

His expression turned sour. "I hate to say this, but he now works for the police. The prosecutor is going to call him as a witness to your radical activities."

Asad? The police? Wahid again recalled Asad during the protest; he was a blur of white in his cap and *kurta*, raising his fist in front of the cold grey American Embassy, shouting for peace in Iraq, adherence to Islam and against American domination. The police were stoic figures at the periphery, wearing dark blue wool uniforms and florescent vests, speaking quietly into radios about the nature and behaviour of the crowd. But Wahid had raised his fist and shouted in agreement with Asad, though to his ears, his voice seemed drowned out by the others. He remembered how Shehnaz's eyes were focused on

169

Asad, whose breaking voice floated above them all and was so much clearer than the other speakers, even those from the LSE.

But Asad now worked for the police. Wahid tried to mentally transpose Asad's bearded face onto one of the policemen that had surrounded him and his fellow students at Grosvenor Square. The juxtaposition was difficult. But there it was.

"Oh my God," Wahid said.

"Don't worry." Hassan reassured him. "All will be well. Just tell the truth."

Asad and the police...what was it that one of the Trotskyite students had said at university? It was in a Political Science class; the Trotskyite student had long stringy brown hair and wore a filthy olive green US Army shirt, which had Communist and Anarchist buttons all over it. In a voice heavily accented by cigarettes and cheap lager, he blurted "In the breast of every revolutionary beats the heart of a gendarme", when the lecturer mentioned Stalin. Wahid, bent over his notebook and trying to remember the difference between Beria and Molotov, had wanted to retort something along the lines that he expected to see him become a Conservative Member of Parliament some day. However, the Trotskyite students had a habit of ignoring his existence.

Asad had become a gendarme. Perhaps Wahid should not have been surprised but the news resonated like a rock thrown into a large, empty metal barrel. As each echo sounded in his mind, Wahid laid his head down on the table, not caring for the moment that it hadn't been wiped with antiseptic. He was back on the floor of the cosmos, staring upward into a black sky with so few spots of light. Betrayal on top of betrayal. Ahmed was going to hell and Asad now too. The celestial comedy was running now in double quick time. Was God laughing in the distance? Father once told him that on His throne, it was written, "My Mercy takes precedence over My Wrath." Did His sense of humour take precedence over either? How many more gags were there still to come?

170

What was left for him to hold onto if the truth was so elusive?

"We can puncture Asad's testimony," Hassan said.

"How?" Wahid said.

"Well he obviously changed his opinions dramatically over time. You haven't."

"You can't change what you don't have..." Wahid mumbled.

"What?"

Wahid sat up. "I just followed him. I was scared not to."

Hassan wrote more in his notebook. "That helps...but the prosecution can say you are following some radical imam now."

"*Our* imam is not radical."

"No, he isn't. But both you and he prayed at mosques that had radical preachers. "

"I never heard them."

"But you were there?"

"I never heard them."

"Are you deaf?"

"No....I was listening to my iPod."

"What?"

Wahid sighed. "I occasionally listen to classical music on my iPod while I'm at the mosque." *Denn alles Fleisch, es ist wie Gras*, the chorus echoed in his mind. How often had he been listening to Brahms, Sibelius or Mozart when he should have been listening to what was being said?

But would he have had the sense to run? Or would he have followed them like he followed Asad? He recalled one of the preachers at Finsbury Park; the preacher's hand had been lost long ago, replaced with a metal hook, and one of his eyes was blind, the iris and pupil having gone a milky white. Wahid recalled him speaking with some force and passion, the light glinting off his hook as he waved it up and down as he spoke: without sound, he could have easily been mistaken for someone trying to sell artificial limbs. Wahid tried not to smile. Rather, he had mimicked the people around him in raising his hands in acclamation of what was being said; it seemed out of sync with

171

Eine Kleine Nachtmusik, which spoke of ballrooms in a place like Lausanne, with crystal chandeliers and people dressed in frilled suits and dresses with powdered white wigs, dancing in circles around each other.

Hassan was writing furiously. "How often do you mean by 'occasionally'?"

Wahid tried not to wince. "Nearly all the time."

Hassan smiled. He punctuated a note he was taking with an exclamation point and shut his book. He quickly shoved it into his valise.

"Where is your iPod now?" Hassan asked.

Strange. "I don't know. I guess it was on me when I was taken to the hospital."

Hassan nodded. He stood.

"Are you leaving?" Wahid asked.

"Yes, I've done enough for now. But don't worry, Wahid. All will be well."

Doubt still tugged on his heart. Quick quick slow. Quick quick slow.

Twenty-Six

Wahid could not sleep.

He tried to calm his mind by thinking about Lausanne. He had hidden Dr. Blanchard's gift underneath his mattress, tucked inside a fold of his blanket. He was sufficiently light and his fingers were slender enough for him to be able to reach underneath, extract the postcard and to hold it up for scrutiny in the limited ambient light of the room.

Somehow the image was more magical in the dark; the shapes were fuzzier and Wahid's mind rearranged the lines of the buildings into sharper, more corcise patterns.

He looked at the image, and then looked out the window. Dirty grey clouds passed over the moon, hiding its light behind muck and pollution. Then the wind picked up; they passed, and the white light gave greater focus to Lausanne.

Where was Lausanne, five hundred miles away? That didn't seem too distant in comparison c Karachi. One merely had to board a plane at Heathrow or G twick; yes, he would be crowded in with a bunch of tou ists, some with runny noses, and others coughing due to the bad ir for the duration of the flight. As the plane took off, Wahid would have to grip the armrests tightly, shut his eyes and wait for his ears to pop. No doubt the stewardess would come by, her cart smelling of rancid mayonnaise warmed up in a microwave and coffee made from dirty dishwater and burned pearuts. The torture chamber of the flight was a means to an end. An hour, maybe two, and the plane would touch down in Lausanne The contaminated air would

173

disperse as soon as the door was open; the sharp metallic scent of disinfectant would flood in, banishing the pestilence of Britain.

Wahid cast his gaze at the postcard again. No, it was not far away. There was merely the Channel, a brackish, grey barrier to the Continent, and then France, a nation enamoured of cultivating bacteria in milk and consuming it by the kilogram. Besides, there they shot Muslims with rubber bullets and tried to suffocate them with tear gas. Asad said so.

Switzerland was tucked away almost like a secret. It was the pristine picture postcard hidden in the folds of the world, the beacon of safety, the lighthouse by which to navigate. God had put it there for that reason.

Wahid sighed and tucked the postcard back into its place. If only Rania had fled to Lausanne instead of Karachi. Karachi was more decadent, messier. It was the difference between a fondue and a Balti, the latter had a richer taste perhaps, but the former was safer, blander, cleaner.

"Quiet now," Wahid tried to tell himself. His mind was so reckless, so ill-disciplined. He shut his eyes and envisaged the traffic in Karachi, Uncle Naseem behind the wheel of his Peugeot, beeping at the teeming crowds in front of him. Ahead were buses painted in bright shades of yellow, puce and blue, with wooden crates and old leather trunks strapped to the roof. Taxi drivers in their black, dusty Peugeot saloons sat stoically in their cars. People walked alongside the road, carrying baskets, shopping bags, plastic gallon jugs filled with water. The miasma of engine fumes rose over the jam and shimmered in the heat.

"Quiet now," Wahid told himself again.

How much better it would be to have thoughts that ran in a straight line like the gentle waves of Lake Geneva. No doubt the movement was as smooth as Dvorak's Serenades, sweetly washing against the shore, smoothing rough stones through centuries of erosion, softening the air by cooling the breezes which kissed it.

Yes. This is what God intended, no doubt. To have action, thought and deed work smoothly and erode the rough edges of

174

the world. Perhaps Asad had been wrong to try and make the waters rush up into waves and crash against the shore; perhaps it was better for sweetness and truth to wash gently downstream.

Wahid rolled over. He placed his hand over his heart. Quick quick quick. He was not going to get to sleep anytime soon. He sighed.

Why had Hassan wanted his iPod?

Not that question again, Wahid argued with himself. The thought kept on popping up like a jack in the box: his mind was unable to let the question go until an answer was found.

Hassan had his own ideas, his own purposes, no doubt. Perhaps he saw Wahid as just another case.

He was very young, and he probably still had to make a mark on the world. "The London Four"! No doubt that was a going to put him in the newspapers. Other Muslim clients would respond to a brave defence; Wahid could picture Hassan sitting in an office somewhere in London, the office panelled in dark oak, a parchment coloured globe sitting on the desk, and Hassan himself seated on a stuffed red leather chair. Wahid pictured the new client sitting on a hard wooden chair in front of Hassan's desk, nervously twisting his hands as he explained his case while Hassan stroked a long-haired white cat like a villain in a spy film.

"I must be falling asleep," Wahid thought. "My ideas are getting stranger."

The client would be someone like Wahid, who had lost everything due to injustice but in this instance, he had a lot of money and could pay for Hassan to make it all right, or at the very least to be "just as brave" as he was in facing down so-called British justice in the London Four case.

Meanwhile Wahid would no doubt be confined in some cold corner of the country, perhaps somewhere like Scotland, where the sun only shone for several hours a day. Did they have a prison in the Outer Hebrides? They would send him there, as far away from any connection to comfort as they could make it. No doubt they would send Arnold Arkwright there too, put him in the same cell, and he would greet Wahid with an acid smile, his sour milk breath spreading out like a cloud of noxious gases and he would say "Hello, girlfriend."

Wahid curled up into the foetal position.

"Stop it," he told himself. "Stop it right now."

Quick quick quick slow.

God had denied him entry through the barrier once. If Wahid ended up in a place where cold damp winds penetrated the cells and chilled him to the bone, and all the daylight shone through a dark grey filter, and he was nothing but a plaything for vicious men, he would have to force the gate to eternity open.

Would he be forgiven for such an act? Wahid rolled onto his back as if lying in that position would ease the query's ascent to God's throne. The words "Would you forgive me?" floated through the ceiling, over the prison, out of the atmosphere and towards the foot of God's throne.

Wahid listened. Silence. The answer perhaps was in the absence of one.

He rolled over onto his other side. Father had told him that God had made man of clay, and one of the reasons that Iblis, a spirit made of fire, had turned to evil, was because God had said man was superior. After all, man knew all the names of creation.

But man was still clay. *Denn alles Fleisch, es ist wie Gras.*

Surely he would be forgiven. He had to be forgiven. To bear living in the Outer Hebrides, and being served some dun coloured stew with dried but not reconstituted vegetables and meat that came from some unidentifiable animal, and to endure that for forty years, was that his fate?

Did he dare cross God if it was? Could he stomach the idea of sitting in a cell and receiving an envelope from Rania, the vanilla scented parchment yielding a document in Urdu with an official seal, saying they were now divorced? There would be a single slip of paper in the envelope with her fine writing in black ink, no doubt. Wahid pictured there being one word, "Sorry."

Was that his fate? Was that what he was meant to endure? Wahid recalled watching a documentary one evening about

176

George Orwell. He apparently lived in a mining town in abject poverty in order to write his books. Rather like a nun who had swallowed a bowl full of pus, he tried to prove that there was nothing that was totally disgusting about humankind.

Madness. Of course there was plenty that was disgusting, and scratch the surface of one evil, there was always a baser one beneath. Men were disjointed in their good, just as he was, and the contradiction led to evil.

Wahid rolled over. "Please be quiet," he whispered aloud. His ears perked up to try and hear his compatriots. Basir was softly snoring, as per usual; he was one of the few untroubled souls. If he was imprisoned, he would blindly ascribe it to the will of God, and smile when he got simple kindnesses; Basir had smiled that day when Watson had brought them fresh apples. The apples were appealing: bright red, firm flesh, marked with a sticker saying they had come from France. Basir wiped one on his boiler suit, presumably in an attempt get the best shine out of the wax that likely covered its surface. He smiled, opened his mouth and sank his teeth in.

The crunch was loud. Basir's eyes were shut, he sucked in the sweet juice, engorged himself on the lingering hint of apple blossom, the satisfying way that the fruit yielded to the bite.

Wahid thought he had never enjoyed anything quite as much as Basir had relished that apple. The germs on the surface of the apple, left by unsanitary Frenchmen, were enough to diminish any delight.

Wahid opened his eyes; directly on the other side of the room, the imam rolled over and coughed. He said a few words that were unintelligible and fell back asleep.

If they were convicted, the imam would find delight in other things. How odd he was, it was as if he was not there with them. It was as if he had studied God for so long that a large portion of himself was on deposit in heaven. Walking, speaking, relating to everyone on earth was of secondary importance: he was removed from dealing with the dangers of day-to-day existence. Only seeing sin seemed to bother him. Otherwise, so

177

long as he had a place to kneel and the Holy Book, long imprisonment would not harm him. All he had to do was wait for reunification of his body and soul after death. Had Arkie raped him, he would have been disturbed, but not just for himself. He would have said that Arkie had committed a grave sin and perhaps would not be saved by the Merciful. But, the imam would add, brightening, the apportioning out of fate by the Lord could mean that he could reverse course and find the way.

Father would have admired the imam. Forbearance personified.

"Would Father be proud of me?" Wahid wondered. He shut his eyes again.

"I am weak," he said softly. There were Basir and the imam, probably in God's embrace in their dreams. God likely sent Basir a dream of Dina and him sitting in their new home in Pakistan. Basir spoke of wanting the colours of home; it was not beyond him to paint the walls of his house a bright saffron and hoist a large Pakistani flag over the roof. In his dream, perhaps Dina was stroking his hair and they were drinking tea while the glass doors to the balcony of their home were open, and the sounds and scents of Karachi washed up to them.

God had the imam in the grip of ethereal light, to be sure. There was no substance to his dreams, just witnessing that which could not be witnessed in terms that man could understand.

Wahid exhaled. "Come on, sleep," he told himself.

Come on. Slow, slow, slow.

Slow, slow, slow.

Twenty-Seven

It was difficult to read omens in British weather. As Mr. Watson opened the door, Wahid noted that it was being indecisive yet again. There were a few scattered drops of rain, falling past him like sparse, miniature streaks of silver.

Wahid followed behind the imam and Basir, proceeding towards the back of an open van, which was due to take them to court. His hands were cuffed; no matter, the suit he was reluctantly wearing chafed against his skin. The little fingers, used to pushing through thread and needles, were poking him in the legs and groin. It took a good deal of concentration to tune out the sensations, not feel the polyester rubbing up and down against his legs; the cold steel of the cuffs around his wrists helped.

In contrast, the imam was walking calmly across the gravel courtyard. His shoulders were square and his posture was erect. His suit, although identical to Wahid's, seemed to fit him perfectly: not a single fold or crease was out of place. Each stride was of an equal length, each foot rising and falling as if he was merely taking a stroll.

"Come on," a policeman urged them.

Ginger haired, freckled, and wearing a dark blue wool uniform, the officer's face was locked into a sideways smirk, the kind which Wahid could envisage having if he was sitting in a room as the lone adult full of grubby children coughing and sneezing. He would want to run for the hills, but the obligation of maintaining order had its own restraints.

What was it Dr. Blanchard had asked? Yes, she had wanted

179

to know about his childhood. He had told her about Father and Mother and the Qur'an on Saturdays, and the rides on the Tube.

This hadn't pleased her, he could tell. She had put the eraser end of her pencil in her mouth (how filthy and disgusting, who knew where an eraser might have been), her eyes focused on the back wall and her lips pursed in concentration.

"You must remember more," she said. It was almost a plea.

He told her about school and hiding in the bike shed from the storm. That pleased her more for some reason; the lips straightened, the chewing stopped.

He could resist no longer. "Why are you asking me about this?"

She looked him in the eyes, the clear, blue, magnified gaze was particularly penetrating, as if she could see past skin, muscle, bone, right into the core of his being.

"There has to be a reason," she said.

A reason? Wahid's mind was blank.

"For your fears," she explained.

Wahid thought for a moment. The imam had asked it, now Dr. Blanchard: why was he afraid of so much? Well, surely it was rational, there was so much to be afraid of; anyone with a heightened sense of awareness of the world knew how danger lurked within every nook, cranny, alleyway and street. Go into someone's home, and there was invariably a surface that hadn't been dusted, and dust mites were contained therein, eating away on the dead skin cells shed by the occupant. Mites carried bacteria, and bacteria carried viruses, and all multiplied and expanded on the basis of what animal and human tissue they consumed.

"It's right to be afraid," Wahid said.

Dr. Blanchard said, "Then how does everyone else function? How can I..." - and she picked up the pencil - "do this without being afraid?"

Once more she started chewing on the eraser. Wahid flinched.

"Stop, please," he said.

Dr. Blanchard was a good woman after all, a kind woman, who had helped him put behind so very much with their chats. He was no longer filthy, the hand that was dipped in mud was made clean again, but still the world was dirty, a crushing mass that would one day collapse in on itself due to the weight of its imperfections.

"I am just aware..." he said.

Dr. Blanchard stopped chewing for a moment. "But how did you become aware? How did you get to be this way?"

Now there was a question. Wahid focused his thoughts on the answer but could only again envisage the dark iron ball floating in the midst of starlight. Within the ball lay the answer, to be sure. It was hidden knowledge, like where one could find the presence of God. Her question made the ball not only visible but crack, and orange light stream out from the heart of the answer.

They had ended the session, but Wahid dreamt of the ball, the vessel of knowledge. He dared not tell Dr. Blanchard about it; did he want her to think of him as mad? No, she probably already did, there was no use trying to aggravate the situation and have himself put in a confined space, in a straightjacket, pumped up so full of drugs that this knowledge would slip out of his grasp.

He climbed into the back of the van and took a seat next to Basir, his leg accidentally bumping into his. Basir looked at Wahid with slight surprise.

The policeman let his smirk fall into a smile. He exhaled and shut the doors behind them.

"What blessings of your Creator would you deny," the imam said under his breath. His eyes were shut and he kept his breathing regular and low. Wahid could not control himself; the exercises were useless now, but he did them anyway. Quick quick quick.

Basir put his head in his hands, as if the position was intended to secure his head over the various bumps and jolts they experienced in their journey. Where were they going? The

181

Crown Court, Hassan had said.

"There will be a lot of media around," he had warned. He had said this to Wahid, Basir and the imam in the visiting room. The bags under Hassan's eyes were growing deeper and more entrenched. His suit was still sharp, but there was a fade to the edge, like a knife that was growing blunter with use. Was he using himself up too much on this case?

"...the police, however, will bring the van up to a private entrance, and I will be waiting there for you. You will be handcuffed until you reach the door."

The imam had nodded.

Basir asked, "What are our chances, realistically?"

Hassan smiled.

"You smile?" Wahid asked.

"Yes."

"Why?" Basir asked.

"Because I have retrieved Mr. Shah's iPod."

The imam spoke up, "I don't understand. What does that have to do with anything?"

Hassan rubbed his hands and stood. "All will be revealed."

Until that moment, Wahid hadn't realised that Hassan had a streak of a conjurer in him.

The van stopped short. Wahid heard a familiar sound: *click, click, click.*

Ah yes, the press again. Fortunately there were no windows, otherwise Wahid was sure that he would have seen all the lifeless glass eyes of the reporters' cameras, some of them from telephoto lenses, others from television, all pushing their way at them, like the tentacles of a hydra, to poke, to prod, to condemn.

Click, click, click

"Come on," Wahid said aloud.

As if the driver had heard him, he accelerated forward.

Quick quick slow. The van halted; Wahid heard the front window open and the voice of the driver, "Yeah, mate, I've got 'em....open it up."

The sound of squeaking metal resonated through the vehicle. The vehicle accelerated forward once more and came to a halt.

Wahid heard the driver open the door, get out, and slam the door behind him.

He shut his eyes. "Think of something pleasant," he thought to himself.

Rania. In his mind, the image of her had become blurred; she was more ethereal than real now. She was surrounded by a halo comprised of waves of golden silk which flowed back to her body. He dreamt of her that way, the trails of silk following her through the garden, or in long flowing ribbons carried on an unexpected breeze as she walked through a grocery store in Karachi, a basket in hand which was full of fresh coriander, peas, and spinach for making a vegetarian meal, the green of the vegetables all the brighter for being in her possession.

"Dearest Wahid," her letter had started, as always.

"Hassan has written to me to let me know that the trial will start soon, and that he is confident of victory. My heart beats faster at the thought."

Really? Wahid looked down at himself; the poor diet meant he was even skinnier now. The last time she had seen him she had said he hadn't looked like himself; indeed, looking in the mirror, he could see the grey strands of hair on his head and in his beard increasing in number and density. He was weak, and he was ill, and while he had been made clean, he still felt the effect of having been made dirty.

There was endless logic in loving her; it could be explained as simply as seeing her eyes and the modest blush on her bronzed cheek. What was the logic in loving him?

Perhaps it was a form of madness. "God forgive my selfishness," Wahid thought, "but let her insanity continue."

He had swallowed and looked at the letter. "When you're set free, I hope you will give some thought to coming to Pakistan. I think Dina and Basir are right to want to live here."

183

Live there and undo all of Father's dreams, he thought. Father who was such a gentleman, so polite, so suave, that he needed to move to a larger stage upon which to perform all the acts of his life. The grey and the cold only served to highlight the splash of vibrancy he brought to the scene. Old monochrome Londoners would buy newspapers from an aged man on the corner who wore woollen navy blue gloves that had holes in the fingers. Conversation would run, "How are you today, mate?" and the reply was inevitably, "Mustn't grumble". Then Father would walk by, smiling, the cold wind catching the forelock of his hair but not disturbing it, looking as if the camera was still rolling on the film of his life.

Wahid smiled. However, the reel had ended. What was the sequel? The cold and the grey were fine so long as they killed germs, but in this city, the cold hit the young girls who insisted on wearing denim miniskirts and tight white t-shirts that said "Slut Bunny" on them in January. From there the pneumonia spread to all the young men they slept with and so on.

Go to Pakistan like Basir? While the young disease carrying girls were not there, the flies and mosquitoes were, and the paradise he saw of colour and flowers and Uncle Nassem's house only held force so long as he was not there and Rania was. Pakistan for him would be the ride through Karachi in Uncle's old Peugeot, a difficult, bumpy journey with too many people in the way.

But Rania was there.

Wahid had reached under his bed and retrieved the picture of Lausanne from its hiding place. Yes, this was paradise – clean, blue skies, hygienic, fresh air. Perhaps without fear then Wahid could smile and the film would roll again on his life as he brought a splash of colour to Switzerland. Not that it needed it.

He had read further. "When we're together again, we must have a child. We shouldn't wait any longer."

He had swallowed. It sounded like a condition. The magic spell that placed this beautiful woman at the centre of the maelstrom of golden silk would only continue to work if he gave

184

in to this demand, otherwise it would dissipate and she would realise he was a scrawny accountant from North London and she could be with a muscle bound colonel from the Pakistani army who no doubt could kill, and had killed, fifty Indian commandos with his bare hands. The charms of raw testosterone versus whatever he had...no doubt, he would be found wanting.

Unless he gave her a baby. He could picture lying with her again, and in fits and starts achieving the act. However, the morning sickness aspect of it made him queasy. No doubt he would find her leaned over the sink, regurgitating the contents of last night's dinner, sobbing and crying.

God. But do the right thing. He would stroke her back, comfort her, wipe her face.

Then what? The bulge would continue to expand in her stomach. He had seen Basir's face when Dina was pregnant. He looked haggard, the smile temporarily deserting his lips, and the glow in his eyes diminished. Wahid had asked him what was wrong, Basir had replied, leaning over his paper-strewn desk, "Pregnant women all believe they're fat, but they want to know they are still beautiful."

He had left it at that. Wahid pictured himself stepping into the bathroom and seeing Rania standing naked in front of the mirror, looking at her distended breasts, and caressing her belly. Was that attractive? To think of another living creature being locked inside her womb, and pushing out her belly?

Wahid was reminded unpleasantly of science fiction films in which the embryo of an alien was expected to bust out of one's stomach.

"Western culture is poison!" Asad had said, "We need only God and Islam!"

Wahid was inclined to agree at that moment. He should have felt joy at the thought of being able to put his hand on Rania's belly and feel the new life kicking out at him, knowing that it was his child. "What blessings of your Creator would you deny?"

No doubt, however, he would fail. His mouth would turn

down, she would see herself as fat and hide in bed and be angry at him for days on end. He had denied blessings of his Creator with a single facial expression and the consequences would be severe.

He had picked up the letter again. Here was the price of admission: to be with her meant having a baby. To do that, he would have to overcome his fears. The dark ball containing the memory was still as locked as ever, the surface of it looking ever more like cast iron in his mind's eye. Cast iron seemed like dense granules of filth, locked together in an inseparable bond, the only thing worse being rust.

"I love you...God be with you" she had written at the bottom of the letter. The flowing ribbons of golden silk, no doubt, were reaching out towards him as far as they could go. Too bad that dominion of colour and light could not extend to within reach.

The doors of the van opened. A guard, wearing a white shirt and a black bulletproof vest stood before them. A blue cap obscured his dark brown hair; his dark eyes regarded them with disinterest. After all, Wahid reasoned, they were probably just one in a longer caravan of prisoners.

"Come on, get out," he said calmly.

The imam opened his eyes and climbed out first, holding out his hands to the officer. For a moment, it appeared to Wahid that time and space coalesced around the imam. His arms were still, his head held steady, his gaze directly aimed at the officer and without a flicker of doubt.

Time returned to normal as the officer took off the cuffs, placing them in a pocket of his vest.

"Thank you," the imam said, flatly. He turned and nodded to Basir and Wahid.

They got out and the officer undid their cuffs. Wahid flexed his arm muscles. Scrawny indeed. At least, however, he was free. The sensation temporarily overrode his awareness of discomfort from the clothing.

"Good morning!" Hassan's voice said.

The imam, Basir and Wahid turned.

The back of the courthouse was made of solid red brick. In front of a plain white door, was a metal railing and a set of concrete steps on one side, and a concrete ramp on the other. Hassan stood right in front of the door, smiling as he leaned on the railing, his hands gripping it tightly. A mistake: God knew how many of the boyfriends of the miniskirt girls had come this way too. The last thing they needed was for Hassan to get ill by catching their germs from that dingy, grey rail.

"Come this way," Hassan urged. He opened the door.

Wahid coughed and followed the imam and Basir up the stairs. Wahid cast a glance at the ramp as they climbed. He wondered momentarily how many disabled prisoners had to be rolled up to the courthouse. Was there ever a gang of disabled bandits, rolling into banks on their wheelchairs and then motoring away?

Wahid shook his head to clear his mind of the clutter. It would not go; the image of a disabled man in a balaclava holding a gun to a bank teller's kneecap was stuck in his overactive imagination.

Quick quick quick slow. They stepped inside the courthouse. Hassan said, "Wait here, please." He walked down the dimly lit corridor and disappeared behind a dark oak door.

Basir, the imam, and Wahid stood in a small circle. The imam looked impassive. Basir put his hands in his pockets. Wahid couldn't stop thinking about the wheelchair bandit.

"Come on, get serious," he told himself. An inopportune smirk was difficult to suppress.

"What's so funny?" Basir asked. The look in his eyes carried an unspoken question: "Are you going crazy again?"

"Nothing," Wahid said. Quick quick quick slow. The smirk faded.

Hassan reappeared. "Come this way, gentlemen."

Quick quick quick. Slow.

The doors of the courtroom, theoretically, were only about a foot or so higher than he was, but to Wahid they appeared much taller. Made of polished dark wood, with brass handles, Wahid wondered if Satan was waiting for him beyond them. If God could be on the other side of a prison wall, surely, the Evil One could be just as immanent.

Hassan touched him on the elbow. Wahid turned. Hassan had put on a white wig which contrasted poorly with his natural hair. He also wore a long dark robe which completely hid his suit. A young woman stood behind him; Wahid disliked the look of her instantly. She had long straight hair that was dyed an unnatural red, and fell to where her neck joined her shoulders. She had large blue eyes that put him in mind of Dr. Blanchard as they too were magnified behind a set of glasses; unlike the good Doctor, however, her spectacles were steel framed and all sharp corners. She too wore a robe, but its dignity was diminished by the five ornate silver earrings she had in her left ear. A scent of cigarettes and cloves drifted from her, which made Wahid involuntarily wrinkle his nose.

"Freak," Wahid thought.

He must have looked at her too long.

"My assistant, Miss Woods," Hassan explained.

Oh.

"A pleasure," Miss Woods said. Her accent was North American: Canadian?

Wahid nodded. Out of the corner of his eye, he saw Basir nodding in time.

"We're ready," Hassan said.

Wahid nodded. Quick, quick, quick, slow.

Perhaps evil did not sit in that courtroom, but certainly Justice Hastings did. Neither good, nor bad, Wahid recalled. Certainly Willows would eventually be there, if he was not already; Wahid shut his eyes for a moment and prayed to the Compassionate, "Please let him not be, so he is not." But Willows was there, so he had to be.

Hassan pushed the door open; the darkness of the hallway

188

was illuminated by the lights of the court. The contrast blinded Wahid for a moment, then his eyes focused.

There was a narrow path between two sets of benches, leading to a wooden parapet with a railing: Wahid had seen enough crime dramas to know that this was the "dock", a dock in which he, Basir and the imam were meant to be confined.

Behind the dock on either side were two desks, one for the defence, presumably, and the other for the prosecution. A set of chairs were nearby, again, possibly there for Wahid and his colleagues to rest. His feet ached at the thought of standing the entire time.

"Come on," Hassan said.

Miss Woods held out her hand, motioning for the party to move along.

Time slowed down as Wahid took a step. His feet felt heavy, leaden, as if he had a burden that he was carrying on his shoulders, and the increased gravity communicated down to the tips of his toes.

Step, step, step. Wahid exhaled.

He cast a glance at the far end of the courtroom; in the middle was a large bench which towered over everything. Behind it was the symbol of England: the lion, the unicorn, "Dieu et Mon Droit". Father had told him what it meant, "God and My Right": they had been in a museum looking at a painting, and Wahid was seven years old. He tried to get his young mouth around the peculiar words.

"It's French," Father had explained.

God and My Right. Wahid had God, he thought, but as for "my right"…well my right to what, he wondered. If he had rights, would he be there?

Wahid exhaled again as he got to the front of the court. Hassan swung open a small wooden gate to let them in, took his place at the defence desk and opened his briefcase. From this he extracted a manila folder, which was bulging with papers. Miss Woods stood next to him, opening her briefcase and handing him a folder. Wahid noticed how she leaned quite close to Hassan as she whispered something in his ear. It might have been an illusion, but Wahid thought he saw a flicker of light in her eyes as she leaned in close, a slight upturn of her lips as she breathed out her message.

Hassan showed no signs of distraction though; his shoulders remained frozen in place. He nodded to Miss Woods and motioned to Wahid, Basir and the imam to take a seat, indicating the chairs behind him.

Wahid focused all his energy on resisting the impulse to ask for an antiseptic wipe before sitting down. The chair was made of metal, with a black vinyl seat. God knew how many criminals had sat there, and what had they carried in. Could venereal disease be transmitted through cloth to vinyl?

No no no. Wahid visualised the black iron ball in his mind again. More fissures had appeared, more light was streaming out, but the memory it contained was still tantalising.

He swallowed. He looked to his right. There, presumably, was the jury bench, two rows of chairs in a wooden box. They were empty for the moment. A thin wisp of a breeze floated through the court, the scent of dust and cough drops contained therein. Wahid felt slightly nauseous.

"Are you all right?" Basir asked. The question contained a slight hint of fatigue.

Wahid nodded and again focused on the symbol, "God and My Right".

Father had believed in this country. He voted in every election, Wahid recalled. He remembered 1979; Wahid was very young and held his father's hand as they went to the polling station in a local school. The school seemed massive to him: made of grey stone, with a bell tower and a plaque that said "1888". Father tested Wahid's reading skills by making him work out the letters in black on the white sign in front of it. "Pooling Station", he had said at first.

Father looked down, his black hair fluttered slightly in the breeze and smiled. "Close enough," he replied.

A red pin was on the lapel of his grey coat; Father always

voted Labour, particularly after he heard that Enoch Powell suggested that his presence would lead to "Rivers of Blood".

"Rivers of blood, indeed," Father had said. He sometimes thundered at the dinner table about the "punk rockers" that were "ruining the country" and that the country needed "much more, many more Pakistanis" who actually understood what Britain was about and appreciated living in a democracy.

Democracy was strange though. In 1979, Wahid stood at the end of a gymnasium, while Father marked up a piece of paper on a desk and stuffed it into a metal box. Later, he found out the Conservatives had won. What had been the point? Perhaps Asad had been right when he had squeaked in a loud voice, "We need Islam, not democracy." It was a strange thing to say over lunch; Wahid was eating his chicken *biryani*, no doubt laced with pesticides, when Asad was seized by such a sudden passion that his statement shook all the trays on the table.

"There is no law but God's law!" Asad concluded. He then smiled, and resumed eating.

Oh.

Wahid looked at the symbol again. "God and My Right."

The doors swung open once more; outside, Wahid heard the insoluble chatter of people, the snap of cameras, a statement soaring above all others: "I am confident that justice will be done."

Wahid winced. The voice was familiar. Willows.

Justice Oliver Pendleton Hastings. Wahid tried not look around as the procession for the prosecution entered the room; just thinking about their presence gave him a cold chill. The people that were a few feet to his right wanted him and his friends to go to prison for a very long time.

No, mustn't think about it. He attempted to amuse himself with the judge's name, trying to dissect its origins. It sounded nothing but English; he was probably related to the Puritans of the seventeenth century, lessons about whom Wahid had to endure when he was in secondary school. On one page, he remembered, there was a picture of an oil painting of a Puritan commander. He was middle-aged, had a neatly trimmed moustache and close-cropped hair. There was no joy in the man's eyes, rather the artist made them look as if they were rapiers pointing out accusingly at the viewer: "What are you doing, wasting your time on decadence such as art?" the painting stated. "Get on your knees and worship God!"

In some ways, Wahid supposed, these people were little different from Asad. In light of the failure of the march on the American Embassy, Asad assumed that God's parcelling out of fate had gone against the Muslims. It was time for repentance, prayer and isolation.

The first Iraq War ended quickly, Wahid remembered. Most students had gone back to class. Asad's devotions had a consequence; he had difficulty fitting in prayer around his schedule. Wahid's impression of him was as a white blur, running out the doors of the university to the Finsbury Park mosque, to purify and pray, then the doors banging behind him again as he ran up four flights of stairs to his Information Technology class.

After Asad's lunchtime outburst, Wahid tried to speak to him only once more. It was third year, and they were in the computer lab; Wahid needed help with a spreadsheet programme which had just crashed on him. He had spent hours trying to dissect an assignment regarding the tax implications for the self-employed, and the formula he inserted caused the computer to surrender to the complexity of the equation.

After banging on the Escape key helplessly for a minute, he sighed. He got up and walked along the rows of peeling veneer desks and their large white personal computers, looking for assistance. It was after seven p.m., the room seemed empty, though Wahid could hear clattering from some part of the lab. The sound was distant but definitely not a hallucination.

Wahid tread carefully. Ah. At the back row, there was Asad, hunched over his keyboard, black plastic framed glasses perched

192

on the end of his nose as he frantically typed away. Wahid approached slowly. Sweat was pouring down Asad's head as he pounded in letters and numbers; Wahid wondered what he could be possibly typing with such intensity. The keyboard sounded like it was buckling and straining under the effort.

"What is it?" Asad said without looking up.

"I wonder if you can help me...." Wahid began.

"Only God can help you, brother."

Fix a spreadsheet? "I don't think you understand...."

Asad turned to him. His face was dripping with perspiration, his black hair sticking to the top of his forehead. He stank of the coffee he had consumed over a number of days; the stale brew obviously had continued to percolate in his stomach. His eyes glistened as if they contained the points of sharpened daggers; his head was at a level where such lethal stilettos felt as if they were penetrating Wahid's heart.

"No, you don't understand! We must all prostrate ourselves before God, and beg for His mercy. We are all sinners."

Asad turned back to his computer.

Wahid thought it best not to ask anything further.

Wahid swallowed hard. The idea of a judge like Asad was an unpleasant one.

A door next to the bench opened and a young clerk stood forward. The clerk was dressed like every other officer of the court: same white wig, same black robe. However, the robe was baggier around the shoulders, the wig was cockeyed, his cheeks were slightly flushed, perhaps revealing the enthusiasm of youth.

"Please rise for Lord Justice Oliver Pendleton Hastings!" he shouted.

The door opened, and an old man, no more than five and a half feet tall, stepped out, wearing a red robe. His wig was long and draped over his shoulders. He carried a cane as he approached the bench. He looked up, sighed, and grunted slightly as he climbed up.

Wahid breathed a sigh of relief. This wasn't a Puritan, it

193

was a pensioner. After court he probably went home and had a pot of tea and a plate of digestive biscuits in a living room full of a floral chintz pattern. Wahid could envisage him dressed in a pinstripe suit, sipping the tea, munching the edge of a biscuit and a small smile shining like a glint of daylight across his stony face. All the pleasure he needed.

Wahid again forced down a smirk. Hassan tapped him on the arm. Wahid looked the solicitor in the eye. Hassan shook his head.

Hastings had taken his seat and leaned over the bench, staring down at the rest of the court. Wahid swallowed. While his stature outside of court was not impressive, the old man had a sharp pair of blue eyes; "ferocious" was the word that sprang most readily to Wahid's mind. The long wig, the red robe, "Dieu et Mon Droit" hanging over him, it made it seem as if the court was a creature in two parts, the building, the structure, the polished wood, and then the brain and spirit of the law which resided in the tiny man whose gaze swept from side to side. The court was a vast ship of state sailing through stormy seas: there was no doubt as to who was the captain.

Justice Hastings raised a bony finger. The murmur which had previously filled the court fell silent.

"Before we begin," the judge said, his voice ricocheting through every nook and cranny of the room, "I would like to make it perfectly clear that I will not tolerate any nonsense in this trial."

Wahid swallowed again. Father had lectured him sternly from time to time, but it had never had quite that edge.

Get outside to play? Wahid remembered being eight, sat on the leather sofa in the living room and Father in his white shirt and tan trousers telling him in a sharp but honeyed voice, that he had to have a healthy mind in a healthy body, why didn't he go out to play. He used to go out to play, why didn't he any longer?

Wahid recalled having a pang in his chest, and looking down at his hands, wondering if the slight discolouration underneath his fingernails represented residual dirt. Oh God, he would get sick and he would die.

"No flim-flammery!" Hastings continued.

Wahid snapped his attention back to the judge.

"No media tricks, no trial by tabloid will be tolerated."

The justice paused, inhaled and straightened his posture. "We used to be well known for the fairness of our trials. British justice was considered the gold standard of jurisprudence."

Justice Hastings' eyes fixed on the prosecution. "In my courtroom, so shall it remain. Now...read out the charges."

Wahid bowed his head and shut his eyes. All he could imagine was Father asking again, "Why can't you go out and play like you used to?"

Wahid thought of the cast iron ball that contained wisdom, terror, memory or all three, and the orange light seeping out its cracks. The cracks widened slightly.

"Because I can't," Wahid whispered.

The prosecution was led by Sir Michael Roberts. Wahid first noticed that his robe was of better quality than Hassan's.

Hassan's robe was clean and tidy, but there were defects of age that could not be covered up through tender loving care. It was like watching an actress on a late night film on BBC Two, where any close up had a soft focus around the edges. There was a fine blur, a filament of age around Hassan's garment.

Sir Michael's robe, however, looked as if he had bought it that morning, and it had been ironed and starched. The lines of it did not move or falter as he gestured and spoke.

"We have a star witness," Sir Michael said, "who has agreed to turn state's evidence. He was one of the plotters, who knew Wahid Shah and the others and knew what they intended to do. However, he has since had a change of heart about their dastardly plan."

The incisive way that facts were laid out reminded Wahid slightly of the sums on his spreadsheet. Click, click, click, they all came together, added, multiplied, subtracted, divided.

"We will prove conclusively that these four suspects are

195

guilty of plotting the most horrendous crime...using weapons of mass destruction...on a crowded, busy, London Underground train!"

Yes, yes, subtract, divide, down to zero, to negative.

Weapons of mass destruction. Wahid turned to look at Basir and the imam; the imam had his hands folded across his lap and was looking straight ahead. Basir's arm twitched; Wahid gathered that Basir wanted to raise his arm up to cover his eyes, as if this could shield him from the accusations flying around the courtroom.

Fly around they did, however. Wahid heard a woman coughing behind him. Accusations and germs now; miniature trolls accompanied by miniature goblins with large teeth, laughing and accusing, ready to deliver the final blow to Wahid, to take him out, to put him away.

Wahid looked at the imam again.

Unless God intervened.

"Thank you, Sir Michael," Justice Hastings said, his voice sounding fatigued.

The judge raised a bony hand and stretched it outward. "Mr. Iqbal."

Hassan stood; Miss Woods turned her head to watch, her bright red hair following the motion in a flourish. Wahid heard him swallow and take a deep breath.

"If it please the court, m'lud," he began, "the prosecution makes an impressive attempt to paint my clients as being guilty of some terrible conspiracy. Nothing could be further from the truth."

Quite right, Wahid thought.

"My clients are all innocent, upstanding citizens who have three things which unite them: their ethnicity, their faith and a total lack of a criminal record."

Hassan leaned forward, grabbing hold of the lectern in front of him, as if he needed its additional strength to push on. Wahid noticed that Hassan's knuckles were turning white from the tightness of the grip. Miss Woods' breathing became more rapid,

Wahid noted. Hassan looked at her for a moment, and gave her a small smile; he then continued: "The defence will show that all three of my clients are innocent of the charges, and that the entire case rests upon a faulty premise – the actions and intentions of my client, Wahid Shah."

Wahid sat up.

"The defence will show that Mr. Shah is hardly a radical...in fact, he's not much of a Muslim. He regularly doesn't pay attention to anything that is said in mosque."

Wahid's eyes opened wide. He looked at Justice Hastings: no help. The old man was utterly impassive.

"...and furthermore, we will show that he is an incurable hypochondriac, which is how the materials for the so-called 'weapons of mass destruction' got into his case in the first place."

Hassan stood up straight again, and grasped the edges of his robe, peering down for a moment as if a profound thought had passed through his mind. "Without Wahid Shah as the doer, the man who was going to carry out this operation, the entire case for the prosecution becomes less than circumstantial. Abdullah Basir is guilty of nothing more than being Mr. Shah's friend and business associate. As for our esteemed imam...well he is *my* imam at *my* mosque. I know this man...he hasn't an ounce of hatred in his body, he is far too consumed with the idea of God's love."

"His mercy takes precedence over His wrath," the imam whispered.

Wahid resisted the urge to tell him to shut up.

"...as for Sir Michael's witnesses...once we are done, I will highly recommend that the Crown Prosecution Service brings Ahmed Mirza back on charges of perjury."

"Mr. Iqbal!"

The entire court froze. Justice Hastings pointed an accusing finger at Hassan. "Keep your opening statement limited, Mr. Iqbal," he cautioned.

Hassan nodded. "Forgive me, m'lud. No grandstanding."

The old judge nodded.

Wahid held his head in his hands for much of the journey back to the prison.

"What did he mean, you're not much of a Muslim?" Basir asked.

Wahid looked up. Basir's countenance was puzzled, his eyes slightly wider than usual, his full lips distorted from a straight line. His face rocked back and forth as the van bucked and swayed over the bumpy roads.

Wahid sighed.

Was he much of a Muslim? He had learned his grip on the uniform from Asad, learned his grip on the rituals from the imam. But was he actually a Muslim in his heart? He knew that God was there, but had he truly submitted?

Again, motive: was it out of fear that he obeyed the rules, or was it genuine love?

Wahid's eyes shifted to Basir's left. The imam sat there, impassive as usual. No, impassive was the wrong word: rather, he was calm. Love of God made him so.

Wahid cast his mind back to the house in Hackney, and climbing into bed at night during the winter. To prevent catching pneumonia, he usually changed in the bathroom just after having a shower: the steam kept the room temporarily warmer than the rest of the house. He had white cotton pyjamas that Rania always ironed for him; they were laid out, hanging over the heated towel rack. Wahid put those on quickly, took a deep breath, and then ran into the darkened bedroom, climbing underneath the white, hypoallergenic duvet as fast as possible. Rania was always there already, and the scent of her perfume and the spices she had used in her cooking, along with her warmth, permeated that sealed little universe of the bed. Wahid lay back and luxuriated in the warmth.

Quick, quick, slow, slow.

"I love you," Rania often said.

He often did not reply. His tongue, along with the rest of

198

him, was too comfortable to be stirred.

The imam had a similar sense of calm with him all the time, perhaps.

"Answer me," Basir said. "What did Hassan mean?"

The imam shut his eyes. "Brother Wahid often listens to music while at prayer," he said.

Basir looked as if someone had punched him in the solar plexus, hard. "But, you look so devout...."

"Appearance is not all," the imam continued.

Basir nodded. His eyes were full of tears. "So you don't really believe?"

Wahid shrugged. "I believe, Basir...just I thought I had heard it all before."

And was there none of God's beauty and glory in the music? Basir and the imam perhaps could never understand, but the rippling flow of notes surely was part of the fabric of Creation. Wahid once wanted to learn a musical instrument; as a boy, he stole into the music room at his secondary school after class. The chairs were arranged in a semi-circle, all facing a dark metal lectern, where Wahid presumed the conductor would stand. Wahid found a blue folder on the lectern. It was old; the corners were bending upwards from years of use and the folder had a multitude of wrinkles along its formerly smooth surface.

Wahid stroked it and opened the folder up. Ah ha, in clear black letters, it said "Dvorak: Slavonic Dance No. 3"

Beneath the words were the notes, all looking like p's and d's to him, arranged in between lines, notated with signs. He could not read the music, but there was a precision in the arrangement of the notes along the lines, a beauty in the swooping curve that linked a set of notes to another, and there was an implied force in multiple notes being stacked up.

God was in that, surely. Wahid was not bad; he remembered, after all, that God was in everything.

"We should be thankful," the imam said, opening his eyes.

"Oh, why is that?" Basir asked. The reverential tones Basir usually used in speaking to the imam had disappeared.

199

The imam shut his eyes again. "For whatever reason, Brother Wahid being a bad Muslim is the key to our freedom. If God wills it."

Twenty-Eight

"I thought it best not to tell you," Hassan explained.

Wahid, Basir and the imam were waiting with Hassan and Miss Woods in the courthouse's anteroom. The trial was going to begin again in fifteen minutes. Wahid looked at the basic white clock hanging on the olive green coloured wall: tick, tick, tick, the hands moved slowly towards the inevitable destination of nine a.m.

"It *was* something of a surprise," the imam replied.

Miss Woods was entirely impassive. Her blue eyes did not blink.

"Sometimes it works out better that way," Hassan continued, "Besides, would Mr. Shah have gone along with a defence that questioned his faith?"

The imam and Basir looked at Wahid.

God, what would Father say? Years of Saturday recitations, fasting at Ramadan, paying alms and performing prayers; the son had been worshipping at the celestial temple of Beethoven and Bach rather than paying due homage to Allah's holy words.

He should have known better. No part of his life was ever going to be hidden from God's scrutiny. God was distant but immanent at the same time. If Wahid took pleasure in a sticky toffee ice cream, like he did when he was little, the caramel and sugar flavours bursting in his mouth along with the ice cold sensations, God would be there, and his teeth would rot and he would get diabetes.

201

What would Father say?

"Are you a good man?" he would ask.

Wahid could picture him in his usual stance when he wanted to discuss a serious topic; his arm was draped over the stone mantelpiece above the gas fire in the living room, his eyes serious, the eyebrows nearly intersecting at the middle of his forehead as he stared him down.

Was he a good man? Dr. Blanchard had said so, Rania said so, but here was the accusation that he was not a good Muslim. How could the two be separated?

"I would have objected," Wahid said quietly. He looked deeply into Miss Woods' cold blue eyes for the first time. He thought he detected a trace of her expression softening.

Hassan looked up at the clock.

"Time to go back in."

Wahid noticed that Justice Hastings walked with a firmer stride than he had the previous day. Each step he took had an added element of force, projecting his slender, frail frame upward. Unity with the courtroom obviously strengthened him, Wahid reasoned.

The court fell silent as the old judge took his seat. The gold-rimmed glasses sat further down his nose, the blue eyes were slightly warmer.

Wahid swallowed.

"Now here comes the awkward bit," Hassan whispered.

Wahid cast a quick glance over to the solicitor, but Miss Woods was acting as a barrier between them. Her gaze, unflinching, fixed, was focused on the judge.

Justice Hastings picked up a glass of water which was resting near his right hand and took a gulp. The court remained silent to the point where Wahid could hear his throat making faint sounds as he swallowed.

The judge put the glass down and fixed the court with a stare. "Call your first witness, Sir Michael," he said.

Sir Michael stood; Wahid noticed that his shoulders

trembled slightly as he pulled himself up.

"I call Inspector Fredrick Willows."

Willows had gained some weight, Wahid thought. The hair was the same, the saliva-stained lips were the same, the eyes were just as beady, but the jowls of the hound had obviously gotten larger. It looked like his waistband was under some pressure as well, as he waddled his way to the stand.

Willows swore an oath to tell the truth and sat down.

"Now, Inspector....you are the officer who was in charge of this investigation?"

Willows' eyes shifted in a circuit of the courtroom, from side to side. "Yes."

"Pray tell us the sequence of events on the day in question."

The inspector looked down. "Mr. Shah, formerly a respectable accountant, first went to pray at the Al Huda Mosque in the East End of London. There, he met with Ahmed Mirza, an accomplice, and received final coded instructions from the imam through his sermon."

Sir Michael pursed his lips and clutched the edge of his robe, giving him the appearance of thoughtful repose. Wahid fought down a wave of nausea.

"How were the instructions coded?"

"Through a citation of the Qur'an. If I may?"

Sir Michael extended his hand. "By all means."

Willows pulled a folded piece of paper out of his breast pocket and opened it.

He coughed: "It's from Sura 18: *He hath made it Straight and Clear in order that He may warn the godless of a terrible Punishment from Him, and that He may give Glad Tidings to the Believers who work righteous deeds, that they shall have a goodly Reward.*"

Sir Michael nodded. "So what do you think this means?"

"Obviously Wahid Shah was considered the Believer who worked 'righteous deeds'."

The imam suppressed a cough; it sounded like an explosion

203

trapped under glass. Sir Michael turned briefly and cast a look at the imam. A pause: the prosecutor returned his attention to Willows.

"So what happened?"

"Wahid Shah then went to visit Abdullah Basir at his garage near Holloway Road; this is near the notorious Finsbury Park Mosque."

"Enough!"

As one, the entire court looked at Justice Hastings. The sound of his voice echoed for a second throughout. Willows looked at him, his eyes wide.

"Keep your remarks confined to the facts of the case," the judge warned.

Willows nodded. "Yes, m'lud."

Sir Michael's thin lips twisted into a small smile. "Continue."

"We suggest that Mr. Shah visited Mr. Basir in order to confirm the plot was underway, and to check the precise combination of chemicals required to make chlorine gas."

"Chlorine gas?" Justice Hastings asked. His forehead was deep with furrows.

"Yes, m'lud," Willows said, "we found ammonia and bleach in Mr. Shah's case – mixed properly, they combine to form chlorine gas."

Justice Hastings sighed. "Continue."

"Mr. Basir is a graduate of Imperial College, London, and knew how to make this gas."

Justice Hastings looked over at Basir. "You there, Mr. Basir....is this correct, did you graduate from Imperial College?"

Basir stood. Wahid could see that his knees were shaking. "Yes, m'lud," he replied.

"Are you a chemist then?"

"No, m'lud, I specialised in mechanical engineering."

The judge waved his hand at Basir indicating *sit down*.

Basir fell back into his seat with a thud. He fixed Willows with a sharp stare.

"I went to Imperial College as well, Inspector. Nowhere was 'How to Make Chemical Weapons' on the curriculum," Hastings warned.

Willows coughed. "Surely, though, that is an indication of his chemical knowledge?"

Justice Hastings nodded. "It's an indication he is intelligent. But don't even begin to try to portray Imperial College as being an Al Qaeda finishing school." The judge fixed Sir Michael with another stare. "Carry on."

Sir Michael nodded. "Yes, m'lud."

Hassan leaned forward, lowering his elbows onto the desk in front of him. His hands were folded, and he rested his chin them. Wahid wondered what the gesture meant.

Hope?

"We are winning," Hassan told them after court was adjourned.

Winning? It was obvious that Justice Hastings was a stickler for protocol, Wahid thought: he wasn't going to tolerate any nonsense. Willows tried to add emotive words like "suspiciously", "secretly" and "dastardly" into his testimony. Hastings stopped him every time, told him that it was rhetoric rather than facts, and said that a police officer should know better.

"Willows was less than pleased that Hastings was chosen," Hassan explained.

No doubt. When Hassan questioned Willows in turn, he asked the following question:

"Did you ever consider any alternative theories?"

The court was silent for a moment; Hassan's erect bearing made him stand out like a beacon in the courtroom, as if he was a lighthouse radiating a penetrating beam right onto Willows. The inspector shifted in his seat uncomfortably.

Willows said, "Certainly. We try to avoid accusing innocent people."

"Oh?" Hassan asked. "Can you tell us about any of these theories?"

205

Willows shifted again. "They are not worth mentioning...they were discarded at an early stage."

Hassan voice added a note of mockery. "Surely, though, you have at least one theory you can share with us?"

Willows shifted once more; he looked up at Hastings, who gazed at the policeman intently.

"Answer the question," Justice Hastings instructed.

"I ask again, do you or did you have any alternative theories?"

Willows smiled, his upper lip was twitching, and beads of sweat were glistening in the courtroom lights. "No."

Wahid inhaled sharply.

It was all so calm and precise, Wahid thought; he began to understand Father a bit more. Pakistan was a land of passion, where waves of fortune could elevate people like Uncle Naseem to the heights of opulence. At the same time, at the base of the tide lay the majority, who were rolled over in the silt with each passing current.

Justice Hastings, however, was like a sheet of ice. The ice lay flat over the currents and tides. It was smooth. Wahid recalled going to Regents Park on a cold winter day with Father and reaching out his foot, clad in a dark green Wellington boot, to touch the ice on the duck pond. There was nothing but the slight scraping sound of rubber against frozen water. Nothing moved beneath it; it was still. The sediment remained undisturbed by the motions at the top, nothing roiled or rolled.

Predictability, reliability: these were traits that Mother had loved about Father. He was always home by six p.m. and ate his meals in the dining room while listening to the news on Radio Four. Wahid loved how he always looked over to him at precisely a quarter to seven and asked: "How was your day? Did you learn a lot at school? What did you learn?"

As he rode in the van back to their prison, Wahid envisaged Justice Hastings and Father having a drink together. One diminutive and elderly in a pinstripe suit, the other, handsome and debonair, but at the same time, laughing and enjoying each other's company.

"I always vote Labour," Father would tell him in an almost apologetic tone.

"I don't blame you," Justice Hastings would reply. "I would if I were you."

They'd laugh and talk about constancy. Yes.

The same standards had to apply. No "flim-flammery", no deviation, no breaking of the etiquette, no breach with standards. Anything that was "spin" had been thrown out.

Pure justice, Wahid thought, as the van sped over a pothole, tossing him up in the air like a flipped penny. He imagined that a large enough dip in the road might turn him upside down, and then cause him to crash on his skull. Death. Peace.

"Pure justice," he whispered. His hands were sweating.

Twenty-Nine

The prosecution called Asad next.

"We intend to establish that Mr. Shah has had a long involvement in radical Islamic politics," Sir Michael had said.

Wahid felt his stomach tighten. He had not seen Asad for sixteen years. How different would he be? What made the radical turn into a policeman?

Wahid felt sweat cover his brow; droplets slowly worked their way through the forest of his hairline.

False witness. Wahid could recall that as one of the Ten Commandments, which he learned at school. He was very young, and the teacher had written them out in white chalk on a blackboard. "Thou shalt not bear false witness against thy neighbour."

But that implied deliberate lying: true, Wahid had joined up with Asad. Asad was radical, at least to a point. Obviously his radicalism stopped where the straps of Shehnaz's brassiere began.

Asad now wore a blue policeman's uniform; the line and cut of the garments suited him. Long gone was the beard of the student radical; it had been replaced with a neatly trimmed moustache, which had some grey in it. He took off his cap as he took the stand, revealing that his thick hair had also been a victim of the years. He had tried to cover up his emerging, glistening dome by combing over stray locks of wispy black hair.

His accent had changed too; Wahid recalled Asad trying to speak Urdu to the student demonstration to finish off his speech. He sounded more North London than Islamabad, and he managed to mangle the sentence order. When he attempted to say "All glory be to God", it came out as "All gloomy be to God".

Asad had then tried to settle on a strong South Asian accent, which made him sound like a television caricature. Speaking to him became painful: upon entering conversation with him, Wahid wondered if Asad was going to preface his reply with "my goodness gracious".

But that was all gone. The callow youth had become the officer of the law. There was a flicker of recognition in Asad's eyes as he looked at Wahid, and a hesitation as he sat down.

"You are Sergeant Asad Choudhry?" Sir Michael asked.

"Yes, sir," Asad replied.

Wahid was stunned at how deep his voice had become over time: he half expected the reply to contain a squeak or two. Asad now had a baritone worthy of a BBC radio presenter.

"How long have you served with the Metropolitan Police?"

Asad's eyes shifted to the left and upwards. Wahid recalled a radio programme stating that such eye movements indicated the quality of the thought behind them. Shift one way and go up, that indicated recollection, the other indicated telling lies. Which was it?

Damn. Wahid could recall everything else on that day; he was in his office, it was early spring, and Rania had given him a small terracotta pot with a single blooming daffodil in it, to brighten up his workplace.

The flower rested on the bookcase in front of the poster of Switzerland. Ah yes, Switzerland.

Wahid wished he could fish the postcard of Lausanne out of his breast pocket without being noticed: to see the world in *order*.

"Fifteen years," Asad finally replied.

"You knew the defendant, Wahid Shah?" Sir Michael asked.

"Yes, he and I protested the first Iraq War together."

"What was your role in these protests?"

"I was the organiser. Mr. Shah was one of my followers."

"Was he particularly active?"

Asad shrugged. "He attended all the meetings and the marches, but never said much. Outwardly though, he seemed to be one of us."

"Outwardly?"

"Shortly after joining our group, he shed Western clothes for more traditional garb...cotton trousers and a *kurta*, which is sort of a long shirt."

Sir Michael outstretched his hand to indicate Wahid.

"Does it surprise you, Sergeant Choudhry, that Mr. Shah remained a radical?"

Asad shifted his head from side to side. "I can't say that I had a strong sense of his commitment...but then again, he did ask me for guidance."

Wahid's eyes opened wide. "To fix my spreadsheet, yes!" he thought.

"Did you give him this guidance?" Sir Michael continued.

"I told him to embrace God," Asad replied. "I wish..."

He trailed off.

"You wish what?" Justice Hastings asked.

"I had given him the advice then that I would now."

"And what would that be?" Sir Michael asked.

Asad looked directly at Wahid.

"Wahid, the Prophet said to honour all treaties and contracts, to do otherwise is a mortal sin. Being a citizen of this country is a contract, never violate it."

Justice Hastings looked at Asad thoughtfully.

"You say that Mr. Shah was part of your group, and he was a radical?" Hassan asked.

"To be honest," Asad replied, "my group was radical, and Wahid was a part of it."

"Have you spoken to Mr. Shah extensively...ever?"

Asad's upper lip twisted. "No...he was difficult to get to know."

Hassan smiled and nodded. "Did you even make an attempt to get to know him?"

Asad sighed. "I was rather...preoccupied at the time."

"Ah yes," Hassan said, "we understand that you were involved with a Miss Shehnaz Massoud."

Asad's lips set into a firm line. "That is not relevant."

"Ah, but I think it is," Hassan said.

Wahid wondered: was Hassan actually being playful?

"I ask again, were you involved with Miss Shehnaz Massoud?"

Justice Hastings spoke up. "Answer the question."

"Yes," Asad admitted.

"She is a person of some fame and importance now, isn't she?" Hassan asked.

"Look, don't drag her into this, she has nothing to do with the case...."

"It's to establish credibility, m'lud," Hassan explained.

"Answer the question," Justice Hastings said. "However, Mr. Iqbal, keep your speculation on a short leash."

Hassan audibly gulped. "I will, m'lud. Again, Miss Massoud is a person of some fame and importance, is she not?"

"Yes," Asad replied.

"And her son, is he not yours?"

Asad looked down. "Yes."

"Do you know what the Islamic term for sex between unmarried people is?"

Asad began to answer with a "but": Hassan stopped him. "It's *zina*. In some countries with sharia, it's punishable by death."

Asad put his head in his hands. His shoulders slightly shook.

"I suggest, Sergeant Choudhry, that you weren't really a radical at all. You were just playing at being one."

Asad looked up. "Yes."

"And thus, you're in no position to judge whether or not Mr. Shah was a radical or otherwise."

Silence overtook the courtroom.

"I have no further questions," Hassan said. He turned and

walked back to the desk for the defence.

Wahid thought he saw a hint of a cricketer's gait, as if Hassan had just delivered a magnificent over. He could picture Hassan in cricket whites on a summer's day, holding the red ball in his hand and polishing its surface on his trouser leg. Yes, Hassan could defeat the Isle of Man by himself.

His smile grew as he reached the desk. He looked at Miss Woods directly, as if she was the only person in the room; her hard countenance softened; her lips stretched up into a smile. Wahid raised an eyebrow.

Feeling somewhat embarrassed, Wahid shifted his gaze to look up at the Justice, who was drinking another glass of water. A flicker of a facial movement: did Hastings wink at him?

Perhaps there was still hope, Wahid thought.

Quick, quick, quick, and slow. The pulse steadied.

Thirty

"The prosecution calls Ahmed Mirza," Sir Michael said.

His voice was tired, as if he had spent the night reading in bed. Wahid pictured him wearing striped pyjamas and lying on a soft feather bed with folders lying all around him. The endless search for an answer must be consuming him, Wahid reasoned.

Hassan visibly trembled for a moment, then his shoulders squared up. Wahid cast a glance at Justice Hastings; the old man appeared to be as energetic and chipper as Sir Michael was downcast.

Pure justice, Wahid thought. Pure justice, pure God?

The doors to the courtroom opened, letting in a rush of air. Wahid did not dare turn to look at Ahmed: the sound of his footsteps grew louder as he approached.

"*The prayer that man should make for good, he maketh for evil; for man is given to hasty deeds,*" the imam whispered.

Wahid stopped himself from nodding in agreement.

Ahmed arrived at the front of the courtroom.

He looked as if incarceration had agreed with him. Wahid supposed that his ideas about Ahmed's imprisonment were correct: surely, he had been held in a hotel rather than a prison. He wore a brand new grey wool suit, which didn't shine and sparkle like Wahid's polyester garb. His beard had been trimmed back, his hair precisely combed and slicked into place. Wahid also noted that the dried blood had been removed from underneath his fingernails. Strange that this would be the first time he'd dare shake the man's hand without worrying that he risked catching some bovine disease.

215

Ahmed swore to tell the truth before God. The imam's breath audibly caught. Wahid wished he could reach over and hold his hand for a moment to comfort him. However, the imam was with God; the need for comfort was surely temporary, because no matter how far he was pulled into this world, God wrapped His arms around him and pulled him back to the foot of His throne.

"Think only of God and heavenly things," Wahid thought for him.

The imam exhaled.

"Sir Michael, continue," Justice Hastings said.

Wahid wondered: was the judge bored? Wahid tilted his head slightly to the left, to look at the judge at a new angle: did the old man just roll his eyes?

Did Justice Hastings think this was a farce?

Quick quick quick, slow. The pulse raced nevertheless. Hope. Hassan had it, now so did Wahid. He felt a slight flush of fever in his cheeks.

He could be free. He could be told that there was no case to answer and he could go. There would be no more police officers to push him into the back of vans, no dreary rides back to the prison hospital, where Mr. Watson would have tea waiting for them, no staring out of scenes of concrete and grey skies that were blocked by iron bars. None of it, nothing more, he could go back to Rania and their home and his life.

Or could he? Would it be the same?

"Please state your name," Sir Michael said, "for the record."

"Ahmed Mirza," Ahmed said.

"What is your profession?"

"I am a butcher; my shop is near Brick Lane."

"Do you recognise these gentlemen?" Sir Michael asked, indicating Wahid, Basir and the imam.

"Yes, they were my friends and colleagues."

"But no longer?"

"No."

"Why?"

Ahmed let his eyes fill with tears. "Because they plotted a terrible crime."

Quick quick quick, slow.

The questions about the nature of the plot were mundane. The plan to release chlorine gas was confirmed. The religious aspect was also confirmed; the "go phrase" as Ahmed put it was from Sura 18.

Wahid? Well, he was a skinny little fellow, a little weird, but he was a true radical: he didn't dress in a suit all the time, rather, he wore traditional clothes. Everyone knew that was the mark of an Islamist.

Wahid felt the clothes pinch and poke him accusingly once more. The Indonesian children were speaking, perhaps telling him that anything based on their labour would not come to any good. "You cannot hide behind us," their little fingers said. Wahid tried not to wriggle in his chair.

He sighed.

Ahmed was alternately charming, witty and yet base. The imam grabbed the edge of the table so tightly that Wahid wondered if his fingertips would leave indentations on its surface. The imam's neck muscles were taught, his eyes glassy: Wahid knew that the imam was not enjoying the spectacle of someone going to hell.

"Of course," Ahmed continued, "Mr. Shah was always the most devoted, in terms of going to mosque. Everyone knew that: he never missed a prayer."

Hassan stirred. Wahid cast a quick glance; the solicitor was trying to look grim, but the upturned corner of his mouth gave it away.

What was he planning, what was he doing?

Hassan pulled a pencil out of his briefcase and wrote quickly on a pad. Wahid's eyes weren't fast enough to catch what was being written, but the pencil flowed elegantly, like Hassan was conducting a Beethoven symphony. He finished by drawing an exclamation point and struck the paper with a loud dot.

"Thank you, Mr. Mirza," Sir Michael said and nodded to the judge.

"Your witness," Justice Hastings said.

Hassan stood.

"Mr. Mirza...." he began, "you are here because you struck a deal with the Crown Prosecution Service, correct?"

Ahmed shrugged. "I did, but then again I am a man of conscience."

Hassan let a hint of amusement enter his voice once more. "Your conscience apparently only troubled you after you were arrested. How do you account for this timing?"

Ahmed gave Hassan an acid grin. Wahid put his hand over his heart; it was beating very fast. Slow slow slow, slow down.

"I was told by the police how many people would have been killed."

"Surely you knew that beforehand? After all, what was the point of the operation as you describe it, if it didn't bring a large body count?"

Ahmed coughed. "I only knew about that as an abstraction...the reality...horrible."

"Yes, I'm sure it was. What have you been offered in exchange for this testimony, Mr. Mirza?"

Ahmed looked at Justice Hastings. No help: "Answer the question," Hastings told him.

"Freedom," Ahmed said softly.

"What was that?" Hassan asked, "I don't believe we all heard you."

"I'll be given my freedom."

"I see," Hassan continued. "Thus, your attack of conscience was rather convenient, was it not?"

"Mr. Iqbal," Justice Hastings said severely.

Hassan paused. "Sorry, m'lud."

"Carry on," the judge stated.

"You say that you know Wahid Shah well. Have you ever

been to his house?"

Ahmed rolled his eyes up and to the right. Wahid wondered: lying or remembering? Had he ever invited Ahmed to his home? Would he have ever invited Ahmed to his home?

Quick quick slow. Why no, no he wouldn't...and hadn't.

Ahmed exhaled. "Well, no."

"Ever invited Mr. Shah around to your house?"

Wahid never would have accepted; but again, had there been an invitation? Wahid scanned his memory.

Ahmed confirmed Wahid's recollection. "No."

"Strange that you two were intimate friends, but never went to each other's houses...."

Ahmed coughed. "That didn't matter, we met at the mosque."

Hassan nodded. "Yes, we'll come to that. You said Mr. Shah is a devoted worshipper."

"Yes, absolutely, I saw him there all the time. That's where we met."

Hassan nodded again. "And you say that he is a very pious Muslim."

"Yes, absolutely."

"Would it surprise you to know...that during prayers, Mr. Shah was generally listening to his iPod?"

Ahmed's eyes opened wide; Wahid fought down the urge to gasp. "What?"

Hassan restated it. "Did you know that Mr. Shah spent most of his time in the mosque listening to his iPod?"

Ahmed sank back into his seat, his bulging eyes staring at Wahid.

Quick quick slow.

"No, I did not," Ahmed said.

Hassan paced in front of the witness stand.

"You do realise," Hassan said, "without Mr. Shah being as devoted a radical as you say, the rest of the story you've just told us, doesn't make any sense...and indeed, you may have just perjured yourself."

Ahmed cast his eyes downward.

Hassan said, "We have proof of Mr. Shah's listening to his iPod during prayers, Mr. Mirza. In light of this, would you like to revise your testimony?"

"Objection!" Sir Michael shouted, "we should have had disclosure of this evidence prior to the trial."

Justice Hastings looked at Hassan. "Mr. Iqbal?"

"M'lud, we were only able to obtain this evidence very recently. We will be happy to disclose this information to all parties for their examination."

"Very well," Hastings replied. "Objection overruled."

Hassan turned to Miss Woods. "We'd like to introduce Defence Exhibit A"

Miss Woods reached into her briefcase and pulled out an iPod. Wahid instantly recognised it to be his: no other had its white surface kept polished to such a high shine, he was sure.

Miss Woods placed the iPod on the table, then reached into her briefcase for a manila folder, bulging with documents.

Hassan strode over to the desk and picked up the iPod and the folder, which he held up like a torch. The gesture reminded Wahid somewhat of the Statue of Liberty.

"Here, m'lud, is the proof."

Hassan stood on his toes and placed the iPod and folder in front of the judge. Hastings picked up the iPod and turned it over in his hands. Wahid noticed that Hastings was obviously not an amateur at using one; he pressed the controls and turned the dial with skill.

"An impressive collection of classical music, Mr. Iqbal, but how does this prove your assertion?"

Hassan bounced up on the balls of his feet; the motion reminded Wahid of a rabbit being allowed to leap for the first time. "Please see the folder, m'lud."

Hastings opened it. "Dates, times, piece of music," he said, "where did you get this?"

"M'lud, whenever a song is played on an iPod, both the date and time are recorded on its hard drive; we hired a technical expert to extract this information. As you can see, the times and dates of this music being played exactly coincide with prayer times. If you flip to the last page…."

Hastings complied.

"…you'll see that the last piece of music was listened to on the morning of the incident in question. Even if there was a code phrase, my client could not have heard it."

Sir Michael stood. "This is all a convenient smokescreen; but this does not explain why Mr. Shah kept the ingredients for chlorine gas in his briefcase!"

Ahmed nodded. "There was a plot! I swear it! This is all a fabrication!"

"Enough!" Hastings shouted, waving his finger reprovingly. "Mr. Iqbal, do you have any further questions for this witness?"

Hassan shook his head. "No, m'lud."

"Fine. Sir Michael?"

Sir Michael's tone was sombre. "The prosecution rests, m'lud."

Wahid exhaled.

Thirty-One

"I am going to call you as my first and only witness," Hassan told him.

Wahid turned Hassan's statement over in his mind as he lay on his bed. It was dark and quiet; the imam and Basir were sleeping peacefully. Basir in particular was more still than usual. Once again, only Wahid was awake.

Hassan had told him the bad news as they proceeded out of the courtroom and back to the van; it was accompanied by the solicitor grabbing him by the elbow, and the statement was harshly whispered in his ear.

Wahid lifted his hands up. While the moonlight was dim, he could clearly see from the outlines of his fingertips that they were shaking.

They were winning, there was hope. But Hassan had just shoved the burden onto him. He would have to testify in such a way as to continue this lucky streak.

Wahid shut his eyes. Again, he envisaged Hassan as a cricketer on a perfectly green pitch with the scent of freshly mowed grass in the air, and the sound of chirping birds in the background. Hassan again wore cricket whites. At the crease stood Asad, wearing a cricketer's helmet and holding a bat. Hassan took a long run, let his arm fly over his body and released the red ball at Asad. The ball spun towards the ground, bounced and Asad swung at it blindly. The ball knocked the stumps and Asad was out. Asad slunk away, trailing the bat in the dirt behind him.

Next Ahmed stood at the crease, wearing his suit, which

223

contrasted oddly with a standard cricketer's helmet. He rubbed his hands together before waving the bat menacingly. Yes, he was going to knock it a long way. Hassan smiled, taking the red ball in his hands and walking backwards. Another run, another bounce, another strike of the stumps: Ahmed was out. Ahmed looked stunned, confused, and staggered off the pitch.

But now it was time for Wahid to take his place. What was the move here, what was Hassan planning? Did he have to surrender or did he have to fight back?

Hassan did not say. All Wahid had to go on was that he was the first and only witness.

If only Rania was with him. She would say something sensible.

Wahid rolled over. The bed was too small for two; the bed in Hackney would have had her lying there, all warmth and comfort when nights were chilly like this one. But she was still in Pakistan; there had been no further letter, Wahid had asked Watson that evening. Had she withdrawn her favour? Were the streams of golden silk pulling back to their epicentre?

No, no, no. Don't surrender to that thought yet. They had been winning, after all. Wahid stood and tried to breathe. Quick, quick, slow. Fall back, fall back, for God's sake.

"God, I run to Thee," Wahid thought. The barrier of Creation perhaps was now in the very air he breathed. Beyond the veil of what could be seen was God in all His Glory; Wahid knew that even if he saw, he could not comprehend. His purposes lay behind all that was happening.

"Islam means submission," Father once said, "but submission to God is only the beginning of what He demands."

God demanded forbearance, decency, character as well as ritual, perhaps. Just like Father had shown.

"I have failed," Wahid thought. Tears built up in his eyes.

"His Mercy takes precedence over His Wrath," the imam had said. Would God be merciful in this instance, could He be?

There were so many things that Wahid did not even understand about himself.

224

"How did this happen?" Dr. Blanchard had asked.

He still looked inward and saw the iron ball of memory locked as tight as ever, despite the gleams it occasionally produced.

Would God be merciful?

Wahid began to pace. Don't run, don't run. That would imply he was falling prey to madness again, and all his thoughts were being allowed to assault him, full force.

Don't run, don't run. He paced, forcing his feet to move slowly across the linoleum.

"Rania, Rania, where are you?" he whispered.

"God, God, where are You?" he added.

Neither was there in the dark and the quiet, except perhaps in his heart.

He did not know what he was doing. He did not know what was required of him. "Answers, answers," he said softly.

He only felt a great blankness within, as if his mind wanted him to be clear of every other thought.

"Give over to God," Wahid imagined Father saying. Was that a memory or was it a whisper from beyond? Was he going mad?

"Give over to God," Wahid imagined Father insisting.

Well why not, God knew what He was doing at all times, which was the complete opposite to himself.

Wahid faced the window and stopped his pacing. He looked up at the moon and shut his eyes.

"I give over to You," he whispered.

The next morning was mundane in its regularity. Watson came in at half past five and said in a strong voice, "Gentlemen, it's time to wake up."

Basir, the imam and Wahid proceeded to the showers and washed themselves with strong lye soap. Wahid put on the suit, which was becoming increasingly uncomfortable due to it having been worn for three days straight. Not only were there accusing fingers, the thin veneer of bodily filth was building up on the

225

garments. Fortunately, his underwear was clean, otherwise it would have been unbearable.

The ride in the van was similarly routine. There was the leading out by the policemen to the vehicle, the ache as muscles pushed him upward into its entrance, the familiar chill of the metal bench beneath him. Wahid sat across from Basir, as per usual. Basir did not meet his gaze.

"I can't believe it," he had said. "I simply can't."

Listening to an iPod in the mosque, how *haram* was that? Apparently in the court of Basir's mind, Wahid had been tried and convicted as a despicable sinner.

Wahid tried to look at his friend again. Basir shifted his eyes to the other side.

Quick, quick, slow.

"Brother Wahid," the imam said, "don't be so nervous."

Nervous? Wahid rubbed his hands; they were almost glued together from perspiration, and made a slight noise as he peeled them apart.

Quick, quick, quick, slow.

His heart was racing. He was going to have to climb into the stand and face questions not only from Hassan but also from Sir Michael. Hassan would no doubt be aggressive, but Sir Michael as well? Those cold grey eyes, could they see right into his soul, and find all the guilt that he had?

Guilt. Wahid felt dirty the moment he thought of the word. Yes, he was guilty of not following in the path of God, guilty of terrible sins of not letting himself be moved by the Word of God. He was covered in muck and filth.

He tried to think of Dr. Blanchard's words, "The hand that is dipped in mud, can be washed clean again." But could such scouring occur in the soul? Would he be able to ever make up for this, his sins dragging others into the same pit in which he resided?

Wahid began to perspire more profusely.

Dirt, filth, muck, the kind that cannot be escaped, forced upon him just as hard as the pestilence that Arnold Arkwright had ejaculated into him.

Wahid shut his eyes. Thinking of Rania, did that help? While the tresses of golden silk wove their way back to her in his imagination, their path flowed through dark London clouds that were lit up by lightning. No, there was no escape, the routes back to her were blocked.

Dr. Blanchard? Well, there was the thought of Lausanne, but thinking of her led once again to the questions she asked. He was asking it of himself now: *Why am I like this?*

"I don't know." he thought.

You do know, his mind responded.

The iron ball of memory cracked further, the orange light pouring out of it increased in intensity. Yes. Childhood, childhood, childhood. Something dirty, something filthy, *Good God, what did you get into.*

Where did that come from?

The van pulled up to a screeching halt.

Wahid opened his eyes, and exhaled. He put his fingers on his wrist to check his pulse. It was distant, but steady. He put his hand over his heart to be sure he was still alive. Too bad, he was.

Basir looked at him; for a millisecond, Wahid thought he might say some words of comfort but the eyes were wide, and the lips that were better suited to a smile were turned down.

"Do not fail," Basir said.

The pulse surged upwards.

Hassan breezed into the courtroom, as if his feet walked on a gust that rolled in from London's streets. He smiled, his tie was slightly loosened, and he was wearing the same suit as yesterday.

"What happened?" Wahid wondered. Hassan hadn't bathed; there was a slight scent of cigarette smoke emanating from him. And what was that beneath? Perfume? Wahid decided not to inhale deeply.

Hassan unpacked his papers onto the desk and was humming. Humming?

Wahid coughed.

227

Hassan turned to look at him. "Don't worry," he said, reassuringly, and resumed unpacking.

He began to hum again.

Wahid turned to his side. Miss Woods entered, her countenance just as dishevelled as that of Hassan's. Her glasses were slightly tilted on her face, and two out of the five earrings on one ear were missing. She nodded to Wahid, the imam and Basir, and then whispered into Hassan's ear.

Hassan laughed.

"Later, later," he said to her. He reached down and squeezed her hand gently.

Wahid felt his heart race. The sweat began to pour off him again.

Quick, quick, quick, slow.

Focus, focus, focus, Wahid told himself. At least the questions from Hassan would now be easier.

Too easy? Was that a hint of liquor coming from Hassan?

He wanted to stand up and yell at the solicitor, "You irresponsible fool!"

But was he? Hassan had not steered them wrong yet. So what if he had done what Wahid couldn't bear to think about; he was still the man in cricket whites, still had the ball in hand, but perhaps he had an additional fan cheering him on.

No, God, how filthy. Wahid saw Miss Woods squeeze Hassan's hand, gently touch his side, lean in and whisper more words into Hassan's ear. His head bent forward, he tilted his neck slightly to be at an optimal angle to take in every last nuance.

Wahid shut his eyes.

"All rise!" the bailiff shouted.

Wahid inhaled, exhaled, could not stop.

Focus, focus, focus.

"The defence calls Wahid Shah!" Hassan said.

Wahid watched Hassan straighten his tie, run a small comb through his hair, and push his glasses back onto his head to at

228

least give some semblance of respectability. Justice Hastings nodded slightly.

Wahid stood, the sinews and tendons stretching and pulling him upward: it was as if he was a puppet on a set of strings that were being drawn taut.

He approached the witness stand, mounting it carefully, and pulling the chair underneath him.

Rania, where are you, he thought.

Switzerland, where are you, he thought.

He knew where they were in terms of geography, but the visions of perfection which shielded his mind disappeared as soon as he sat. All that existed was the stern countenance of the judge, the drawn face of Sir Michael, and Hassan's impish grin, a strange cold breeze that touched him on the back and made him shiver.

Dieu et Mon Droit lorded over him. Here he was, at the Day of Judgement before the Day of Judgement.

Oh to be like the imam, and to be able to take it with grace that came from the utter faith in God.

"You are Wahid Shah?" Hassan asked.

"Yes."

"You live in Hackney?"

"Yes."

"Describe for the court what you did on the morning of the incident in question."

Hassan began to pace in front of Wahid.

Wahid spoke slowly, describing how he woke up, had breakfast, went to the mosque to pray, went to his office, visited Basir, and then bought surgical masks.

"Why did you buy the surgical masks?"

Wahid tried to form the words. He found it was difficult to verbalise his fears: they begged him not to speak out. "No, no, we keep you safe," they urged.

"Go on," Hassan urged.

"I'm afraid of catching other people's germs," he replied.

"It would be fair to say that you are rather obsessive about

229

this issue, are you not?"

Wahid shook his head. "Not obsessive, just careful."

"Oh?" Hassan said.

Hassan pulled a tissue out of his pocket, held it up to his nose and blew colourfully into it. He crumpled it into a ball and put it on the rail in front of Wahid.

"Pick it up," Hassan ordered.

"What?"

"You heard me, pick it up. You don't need to touch the snotty part, just grab one of the dry edges."

"Objection!" Sir Michael shouted, "what is the relevance of this?"

"Mr. Iqbal?" Justice Hastings asked. His eyebrow was raised.

"I'm trying to establish the full nature of Mr. Shah's infirmities, m'lud."

"Proceed...cautiously," Hastings replied. "Objection overruled."

Hassan turned back to Wahid. "Pick it up."

Wahid felt his sweat glands start up again. Fever rose. God, even the proximity of that tissue and all its germs, he felt like nothing but running as far away from it as possible.

"We're waiting, Mr. Shah," Hassan said.

He was smiling. How dare he smile, Wahid thought. He just did the equivalent of blasting him with a biological weapon. The tissue was probably crawling with anthrax, plague, yellow fever, whatever social disease he got from that Woods woman the previous night. Yes, it was permitted for Hassan to marry her, but just to sleep with her? Wahid glanced at Miss Woods again: she was probably a drug addict too, judging by her pallor and almost anorexic figure. Hassan plunged into *that*? Disgusting, disgusting, disgusting.

Wahid focused his attention on the tissue. It would not have surprised him to see a black centipede with poisonous pincers and red glowing eyes crawl out of its depths.

No.

"I can't," Wahid said softly.

"Sorry? Please say that louder?"

"I can't," Wahid repeated.

Hassan picked the tissue up with his right hand and threw it over his shoulder.

"Mr. Iqbal," Justice Hastings said with a note of mild reproach, "don't litter."

"Apologies, m'lud – the relevance will be proven shortly."

"Proceed...again, cautiously."

Hassan nodded. He extended his right hand outward to Wahid.

"Shake my hand, Mr. Shah."

"What?" Wahid asked.

"Shake my hand. It's a very simple gesture."

Wahid forced his arm upward and began to reach his hand outward.

No, no, no, that was the hand that he had used for the tissue. He was covered in filth; don't touch him, he's just covered in germs, disease, impurity. His arm cramped up. Wahid gasped. Quick, quick...no, the breath wouldn't come, the exercises wouldn't work.

Good God, what did you get into?

"Mother?" Wahid thought.

Wahid, you're covered in mud!

"Yes, Mother," Wahid thought. "We played rugby."

You smell as well. Did you have to use the loo out there?

"Well, yes..."

Did you clean yourself correctly? Did you use water?

"No, Mother."

Don't you know that's disgusting? That's unclean in the sight of God.

"What?"

Wahid shut his eyes. The iron ball had crumbled, and the orange light blasted outward behind his eyes.

"So sorry, Mother, I did not want to disappoint God."

Her worried yet stern countenance stared at him. He was

231

young, no more than seven to be sure. He had come in from playing rugby with his friends out in the rain. She stood at the door, regarding him as he was covered in mud and had a cut beneath his eye. He stank of sweat, his own and his friends'. There was also a slight stench of excrement and urine that followed him in.

And he did not care.

Mother wore her brown and gold scarf that day, which was draped over her shoulders. She looked down at him, like a towering giant, the voice of God from on high.

"God commands us to be clean and pure, that's why we wash. Those outdoor toilets are probably covered in germs too."

Germs? Young Wahid didn't know about this.

"What are germs?"

"They are tiny little creatures that make you sick. In fact, not only can they make you sick, they can make you die."

Die? "And God may take a dim view of someone who dies because he ignored His advice."

Young Wahid trembled. "No, Mother, I won't ignore God."

"How did this happen?"

Wahid thought. He had been pushed into the mud by one of the other boys while he was carrying the ball; he tried to duck and dive and wave, here he was, the great rugby captain for England, Wahid Shah. Then the solid impact of another boy around his middle: Wahid was pushed into a patch of mud and water. His face was momentarily submerged. Ugh. The blow had landed so hard on his stomach that he had been squeezed like a bagpipe or a tube of icing.

Wahid sat up; the boy who had tackled him was named Fred, he remembered. He was red haired, had freckles and was twice his size. Fred offered his (dirt covered) hand to Wahid to help him up.

"Where is the bathroom?" Wahid asked.

"Over there," Fred pointed; on the side of the pitch was a small green shed.

Wahid ran as fast as he could to the shed and opened the

door; the stink of urine and human waste hit him. He wrinkled his nose. But he charged in, slammed the door behind him, and dropped his shorts. After he sat down, the relief was near instantaneous.

That was the last time he'd eat before he played rugby, he promised himself. He reached over to where he expected the washbasin to be; he reckoned he would get a handful of water to wash himself, as he had been taught to do. Nothing. The light inside the shed was dim, and only provided by a narrow ventilation hole in the wall above him. He reached around to try and find some paper. He reached underneath. Nothing.

Ugh. But what else could he do? He stood up, and pulled his shorts up.

Mother was not pleased after he related the story. She took two steps back, put her hand up across her nose and lips.

No, Mother, don't be mad. Don't let God be mad at me.

"Go into the shower, you are covered in filth, get it off yourself," she said.

A filthy little boy. Mother was mad. God was mad. Oh no.

Her gargantuan arm pointed upwards to the bathroom. Young Wahid ran up the stairs as fast as his legs could carry him. The bathroom was gleaming white and smelled of disinfectant: it was a heaven of cleanliness. He looked at his muddy hands, muddy feet, muddy face. He was fouled with excrement. A filthy little boy. He turned the shining silver tap on to full and switched on the shower.

He threw his clothes off. Mother was mad, God was mad, hurry up. Get back into Grace.

Yes, Baba talked about Grace when he read from the big green book, Young Wahid thought. Grace was doing that which was beautiful. There was nothing beautiful about him now.

The steam rose from the shower and he jumped in. Young Wahid washed and scrubbed, covering himself in soap, using the washcloth till his skin turned red and raw. He pressed himself up against the cold tile around the shower.

"No, God, please don't hurt me!" he cried.

God was silent. There was only the sound of rushing water, and the sight of clouds of steam rising around him.

Wahid opened his eyes. Hassan was still there, reaching out his hand. Wahid felt tears coming out of his eyes, his breathing was congested: he simply could not raise his arm.

"It's all right," Hassan said, withdrawing his hand. "Calm down."

"What is the point of all this?" Justice Hastings said.

"As you can see, m'lud – my client is an incurable hypochondriac, who suffers from obsessive compulsive disorder. I can bring in expert testimony if so required, but after this demonstration, I doubt it will be necessary."

"Carry on," Justice Hastings said.

Hassan took a deep breath.

"My client was carrying the bleach and ammonia for a very simple reason...to keep surfaces abnormally clean and hygienic, in line with his psychological disorders. He isn't a terrorist. He is an ordinary man with an extraordinary affliction. This has been grossly misinterpreted by nearly everyone around him, who can only see my client's faith and his ethnicity: he has been viewed entirely through the prism of their prejudices. They cannot see the individual human being, with all his faults, his foibles, and yes, his virtues."

Wahid choked as he tried to keep down his emotions.

Hassan allowed a slight smile to curve his lips. "This has been a gross miscarriage of justice, m'lud. The flim-flammery you wanted myself and Sir Michael to avoid has been inflicted on us by the circumstances of this trial. I can only suggest we call for an immediate dismissal."

"Poetic," Justice Hastings replied. "I will take it under consideration. Any further questions for this witness?"

"No, m'lud," Hassan said.

"Sir Michael?"

Sir Michael looked at Wahid for a moment. The grey eyes were not cold: there was no anger. It was as if Wahid was some

234

small animal which had its limb caught in a trap and Sir Michael was a hunter observing him: was he prey, or was he to be set free? The solicitor's mouth twisted into a frown.

"No, m'lud," Sir Michael said.

"Court adjourned till one p.m.," Hastings said.

Wahid could not speak to the imam, Basir or Hassan. Hassan gently guided him to a waiting room, which had a single wooden table and a clock which was loudly keeping time.

Tick, tick, tick.

"I'll leave you here for a few minutes," Hassan said, and he shut the door behind him.

Tick, tick, tick. Wahid looked up at the clock, the hands moving through time, registering the dying of every second with that simple memorial of sound.

Horrible, just horrible.

He put his head in his hands. It had been as if his soul had been laid out upon a table for autopsy, but the examination had occurred on a living patient. Memory was free and clear now.

"Yes, Dr. Blanchard," he thought. "I know why now."

He had been young and sailed carefree through the world, until he knew what Mother and God expected of him. So difficult and so painful, that somehow memory had built walls around it.

"God wants what is easy for you," Wahid thought. Yes, Father had said that during one of his Qur'an readings on a Saturday, opening the dark green leather volume and comforting him. But by then it was too late, nothing was easy, nothing had been easy.

There had been no cosmic gag reel. God had not set him up for amusement. The challenges in life had been there for him to either learn or fail.

Had he learned? Had he failed?

Tick, tick, tick.

Seconds stretched out behind and ahead. He was running along both trails at once, forward to judgement, backwards to home and Mother and Father. Father had not been there on the day he was found to be filthy: what would he have said? God to him was close, was with them, merciful: "My Mercy Takes Precedence Over My Wrath". To Mother, he was distant, stern, just and when necessary, punishing. Was it both? Was it neither?

"Oh Rania, Rania, Rania," he thought, "where are you?" She was wise enough to know that some questions were better ignored by those who couldn't comprehend them. He lived well with her; now he would like to live better with her.

Perhaps in Switzerland.

Hassan opened the door.

"It's time."

Wahid stepped out.

Quick, quick, quick, slow. No, he was not dying, not yet anyway. Perhaps the path of the future was long or it was short, perhaps God was merciful or perhaps He was not. All he could do, was accept, surrender, and try to understand.

Hassan walked by him.

"Justice Hastings may dismiss the case," he said. "Are you ready?"

Wahid nodded.

They re-entered the courtroom. The imam and Basir looked at Wahid as he took his seat. There was no anger in Basir's eyes; he motioned to the chair: sit down.

Wahid complied. He exhaled.

"Have faith, my brothers," the imam whispered.

"All rise!" the bailiff shouted once more.

"I have seen a lot of cases," Justice Hastings began, "but nothing in my fifty years of service matches this."

Good start, Wahid thought. He focused on the emblem. *Dieu et Mon Droit.*

"Never before," he continued, his voice rising, "have I seen a case constructed so loosely on innuendo and prejudice. It is clear that certain members of the police hoped to try this case in the court of public opinion, and use the results to bolster their reputation. Some judges might go along with such flim-flammery, but not I!"

Hastings pointed at the prosecution: his extended finger was accusing, sharp and hard.

"You should have known that this was a ghastly mistake the moment you took a look at Mr. Shah. This poor, miserable man is incapable of hurting anyone: apparently, his inner demons are tormenting him to the point where such an action would be impossible."

Hastings stopped pointing, and took a deep breath. He looked directly at Wahid: Wahid wanted to put up his hands to shield himself from the judge's cold, blue gaze.

"British justice is not served by harming the innocent," Hastings said. "Our efforts in the war against terrorism are not served by inciting paranoia. Mr. Shah is an example of how fear can paralyse an individual; imagine what it could do to a society."

Wahid suppressed a sob.

Hastings motioned to the court. "Please rise," he said.

Wahid, Basir, the imam and Hassan stood.

Wahid shut his eyes. The heart was there, beating. His breathing was fine. Tick, tick, tick, let the path of life lead to the following moment, and see where it goes.

"It is my judgement that any further prosecution would be unsound. Therefore, I am dismissing this case."

Epilogue

"You're free to go," Justice Hastings said. "Court adjourned."

Wahid strained his ears to hear the echoes of the statement. It was difficult to take in the idea that the trial was over. Justice Hastings' clear blue eyes were set behind his gold-framed glasses. His white wig was still immaculate, his red robe hung loosely over his shoulders. However, his forehead was not wrinkled as it usually was when he was concentrating. No, the lines were completely gone; was he just as relieved?

Hastings stood, thrusting himself out of his seat with unexpected swiftness and force. He then faltered slightly as he stepped down, his shoulders sagging as he descended. He proceeded through an oak panelled door beside the bench. It swung open as he pressed on it; he slammed it hard behind him after he entered the darkened portal.

BANG!

The explosion was as big as the bang at the creation of the universe, Wahid thought. From that start all matter and life proceeded outward under God's guidance and formed into the planets, moons, stars, and people. Purple nebulae stretched across the cosmos like a carpet laid in front of God's throne. Amidst such wonders, Wahid was a microbe on a speck of sand hurtling through space. But somehow His mercy had prevailed for the miniscule.

Hassan tapped him on the shoulder. Hassan's expression, dour as the judge had spoken, had given way to a grin as radiant as Basir's. His glasses were no longer firmly pushed up to his

239

face, rather, they had fallen to the end of his nose. He had ripped the wig off his head, his robe was open, his blue silk tie was loose and the collar was unbuttoned once again. Miss Woods allowed herself a large smile and kissed Hassan full on the lips; he lifted her up in his arms for a moment, her bright red hair fluttering slightly before she said in a cheerful voice, "You're hurting me."

Hassan set her down. Wahid again felt a twinge of disapproval; however, allowances had to be made for victory, he supposed.

"Congratulations!" Hassan said, and shook Wahid's hand.

Did Hassan realise what he had just achieved? The Reset button had been pressed on creation. Even the fact that Hassan probably hadn't washed his hands prior to shaking Wahid's meant little. The microbes would take time to evolve now that all had been restarted. For the moment, the universe was sterile, a playground of creation, into which life was pushing out its first feelers.

Wahid turned to look at his friends. The imam had his eyes shut, his mouth moving quietly to the words of a prayer, thanking God for deliverance and freedom. Basir was gasping, his eyes glassy, as if he had just come to the end of a long marathon.

Hassan prodded Wahid on the elbow. Miss Woods was gathering up her belongings.

"Time to go," he said.

He nodded a reply.

Wahid turned and slowly paced towards the dark oak doors, the brass handles glinting in the flickering light of the courtroom. He had to go, yes. The ripples of creation proceeding outward from the courtroom meant he too had to move away from the epicentre, until he found his proper place.

But where was that? Where would he even sleep that night? If he went home to Hackney, would he find that his house was burned to the ground? Maybe not, but he would have to buy a crowbar at the local DIY store before going home; cousin Imran had probably been very thorough in boarding up the place. Did he have enough change in his pockets to get one?

Wahid reached into his pocket. Empty. Well of course, everything was new. Money had not yet been invented in this new life, but surely it would present itself. Hassan had mentioned that he would get some money upon departure: enough to get him a meal and a night in a hotel, if he so desired.

Wahid reached the door and pressed on the handle.

It swung open with a creak. The dark cream-coloured halls of the courthouse were strangely dim and quiet; on a polished dark wood bench sat a single reporter who was writing in his notebook with a pencil. He was middle-aged and wearing a grey fedora. He looked up at Wahid, the imam, Basir and Hassan, nodded, frowned and went back to writing. There was little mileage in a story about innocent men, Wahid presumed. No doubt things would go back to normal and headlines like "Wot a Scorcher" would take precedence over ones stating that the "London Four" had been freed.

Wahid cast a look down the hall at the exit. Wood and glass doors separated them from the evidence that London was going on without them. Wahid could see the bustle of people walking by; he spotted a young man in a dark blue suit and pink shirt with white headphones clamped firmly on his head. A blonde woman of middle age with red lipstick and wearing a fake dark brown fur jacket followed him. In the street, two red double-decker buses lined up at the traffic light, next to a black cab belching out smoke as it idled.

Creation proceeded outward and it boomeranged. Wahid knew he was supposed to step out into that maelstrom and fade into the background once more. He was destined to get rid of the suit, and going against every impulse against waste he ever had, throw it in the rubbish. It was plastic enough, perhaps it could go into the recycle bin, and be used as a tablecloth or tarpaulin. It was strange to think of walking through Green Park in the early autumn sun and seeing a family, no doubt white and English, a new mother whose breasts were just starting to sag from having

241

nursed their first child, a father in a blue and white striped shirt and a baby dressed in pink, gurgling and drooling as it sat in a stroller, all parked on top of a picnic blanket that was strangely familiar in colour and luminosity.

He was destined to go back to his office, such as it was. Presumably the walk down Brick Lane would not be any different, the walking through trash, the nauseating scent of curries from the previous night mixed with cheap lager and hooligans' vomit, the autumn's chill wind penetrating his frail form and forcing him to bundle his green parka more tightly around him. The unlocking of the door, the climbing of stairs would not be any better; his heart would burst doing that one day, he was sure.

No doubt his desk had at least an inch of dust on it. He could see himself getting the yellow plastic bucket out of the closet along with his bottle of antiseptic, and a large sponge. If the court returned his sanitary masks, he'd put one on, and then scrub the floor, carefully wiping between the cracks in the floorboards to get every last bit of muck that had settled there. It would no doubt take most of a morning to get it clean. In the afternoon, he would open his green ledger, and see how badly off he was, and figure out what taxes, if any, he owed. He probably owed some; after all, if the courts couldn't get him, surely Inland Revenue would. The spreadsheet's marching sums would signal defeat, but perhaps, if he was clever, it would constitute only a temporary setback.

Yes, all would be the same; except maybe for Rania.

"Wahid?" Basir asked. The tone was gentle.

"Yes?" Wahid replied.

"We are taking a cab to the mosque. Would you care to join us?"

Wahid nodded.

The mosque was unchanged. As the door swung open, Wahid heard the call to prayer, exactly the same in pitch, tone, duration. The sea of faces and voices flowed into the grand entrance.

242

Some of the entrants turned to look at who was emerging from the cab; after all, it was unusual for a Hackney cab to be in close proximity.

"They're going to stone me," Wahid thought as he emerged. No doubt the word about how he listened to Western classical music when he should have been praying had spread through the congregation. His eyes darted from face to face, looking for frowns, hostility, the narrowing of eyes.

He swallowed. The short fellow to his left, was that Basir's cousin? Obviously so, he was smiling; Basir ran up to him and embraced him, lifting him up in the air. They laughed and jumped up and down.

"Free!" the cousin said.

Wahid looked down the centre. The imam stepped forward, reaching out his hands, the palms facing upward. Men in suits and *kurtas* approached him, grasping his hands, either to give him a Western style grip, or in some hope of getting a blessing from him. The imam bowed his head and said "*Salaam alaikum!*"

"*Alaikum salaam!*", in reply, rippled through the greeters.

To Wahid's right, Hassan also received congratulations from the crowd; Miss Woods stood closely behind him. Unlike the imam, the greetings Hassan received were distinctly Western: handshakes and words in English. With each hearty grip and release, his appearance became more dishevelled, yet his smile more broad. For the first time in their acquaintance, Wahid noticed that beads of sweat had broken out on Hassan's forehead.

Wahid stood behind the imam, grateful for the shield.

The imam turned and looked Wahid in the eye. He smiled.

"My brother, this is your day too."

Wahid felt a smile nervously twitch the corner of his lips.

The imam reached out to Wahid and grabbed him by the hand, pulling him up till they were side by side. The imam wrapped an arm around his shoulders. Wahid tried not to flinch.

No, no, I don't deserve this kindness.

Wahid looked at the faces around them; surely they would

darken, he thought. Surely the shield of his compatriots would not be sufficient to protect him from their anger. Yes, any moment now they would urge the imam to stand aside so they could lift him over their heads and dump him in the street. Yes, he would land on his stomach, and face the black tar and gravel on the ground, and a white Ford Transit van, its driver dressed in an England football shirt, simultaneously consuming a pork pie and shouting "Wanker!" out the window would run him over, pushing him into the ground for the final time: then cold, silence, death and Hell.

Wahid trembled. But the faces did not flicker. It was as if he was invisible and their gaze continued to approve of the imam, Basir, and Hassan, while he did not exist.

"Not be," he had wished. And apparently he was not. Praise be to God: far better to be nothing than reviled.

Slow slow slow. The imam squeezed his shoulder.

"Come now," the imam urged.

With the imam's arm still draped around his shoulder, they ascended the stairs.

The imam said a few words after prayers, speaking into a makeshift microphone that looked as if it were a relic from the 1960's: the silver mesh ball at the tip and the black plastic handle were large and ungainly, and the amplifier squeaked as the imam began to speak.

Wahid knelt on his mat. His miraculous non-existence continued through prayers, the men around him not edging away in disgust, nor saying hello. He pictured that they saw a gap where he was, an empty space in the front row.

No, that made no sense. Surely someone would want to be near to the imam in his moment of triumph. Ah, perhaps it was respect; giving the imam room to pray, and Wahid remained solely seen by those with whom he had been imprisoned.

The waves of creation were surely still lapping outwards. Hopefully in the tidal wave, Watson found a better place than the prison to inhabit. Surely there was a country manor somewhere in a place like Surrey or Hampshire, made of alabaster stone with narrow gothic windows and a long driveway full of pebbles; the manor should be surrounded by neatly trimmed green lawns, rhododendron bushes with large pink blossoms and oak trees stretching as far as the eye could see. In this scene, Watson would be obliged to wear a morning suit, complete with a silver satin waistcoat and would stride with his hands firmly clasped behind his back; he would patrol up and down a line of young women and men standing on the front lawn, pointing out how their dress sense was lacking.

Wahid smiled. The imam spoke of God's kindness.

"Have no doubt, my brothers, my faith has only grown. Even in a place where God can seem absent, He is there; finding Him in the void is the greatest gift of all."

Wahid paused and looked around. The mosque, even in its re-created form should have been a familiar sight, right down to the words of the Qur'an in green against gold plastering the beige walls. The scent of tea and lemon, the carpets, the sounds of breathing contrasting with the imam's voice, all were familiar.

Yet God had seemed so distant for so long; He felt absent from this place as well. But was he Near as well as Far?

Wahid put his hand over his heart. The beat was steady, the rising and collapsing of his lungs continued. Such mysteries were beyond him to answer; wiser, smarter men like the imam knew more, but perhaps they did not know All.

"Not be," Wahid had wished, and so he was not in so far as those around him were concerned. But yet he was. God perhaps was ready to touch him, but if offered such a touch, would Wahid shrink away?

"What blessings of your Creator would you deny?" the imam said, finishing his address.

Indeed. Wahid was alive, which considering the disease and filth that contaminated the prison and its attending hospital was a miracle. He could go home; yes, he would have to pry off the boards and dust the surfaces. But, it was still there. He could still make peppermint tea at midnight to settle his nerves and climb up the creaking staircase to the vast expanse of the bed.

When he stood at the doorway, the gentle light of the corridor softly intruding into the darkness of the bedroom, would Wahid see Rania lying there, the white duvet tucked around her body, her face turned away? Or would she have run off with the colonel by now? His last letter had been so terse and her reply hung in the balance. Surely she knew he was free; it would be a blurb on Sky News, which would then be seen by some young man, a callow youth perhaps, sitting in the control room of a Pakistani television station. Wahid could picture him: the boy would be no more than twenty, with large black headphones clutching his ears. He would be covered in pimples due to eating bad food and his skin would have an unhealthy pallor from being trapped indoors all day.

Yes, on Sky, the phrase "The London Four Freed" would scroll by, and the young man would translate it into Urdu, which would then be repeated by a newscaster, perhaps that middle aged woman who wore too much lipstick and had a weakness for electric blue dresses. Rania, sitting on Uncle Naseem's white and pink floral chintz couch and watching his large plasma screen, might see it and her heart might beat faster, her thoughts racing with the expectation that he would come for her. Or, her lips might turn downward, her eyes shifting away from the screen and her thoughts could turn to what she lost by his not being imprisoned.

Surely she was not that cruel. She was not a blessing of the Lord he would deny.

"Stop being afraid," Wahid told himself. But should he? His fears were not necessarily a problem; after all, did they not indicate that he respected the blessings he had?

"What blessings of your Creator would you deny?" the imam repeated with greater emphasis.

Wahid shut his eyes. No, he would deny nothing.

Wahid borrowed twenty pounds from Hassan and took a cab home, using a minicab firm on the corner next to the mosque. He was hesitant at first; the sign's creator had tried to spell "Star of Karachi Minicabs" but misspelled both "Karachi" and "Star"; the caked on dirt suggested the error was permanent. Worse, the Urdu subtitles were similarly mangled.

The man behind the plexiglass window looked as if he had evolved into the chair from microbes on the seat. He was a brown lump that moved around his narrow confines by pushing himself along using the wheels attached to the chair legs. A stripe of grey in his unruly thin black hair indicated that evolution was leading to his demise.

"Cab to Hackney?" Wahid asked.

The lump looked up and nodded, and spoke into a transmitter. "Car 53, need immediate, come back to base."

He looked up. "Won't be five minutes, sir."

Wahid began to regret it. His nostrils detected a whiff of stale beer, and the plexiglass was nearly opaque with streaks.

A red Ford Escort pulled up outside the door; it was so old that the red paint was not only peeling and chipping, but the sunlight had partially bleached the battered vehicle.

"Your car, sir," the lump said.

Wahid climbed into the back; at least the driver had the sense to use air freshener; that said, there were holes in the brown upholstery and yellow foam was leaking out.

Wahid sat down. He exhaled. Slow slow slow.

The driver was English, his head was bald except for a few strands of grey hair, which had been unsuccessfully combed over to hide his condition.

"Where to?" the driver asked, without turning.

"Hackney," Wahid replied.

The roads gradually become more familiar. Wahid recognised a *halal* butcher on one corner; that was where Rania would go to get their weekend roasts. Wahid was grateful that Rania had identified Ahmed's meat as being substandard a long time ago.

"It's halfway rotten," she told him, holding up a slab of

beef. They were in their kitchen. Wahid had been cutting up parsnips for roasting in the oven. He looked up; yes, it was grey around the edges.

"We're not using him again," Rania told him, her eyes flashing.

Wahid grinned. He leaned forward. Ah ha, there was the florist run by the aged lady from Bangladesh. She was no more than five feet tall, wore a maroon sari, and had been there since Queen Victoria was on the throne, Wahid estimated. She sometimes slipped and referred to Bangladesh as "East Pakistan", saying that it was a pity that two brother nations should ever come to blows and it was all the fault of that damn India anyway.

She had the best carnations in London, however, red and full with petals that appeared so delicate that they would evaporate in a strong gust of wind. Rania loved them; she cut off the blossoms and set them floating in a large, clear glass bowl full of water. She said she saw some designer on television do the same and it was "trendy".

If Rania came back, Wahid thought, he would buy her a dozen of those carnations. No, more than a dozen, he would buy out the shop.

But would she come back now that she knew he was free? Or would he have to go and get her?

He swallowed. They passed the Jinnah Travel Agency, which had a poster for Air Pakistan in the window; the poster featured a smiling stewardess in a beige uniform and a headscarf, with a jet flying at a sharp angle upward in the background. "Visit Pakistan" it read. Jinnah or whoever had left the poster out for too long; it was nearly as faded as the minicab, except that the tint of it was green, giving almost a Martian glow to the idea of going home.

The minicab turned. A sign read "Welcome to Hackney". Wahid recalled the dream that he had about his father crossing from India to Pakistan, and that nothing could stop him. Slow slow slow.

248

"Almost home," he thought.

Yes, almost home to discover the wreckage of his former life. Wahid could picture the house left as a burnt-out wreck, the marks of blackened smoke contrasting with the pale yellow paint he had so painstakingly applied. The neighbours, frightened immigrants though they were, would likely have picked over the wreckage, trying to find anything they could worth taking. The garden was probably denuded of tomato plants, their blackberry bushes, even the tulip bulbs that burst out with orange and yellow blossoms every spring.

Wahid put his hands over his eyes, but peeked out through a gap in his fingers. He recognised the little Tesco; he sometimes walked there when other stores were not open to buy milk, resisting the temptation to buy the kind sterilised at high temperature, because Rania had scolded him about its taste.

"It tastes like nothing," she had said before reluctantly pouring some into her cup of tea. She had wanted proper Earl Grey tea like she had in Karachi; she had taken down the red and white porcelain cups, the good tea leaves from Fortnum and Mason, and had sent him out for the milk only for him to bring back that "stuff" as she called it.

She sighed and sipped. She tried to smile. "It's still lovely anyway," she said.

A lie.

Wahid felt a pain in his chest: a precursor to a heart attack, he assumed, but it quickly faded. If the house was demolished and the red and white porcelain teacups, the garden, and all their furniture were gone, would she want to come back? He had been worrying that she would want to divorce him because he had gone to jail. Now he had to worry that their life had been such a mundane nonsense compared to the jasmine flowers and blue skies of Pakistan that she would divorce him in order to remain there.

"Almost there," the driver said.

Yes, almost there. The terraced houses, built in the

249

nineteenth century to provide living space for the striving middle of Victorian society, combined into a terracotta and pastel blur in front of him. At one point, this was a no man's land for anyone sensible and sane, when the city was lit by gas lights and the soot of coal hung over the city. Father had come when that era was breathing its last and was damaged by war; he had still loved London. Why?

Strange. Wahid might never know.

The street appeared to be the same. The same row of houses in various states of repair and age spread out in front of him like a long tapestry; the car screeched to a halt when Wahid said, "Here!"

Not quite on target, but at least the rear of the car was in front of his home.

Wahid averted his eyes, casting a glance at his feet: he dared not look at what remained. The driver blurted out a sum, Wahid paid and stepped out of the cab. He looked to the side to prevent his eyes from focusing on his front door.

The suit itched again. The little fingers prodded and poked.

"Look," he thought.

He looked ahead.

Quick quick quick, slow.

Cousin Imran had done a good job. The boards, made of a pale plywood, were secure. Someone had put up a black and white poster inviting people down to a club called "The Swamp" to hear a band called the "Deadly Fairies". Next to it, someone had put up a poster encouraging people to earn money working from home: a premium rate phone number was listed. Wahid smirked; that was certainly a way to get money to pour in.

His eyes drifted to the door; solid, painted dark green, it was pristine except for a bit of red spray paint. It took a moment for Wahid to realise that the paint formed a word; the handwriting, such as it was, was skewed and poor, no doubt done by one of those illiterate children who sat on bicycles on street corners, wearing hooded sweatshirts and who used the words "fucking" and "innit" in every sentence.

"Paki," it said.

No doubt the lads on the street corners thought this was clever. Wahid supposed they thought the single word was intimidating enough on its own. There was no accompanying "Go Home", no "BNP" either and oddly not even a swastika: Rania and Cousin Imran must have cleaned those off and they had stayed gone. But perhaps it would have been more surprising if most of the lads who lingered on his street read the newspapers enough to know who the BNP were, and perhaps they argued over the spelling of "Go Home" before taking flight.

"Paki," though. Stranger in a strange land. Father was, but didn't feel it. Wahid was supposedly home, but he did.

Basir. So this was the feeling he was talking about, so long ago.

Wahid reached into his pocket and fished around for his key. He hoped that no one would see him, not dressed like this, not fresh from court. He cast a glance across the street at the lace curtains in the window of number twenty-three. Mrs. Morrison would no doubt have seen him, but she was behind the protective veil in her observations, sitting on her armchair with a cup of tea.

Wahid put the key in the lock and turned it; the door opened with a slight squeak on its long un-oiled hinges. He stepped inside.

On the floor in front of him was a large pile of envelopes, scattered in a circular array spreading outwards from the door like streams of sunlight with the area just below the mail slot as the epicentre. Some of the envelopes were brown, no doubt advising him that he was overdue on some bills, others were bland and disguised, perhaps inviting him to change his mortgage provider or offering new home insurance. The clear plastic enclosures contained catalogues for office supplies. He smiled, bent over and picked one up, tearing open the cover carefully; ah, there had been a special on leather bound ledgers he'd missed. Too bad, the cracking open of a new ledger, the scent of leather, paper and ink was a satisfying experience.

251

Wahid proceeded to pick up the envelopes and put them in a neat pile, arranging each bit of mail by size. There were a few anomalies, there were several folded up pieces of paper amidst the regular mail: some were harmless, it seemed that the Deadly Fairies really wanted him to go and see them in concert. Others invited him to order Chinese food which was reassuringly and certifiably free of monosodium glutamate from a place called Confucius' Garden. However, there were also ones written in a shaky hand on lined paper, each one more vile than the last. "Die Paki", "Go home Paki", "Eat shit, Paki", "We'll kill you, Paki."

Quick, quick, slow.

Enough.

He looked up. The hallway was dim, and the predominant scent that hit his nostrils was damp and dusty. He could hear the faint sound of a faucet dripping; perhaps it was from the kitchen? Rania had wanted him to fix that tap a while ago, but going underneath the sink and reaching his hand into the dark crevasse to switch off the water, and encountering the gooey slime inside of pipes when he tried to replace a washer hadn't appealed to him. He was glad he had been lazy in this regard; now the drip kept time and gave an audible pulse to the house.

Drip drip drip. So slow. The house was barely on life support. A blaze of energy would be required to bring it back to life. Rania would need to return and bang pots and pans in the kitchen and the sizzle of her cooking chicken in a fry pan would need to be heard once more. Indeed, the scents of cumin, melted butter, freshly baked bread and garlic were a necessity. And then she would have to sing some Bollywood tune which he could not name, but was gloriously melodious so long as she sang it.

A smile touched Wahid's lips. He turned to look into the living room. Rania and Cousin Imran had both been thorough. In the darkness, Wahid could make out the outline of white sheets covering all the furniture. As he stepped into the room he detected the faint hint of room deodoriser and the tiniest traces of Rania's perfume.

Rania. Wahid put his hand over his heart. No, she would not

want to see the house like this. Not this sad. Not this way. She had to come back, or he had to leave this all behind.

He stepped up to the couch and grabbed a hold of one of the dust covers, and with a single motion, ripped it off.

The dust flew upward from the motion, and cascaded down like a malignant snowfall.

"Welcome home," Wahid whispered.

Wahid found, to his delight, that all the cleaning supplies were intact. He swept and vacuumed the floors, removed all the remaining dust covers and polished the surfaces.

Wahid also discovered that there were enough packs of Ramen noodles to sustain him on his first night at home; he sat in the kitchen, bent over a large white bowl as he consumed the boiling liquid and semi-soft noodles as quickly as possible. He was sure that by an objective measure, months-old noodles were less of a treat than the *halal* food in prison. For some reason, however, he devoured the dish. The food tasted wonderful, very fresh and completely nourishing. The hot broth, no doubt containing more soya protein than fresh onion or carrot, washed down his throat with ease, and a warm glow filled his stomach which rushed to his extremities with his pulse.

Was it freedom that added flavour to it all? Perhaps. He hadn't eaten noodles like this, a dish consumed out of academically inspired poverty, since he was doing his degree. He recalled that he had bought them just in case there was nothing else to eat.

Father sometimes liked to smoke a cigarette or cigar in the garden after a good meal. Wahid could not understand it. Food was there to nourish, smoking was a pleasure, the two did not necessarily have a point of intersection. Wahid remembered finding Father sitting on a lawn chair, one of his Cohiba cigars glowing at the tip and large clouds of rich smoke blowing out of his mouth and circling his head.

For the first time in his life Wahid wished he had a cigar to hand. He looked out the French doors onto the garden; the sun was setting, the soft purple sky of twilight was draping itself over the city with darkness at its fringe, hinting at the night to come. The flowers that Rania had cultivated were in bloom. Rich smoke in this scene would be like incense rising to heaven, no doubt reaching God's celestial footstool.

Wahid smiled. Would Dr. Blanchard call this sensation "progress", he wondered.

Perhaps sleeping in a dirty bed was progress as well. The hour grew late, Wahid got tired of stuffing dustcovers into the washing machine and finally had to climb up the stairs to bed. The scent of damp was slowly yielding to the sharper smells of lemon and antiseptic with a hint of the vegetable noodles lodged in between. The dripping no longer kept the pulse of the house; he had set the stereo in the living room to Radio 3, and the sounds of Tchaikovsky's Violin Concerto floated through the stairways, all the way to the loft.

The papers were cleared away. He had removed his suit and was now back in his trousers and *kurta*.

"Enough for one day," he thought. He stood at his bedroom window; the shades were drawn. He reached out and opened one of them to look onto the night sky. Across the street, Mrs. Morrison was obviously keeping vigil: her lights were on. The soft sounds of traffic a few streets away penetrated the room.

Rania was no doubt asleep. But would she want to come back to this; should he go and get her?

He shut his eyes. Freedom. There was nothing more to be said. "Not be" and so imprisonment wasn't. "Be" and so he was.

He pulled off his *kurta* and hung it carefully in his white built-in closet. Then, bare-chested, he could no longer resist the urge to sleep and fell into bed.

Wahid awoke late. He let Radio 3 warm the house with Brahms Symphony No. 2 and ate more noodles for breakfast. Their flavour was less miraculous in the light of a new day. Washed down with peppermint tea, it was bearable and he was fully

254

awake.

He thought about phoning Rania. He picked up the receiver in the kitchen; it was a white, plastic Chinese made phone he had bought in a discount store. No tone. No doubt the phone company had cut them off during his long absence; or, had Rania cut off the phone to stop the press bothering her?

He walked into the living room; certainly, he had missed some spots of dirt, but the big problem was the scent of ammonia fumes, which, having no place to go, were coalescing and gagging him. The boarded up windows prevented the noxious mixture from escaping.

There was nothing for it; he would have to go out to the shops.

As he put on a clean *kurta* and cap and his coat, he wondered what would happen. The house was his world; hermetically sealed and locked away from what other people thought with the exception of the peering eyes of Mrs. Morrison, who expressed her disapproval with silence.

He buttoned up his coat and breathed.

Quick quick slow. Quick quick slow.

The trip would tell him something. Would he step out and find the *click click click* of cameras awaited him?

He leaned his head against the door and listened intently. Nothing.

He unlocked the door a crack. No one. The street was empty, except for the sound of a kicked soccer ball echoing from down the street and a young male voice shouting, "Oh bloody hell!"

He opened the door fully. The sun was making an effort to poke through the rolling tapestry of patchy grey clouds; when the sun was able to break through, there was a moment of warmth.

Wahid put his hands in his pockets and shut the door behind him.

Quick quick slow.

"Not be" and so he was not. No one recognised him. Fame was such a fleeting thing; pop singers who were on everyone's lips one day were forgotten the next, appearing on late night programmes on television trying to talk about some new "project" which would get them recognised again.

But Wahid had rejoined the sea of London faces: some like his, most of them not. He was one part of a rolling tide of humanity washing through Hackney. Bits of the wave broke off to go to the cash machine, some rolled into coffee shops to buy a triple *grande latte*, others like him fell across the shoals of the DIY store.

He found a crowbar at the back of the shop, iron, solid and not too expensively priced. The clerk, white and English, told him it was ten pounds and fifty pence. Wahid handed over the money; the clerk handed over the crowbar and didn't give him a second glance.

What blessings of his Creator would he deny? Wahid rolled back into the tide towards home, only slightly conscious of the people on the streets who had colds including the old man sitting in a wheelchair, wearing a beret, dark blue blazer with medals pinned to the breast from the War and coughing painfully into a stained handkerchief. At some point, he had probably worn olive green and charged purposefully at the enemy, with a bayonet drawn, but now he was decrepit and too long in the world. Steering clear of the no-doubt venerable if diseased gentleman, he returned safely home, and gazed at the front of the house.

In particular, he looked at the first, large plywood board which had been nailed over his living room window.

It had to go.

He took off his parka, picked up his crow bar and, with a slight grunt, began to pry it off.

Two days later, Wahid awoke early. The alarm clock went off at six-thirty a.m. and he opened his eyes to find that the shadows of autumn were creeping in. No longer was there a hint of dawn streaming in through the bedroom window.

He reached over to where Rania would have been.

Should have been.

On a normal day, she would have rolled over as soon as the clock fired up with Bach's Cello Concerto or Dvorak's Serenades, as it was apt to do.

He stood, his eyes fixed on the distant join between the London skyline and the sky; there was only a slight hint of orange and blue at the periphery to indicate that the night was not eternal.

Quick, quick, quick and slow. He put his hand over his heart; he knew that it was unlikely that he would die that day, after all, the good Dr. Blanchard knew best, but still, old habits were comforting and comfortable. They wrapped around him like the warm water hitting his skinny body as he entered the shower.

Disinfectant scrub all up and down his arms, and underneath his armpits. Yes. Wash all the delicate areas. Yes. These habits had not changed either. He was careful to lean his head forward as he washed his hair, to ensure that the running soap and water didn't carry any dirt or grit from the top of his body down to places were he was more vulnerable to infection or disease.

He dressed, climbed down the cold stairway to the kitchen, made peppermint tea and switched on the radio. "It's going to be a chilly, brisk day," the radio told him, which Wahid assumed was BBC-speak for "beware of frostbite".

Click, click, click, pop! Two slices of bread Wahid put into the toaster leaped out and he consumed them without putting any butter on. Dry toast was comforting too, and didn't carry the added premium of risking heart disease.

He sipped his tea and looked out the French doors leading out of the kitchen onto the garden. The sun had finally begun to come up over the horizon, and the overgrown plants, the rhododendron, the small apple tree, the wildly growing grass appeared to stand up as it announced its presence.

"Please rise," Wahid whispered.

The golden light flowed through the window and touched his face, a strange warm tingle accruing from its caress which contrasted with the hints of frost on the ground.

Wahid gathered up his briefcase and wrapped a long black wool coat around himself. He sniffed the sleeve gingerly and smiled; yes indeed, Rania had treated this with his favourite disinfectant before she had put it away in the closet. He had found it in their shared wardrobe in the spare room, a piece of furniture which had been made in England, shipped to Pakistan and then shipped back again. Mother said it was made of burred walnut; the brass handles on its two massive doors had become tarnished, and the hinges squeaked whenever Wahid opened them. As a child, its dark vast interior was oddly frightening. Rania however had put all of her exquisite silks in there, along with Wahid's clothes. Specifically, she used it as a dumping ground for his garments that were so threadbare due repeated bleaching that Wahid could no longer wear them. His accountant's soul, however, would not let him throw them out.

In order to make his coat easy to find, Rania had kept it in a black plastic covering which had a zip on the front. That was care. But the disinfectant too, was that love?

Wahid jangled the keys in his pocket and opened the door. He stepped out onto the front porch. Across the street, the curtains in Mrs. Morrison's windows flickered slightly; the closest she would ever get to saying "Good morning."

He shut the door behind him and began to walk.

The first dilemma hit him when he saw the familiar red, white and blue sign for the London Underground. Should he or should he not?

God knew what was down there. He stared into the station: its white tiles glowed alabaster in the dim light of the fluorescent bulbs. He knew that the turn in the stairwell beyond the ticket barrier led into a dark hole. It was still horrible down there.

However, it was only one change at Bank station and he had a clean run to Brick Lane.

Yes, no, maybe?

But perhaps on the train there would be more of the same ugly faces that had crowded around him when he last descended into that particular hell. Wahid put his hand up beside his head, as if it could hold the thoughts back. The faces were angry, distorted, twisted. He felt a pain where he had been kicked so many months ago.

"The hand that has been covered in mud can be washed clean again," Dr. Blanchard had told him.

Who was the Pakistani friend that had told her that, he wondered; was he a Messenger of some sort?

Wahid exhaled. Mathematically, he knew that the probability of the same collection of tourists and the West Indian woman eating fast food being in the carriage with him was next to zero. Ten to the power of ten to the power of ten. Could he risk it? Could he risk anything?

Wahid entered the station.

Trains were still exquisite little tortures. The Northern Line had not improved during his incarceration: its cars remained dim and the wood between the windows still looked as if it was an uneasy mixture of shellac and dry rot. Wahid did his best to avoid other people by sitting at the end of one row. An old man in a Russian fur hat and camel coloured wool coat got on at Angel station and sat next to him. As the electric hum inside the cabin rose, the doors clattered shut and the train sped off into the darkness, the old man drew a handkerchief out of his pocket and began to cough profusely into it.

Wahid fumbled with his briefcase. He had left the bleach and ammonia behind; there were no surgical masks.

"God," he thought.

A surgical mask would be lovely right then, a shield against the streams of disease coming out of the man.

Quick, quick, quick, slow.

259

No, it's part of the past, Wahid thought. If I get sick, I get sick: I can be cured. The hand that is dipped in mud can be washed clean again. But Rania needs to be there to make soup for me and move the television out of the lounge into the bedroom.

Wahid stopped himself from smiling as he pictured himself lying in bed, Rania leaning over him, a washcloth in her hand which she rubbed on his forehead.

The old man sputtered again; this fit was the most explosive yet. Wahid would not have been surprised if parts of the old man's lungs had dislodged themselves and spewed outward.

Wahid could not help but stare. The old man looked at him sheepishly.

"Excuse me," he said to Wahid, "I've recently had the flu."

"Bless you," Wahid replied.

Wahid hoped that his invocation still applied: not be and so he was not. He whispered it to himself as he approached the turning into Brick Lane.

The sun had risen enough to melt the early morning frost. However, Wahid noticed that some people were still digging themselves out: he passed by a man who was similarly dressed in a *kurta* and cap, scraping the windows of his old white Ford Escort, pausing only to look in the direction of the sun and squinting, perhaps looking to see if the labour was no longer necessary.

The man winced, sighed and resumed his work.

Scrape, scrape, scrape.

Wahid turned on the corner.

How little it had changed. It was as if a snapshot had been taken on the day that Wahid was assaulted, and on the day of his release, all the colours and elements of the scene were replicated. God's parcelling out had led to all things being put back into their proper places. The same scent of old curry assaulted his nostrils; the same wet trash and detritus of restaurants lay strewn in his path. The old man in a green parka was still there, sweeping his front step.

Wahid's heart leapt into its familiar pattern. Yes, he thought with a smile, it was time to wonder once again if he was actually here on Brick Lane or if he was dead.

"You might be tempted to slip back into old patterns," he thought. The instinct had the same voice as Dr. Blanchard.

He stepped over an empty gallon drum of vegetable oil that lay in front of him and proceeded to the front door of his office.

He inhaled as he pulled the key out of his pocket.

No doubt, he thought, there would be a load of unread post laying in the hall for him. Perhaps even the electricity and water had been cut off in his absence; no, wait, those were on Direct Debit.

He pushed the key in. However, the gentle pressure caused the door to swing open.

What?

The hinges squeaked as Wahid stepped inside. He looked down – the mail was there, but it was kicked aside, muddy footprints were stomped all over the envelopes.

Quick, quick, quick, slow.

Oh no. Wahid climbed up the stairs as fast as he could; he noticed that a brown glass bottle had been smashed against the stairway wall, the scent of old, stale beer assaulting his nostrils, the crunch of broken glass sounding from beneath his footsteps.

Oh no, oh no.

Quick, quick, quick, slow.

Wahid reached the top, gasped, and stepped into his office.

As he feared, the computer had been ripped off his desk, a slight indentation in a layer of dust indicated where it once sat. Another indentation was on the coffee table, indicating where his radio had been. His books, his ledgers, lay strewn all over the floor. Notes for the 2001 tax year mingled with pages from his old *Principles of Accountancy* textbook, which had been ripped to shreds. This was the confetti of anger, an afterthought to an orgy of destruction and violence.

Wahid turned to look at the wall behind his desk. He

261

swallowed hard.

"Paki". A swastika. "BNP". "Terrorist".

Wahid had hoped to find his office was like his house: dusty but more or less secure. He had envisaged how much fun it was going to be to make this aspect of his life work again: he had made mental notes about going down to the small Tesco Express for disinfectant wipes and glass cleaner. He was going to listen to Radio 3. They said they would play a recording of Barenboim playing Beethoven's piano concertos on at eleven a.m.: perfect music to relish while he mopped the floors. After the place was spotless, he intended to sit at his computer and bring all his accounts up to date. A good day's work. He could then call Rania and say, "Come home, darling, all is well".

All gone. He stepped behind his desk to look at his old chair: someone had slashed it with knives. Yellow foam stuffing protruded out of the wounds. Wahid found that someone had used a crowbar to pry open the drawers. Nothing had been spared: the petty cash box, made of a grey metal, had its lid ripped off, his pair of scissors had been broken in two, and even a box of paper clips had been upended on the floor and stomped on.

Wahid sank into his seat. The sun's rays had reached his windows but the illumination brought no comfort. There was a scent of sour urine and old excrement which only grew as the sun's warmth penetrated the office. Wahid raised his head; it was obviously coming from the office's small bathroom. He didn't dare take a look at it. Not yet.

He swivelled in his chair to look at the wall. He sighed. Well at least the poster of Switzerland was still there, intact, though it was now hanging lopsided. For it to have withstood the attentions of the thugs was something of a miracle: God be praised.

Wahid opened his briefcase and pulled out the postcard of Lausanne that Dr. Blanchard had given him; he paused to admire the scene again, the straight buildings, the clear blue sky, the polished perfection of the streets. He smiled. It had been his intent to clean up the poster frame with a bit of disinfectant, and then stick the postcard in the frame. A lovely pastoral scene contrasting with a tidy cityscape, Switzerland would look more appealing than ever.

Wahid looked down and found that his telephone was on the floor and upended. He picked it up and placed it on one empty spot on the desk, placing the receiver back into its holder. He lifted up the receiver: a dial tone – at least that worked.

Should he call the police? Yes, but what could they do? The vandalism had occurred a while ago, and this was the East End of London and not too far from where drugs were dealt and gang murders happened. One Pakistani accountant who was recently released after being accused of plotting an act of terrorism would not be a priority. Wahid could imagine the studied indifference of the police officers walking around the shattered remains of his office. They would likely all be white, all wear white shirts, blue caps and black vests, and write down notes using a small pencil on tiny white pads. No doubt the shorthand would say, "Paki terrorist, got what he deserved".

Wahid read the words again: "Paki", "BNP", "Terrorist". Perhaps Basir had been right, perhaps it was time to leave.

Perhaps it was time to go to Switzerland. Wahid smiled at the thought of a country full of Dr. Blanchards and open fields, with the air clean and bracing at every turn. There, at last, he could feel comfortable.

But was life supposed to be comfortable? Or was it a succession of events in which one's hand was dipped in mud and then washed clean again?

Was it time to go back to that multi-coloured vision, Pakistan? Rania was probably awaiting his telephone call. He now had the means, he did not have to put it off any longer. He knew the number to Uncle Naseem's by heart. If he phoned, he would probably get an ear bashing from his aunt:

"Why didn't you phone the moment you were released? Rania has been worried sick!"

Then:

263

"You poor brave dear, of course I'll put her on."

That was assuming Rania hadn't run off with the colonel.

Wahid stood and looked out the window. Ten a.m.: London's heart was beating at full rhythm at that point, less Blue Danube than something modern and pulsating like the techno music that greasy teenagers dressed in black leather listened to on their MP3 players so loud that it filled the average London Underground carriage with its peculiar beat.

He sighed.

Heaven of the heart or heaven of the soul: that was the choice laid out before him. He could embrace the ethereal delights of Switzerland or the colours of Pakistan and find his darling waiting.

He had been silent for so long, however: had she run out of patience? Did she understand that all of his concentration had been diverted to such odd purposes?

She had to understand; if anyone could understand it was she. He perhaps ought to see her now, alive and healthy. Yes, he would answer her questions: yes, he loved her, yes he would give her children, yes, he would move to Pakistan.

His mind caught on the last "yes". He had come a long way to be sure, but the idea of dirt and filth grated on him. Too many people lived with disease there.

He placed his hand over his heart. The heart worked, but it was probably still weak from all the trials and tribulations he had faced. Going to Pakistan could kill him as well as revive him. Would his heart be able to withstand the pounding when he saw Rania again? In his mind, he could envisage her waiting at the door of Uncle Naseem's house, the magnificent oak and brass portal propped open to let the jasmine-scented breezes circulate.

He would and could run to her, take her into his arms and look into her eyes, at the soft curve of her nose and lips and tell her, "I love you".

Too much, perhaps. He looked at the phone again. He could just as easily arrange a ticket to Lausanne. Yes, he could leave that very afternoon: he could book a cheap flight from Gatwick

264

and a reservation at a four star hotel. With a bit of luck, he would not be next to anyone, and the bright orange seats of the low cost airline might have been freshly sterilised. He would eschew the items laughingly referred to as food which were offered by a stewardess off a trolley with a squeaky wheel. The plane would land and glide up to a perfect glass structure: stepping into Switzerland, he would be greeted by the scent of disinfectant and miles of polished linoleum stretching out from beneath his feet.

Rapture. The cab would no doubt smell of lemon, and they would race through a perfectly manicured landscape to the centre of Lausanne. With a bit of luck, he'd get a hotel room that captured the exact same view as the postcard. His heart could take that. It was a pity that Rania would not be waiting by that particular door, painted white, and leading into a room with a large bed that had starched and bleached bed linen and a television which showed only programmes about gathering mushrooms.

One or the other, it had to be. He could love or he could experience safety. Dr. Blanchard had made him look at the core of his being and he had seen what lay there. He knew why he loved safety now, but perhaps he loved Rania more.

Wahid opened the drawer of his desk and found a copy of the *Yellow Pages*. He picked it up and put it on the desk with a loud thud. He paged through the numbers, finding the travel agent's office. He picked up the phone and began to punch numbers.

Love or safety, safety or love, quick, quick, quick slow. Which to choose?

Quick, quick, quick, slow.

"Hello?" the travel agent answered. Her accent penetrated his eardrum harshly with its broad East London tones.

He took a deep breath.

Lightning Source UK Ltd.
Milton Keynes UK
29 July 2010

157570UK00001B/3/P